PERFECT ALIBI

a Mike Daley Mystery by

SHELDON SIEGEL

Other books in the Mike Daley Mystery series by Sheldon Siegel:

PERFECT ALIBI

a Mike Daley Mystery by

SHELDON SIEGEL

MACADAM CAGE

MacAdam/Cage
155 Sansome Street, Suite 550
San Francisco, CA 94104
www.MacAdamCage.com

Siegel, Sheldon (Sheldon M.)
Perfect alibi / by Sheldon Siegel.
p. cm.
ISBN 978-1-59692-336-2
1. Daley, Mike (Fictitious character)—Fiction. 2. Fernandez, Rosie (Fictitious
character)—Fiction. 3. San Francisco (Calif.)—Fiction. I. Title.
PS3569.I3823P47 2010
813'.54—dc22
2010014404

Printed in the United States of America
Book and cover design by Dorothy Carico Smith

10 9 8 7 6 5 4 3 2 1

For Linda

1/ YOU AREN'T A CIVIL LAWYER

Friday, June 17, 2:34 p.m.

The Honorable T.J. Putnam Chandler exhales with melodramatic disdain. The Presiding Judge of the San Francisco Superior Court–Civil Division can feign exasperation as convincingly as any jurist in Northern California. "Mr. Daley," he bellows, "why are you wasting this court's time on a beautiful Friday afternoon?"

As if I had anything to do with the scheduling of this hearing. I summon an appropriately deferential tone. "Your Honor," I say, "we are here to contest the defendant's motion for summary judgment."

The three-hundred pound Brahman responds with another pronounced sigh. The fifth-generation San Franciscan firmly believes his appointment to the bench was an entitlement bestowed upon him by birthright. To those of us who have the privilege of appearing before him, it's common knowledge that Putty Chandler is well into the back nine of a thoroughly undistinguished judicial career. The dour bureaucrat has to go through the motions for six more months before he can start collecting his pension and retreat to a cushy corner office in a private mediation firm where he can work a couple of days a week for triple his current salary—as if he really needs the money. His more immediate concern is that he may be late for his regular three-thirty tee time at the Lake Course at the Olympic Club.

Judge Chandler leans forward in the custom leather chair he had to buy on his own dime. The state budget covered the construction costs of the workman-like civil courthouse across McAllister Street from City Hall, but there wasn't much left over for furniture. His bushy right eyebrow shoots up toward his mane of uncombed gray hair. The Einstein look is better suited to physicists. His voice fills with its customary scorn. "You're a *criminal* lawyer, aren't you, Mr. Daley?"

"Yes, Your Honor." I prefer the term defense attorney.

"That means you spend your time representing *criminals*, doesn't it?"

It will serve no useful purpose to remind him that everybody who watches *Law and Order* knows we're supposed to pay lip service to the concept that you're innocent until proven guilty. The Putty Chandlers of the world draw no substantial distinction between people who are accused of crimes and those who are actually convicted—or, for that matter, the attorneys who represent them. "We take on *pro bono* civil matters from time to time," I tell him. "This case was referred to us by the Haight-Ashbury Legal Aid Clinic."

He's unimpressed. "As I recall, the last time you were in my courtroom, you were trying to make the world safe for panhandlers."

"Something like that, Your Honor." A couple of years ago, I filed a civil suit for false arrest on behalf of a homeless man on the theory that the cops had violated his constitutional right of free speech. It wasn't precisely what the Founding Fathers had in mind when they drafted the Bill of Rights, but it seemed like a good idea at the time. Not surprisingly, Judge Chandler ruled against me. That case is still working its way up the appellate ladder.

He points his gavel in my direction. "Mr. Daley," he says, "I trust you understand we try to conduct ourselves with greater professional decorum over here in the civil courts?"

"Absolutely, Your Honor." I don't care how many of your inbred ancestors are living off their trust funds in Pacific Heights—you're still a pompous jackass.

I shoot a glance at my law partner and ex-wife, Rosita Fernandez, who is providing moral support from the front row of the otherwise empty gallery. I met Rosie at the Public Defender's Office two decades ago. I was fresh out of Boalt Law School after a brief and unsuccessful attempt at being a priest. She was fresh off an acquittal in a capital murder case after a brief and unsuccessful attempt at being married. After a string of victories, the *State Bar Journal* boldly proclaimed we were the best PDs in Northern California. Then we made the tactical error of trying to transform a successful working relationship into a more intimate one. We quickly discovered we were more adept at trying cases. The wheels fell off our marriage two years after it started. After a five-year cooling-off period, we formed the tenuous law partnership we've operated slightly north of the subsistence level for the past decade.

"Mr. Daley," the judge says, "I understand the plaintiff is claiming she was injured by a product manufactured by the defendant."

"That's correct, Your Honor." That's why it's called a product liability case.

I steal a look at the plaintiff's table, where my client is staring intently at her jet-black fingernails. Andrea Zeller is a sullen young woman whose closely cropped pink hair, twin nose rings, and gothic tattoos project an acceptable professional image for her day job as a sales clerk at Amoeba Music, a cavernous store in a converted bowling alley in the Haight. When she isn't peddling CDs, she plays bass guitar for a heavy metal band known as Death March. She prefers to be called by her stage name, Requiem. I've tried, without success, to explain to her on several occasions that patrician judges like Putty Chandler tend to have little empathy for people who exercise their right of free expression through body piercings and tattoos.

"Your Honor," I continue, "we have fulfilled our obligation to provide *prima facie* evidence that Ms. Zeller's injuries were caused by a defective product. The defendant's motion for summary judgment therefore should be denied."

This gets the attention of my worthy opponent. The aptly named Gary Winer is a cloying, owl-eyed man with large, horn-rimmed glasses, a horrific comb-over, and a grating nasal voice. He's spent the past thirty years trying to make the world safer for insurance companies. He has also perfected a legal strategy that may be summarized in three words: delay, delay, delay. He nods reassuringly to his client, a greasy, middle-aged man whose ill-fitting black suit matches the bad toupee that he probably bought on eBay.

Winer stands and addresses Judge Chandler. "Your Honor, the plaintiff wouldn't have been injured if she had followed the easy-to-understand instructions included with my client's product."

"She did," I say. Well, more or less. "The on-off switch didn't work properly."

"Your Honor," Winer drones on, "my client has rigorous quality control standards. Nobody has ever complained about the switch."

"There's always a first time," I say.

Winer won't let it go. "This is what happens when criminal lawyers bring civil cases. They don't understand our procedures."

Now *that's* a cheap shot. "Your Honor," I say, "the Civil Code isn't *that* much more complicated than the Penal Code."

"Nevertheless," Winer continues, "if Mr. Daley insists on proceeding with these unsubstantiated charges, we will need additional time to conduct a full structural analysis of this product."

He's stalling. "Your Honor," I say, "we don't need to take up this court's valuable time with expensive experts to prove Ms. Zeller was injured when the defendant's product malfunctioned. We've submitted an affidavit from a reputable engineer attesting to the design flaws in the switch. We've provided a sworn statement from her doctor and copies of her medical bills. Unless Mr. Winer's client is prepared to reimburse

Ms. Zeller for her medical bills and lost wages, this case should move forward to trial." So there.

Putty Chandler's chin is resting in his right palm. "Mr. Daley," he says, "what can you tell me about the product in question?"

"It might be more appropriate to have that discussion in chambers."

"Denied."

Have it your way. "If I might ask the bailiff to bring it over to you."

Judge Chandler's bailiff is a world-weary African American woman with the unenviable job of trying to keep her boss from making an ass of himself—no small assignment. "Your Honor," she says, "counsel's point might be well taken."

He doesn't take the hint. "Is it offensive?" he asks.

"Not really."

"Pornographic?"

"Not exactly."

"Then please deliver it to the bench."

Her eyes dart toward the ceiling, then she dutifully hands him a shoebox marked with an evidence tag. The judge removes a device that's the size of a screwdriver. He takes off his glasses and examines it. "Mr. Daley," he says, "is this some sort of power tool?"

You might say that. "It's a marital aid," I tell him.

"What does it do?"

The same thing as Viagra. "It stimulates erotic feelings."

He quickly sets it down on the bench. "How was your client injured?"

How do I say this? "The on-off switch jammed as Ms. Zeller was, uh, gratifying herself. She sustained bruises in certain sensitive areas."

"I see."

He's getting the idea. Thankfully, he doesn't ask for additional details. A reasonable argument could be made that Requiem didn't use the product in precisely the manner contemplated by the easy-to-understand instructions.

"Your Honor," Winer says, "Mr. Daley has not provided any evidence our product is defective."

"I'd be happy to show you," I say.

"Your Honor—" Winer implores.

The judge stops him with an upraised hand. "Approach the bench, gentlemen."

We do as we're told.

The judge puts a huge paw over his microphone. "We're off the record," he whispers. "It seems to me the most expedient way to decide this matter is to have a demonstration of the allegedly defective equipment."

"Fine with me," I say.

"That would be highly irregular," Winer says.

"I *want* a demonstration, Mr. Winer," the judge says.

It's my cue. "It works just like a flashlight," I explain. I slide the switch to the "On" position and it springs to life.

Judge Chandler's interest is piqued. "How do you turn it off?" he asks.

"That's the problem." I keep my tone clinical. "It's supposed to shut down when you slide the button back to the 'Off' position. Unfortunately, it doesn't."

"Your Honor—" Winer says.

I cut him off. "I don't expect you to take *my* word for it, Mr. Winer." I hand him the pulsating equipment. "Move the button to the 'Off' position."

Gary Winer has many talents, but manual dexterity isn't one of them. He corrals the bucking bronco and holds on for dear life. He makes a heroic, but ultimately futile, attempt to manipulate the switch. "I can't get it to stop," he says.

"Neither could Ms. Zeller," I reply.

Winer loses the handle and inadvertently flips the merchandise in my direction. I snag it just before it hits the floor.

The judge can't contain a smile. "Nice catch, Mr. Daley," he deadpans.

"Thank you, Your Honor." I make a big display of pretending to jimmy the switch. "I think we're going to have to remove the batteries."

"You've made your point, Mr. Daley." Putty Chandler turns to his favorite page in the judicial playbook: trying to broker a quick settlement. "Did Ms. Zeller sustain any permanent injuries?"

I answer him honestly. "No, Your Honor."

"How much were her medical bills?"

"About ten thousand dollars. Her lost wages were another five grand. I've told her she's unlikely to collect punitive damages."

"So you're willing to dispose of this case for fifteen thousand dollars?"

"Yes, Your Honor."

"Are you prepared to keep the settlement terms confidential?"

"Absolutely." Requiem isn't interested in making a statement—she just wants the cash.

Judge Chandler's pleased expression suggests he may make it to the Olympic Club after all. He turns his attention back to Winer. "You can make this go away for fifteen grand," he says.

"If we admit liability, we will be inundated with frivolous lawsuits."

"Mr. Daley has already agreed to keep the terms confidential."

"But Your Honor—"

"Let me put it this way, Mr. Winer. If you don't settle this matter in the next ten seconds, I'm going to rule there is sufficient evidence to move forward *and* that Ms. Zeller may assert claims for punitive damages. A full-blown trial will run your client at least six figures in legal fees—not to mention the possibility a jury may come back with a verdict for a lot more than fifteen grand. You know how unpredictable juries can be, don't you, Mr. Winer?"

"Yes, Your Honor."

"You're going to make this go away, aren't you, Mr. Winer?"

"Yes, Your Honor."

I'm not inclined to quibble about whether Judge Chandler is trying to serve the interests of justice or the interests of getting in eighteen holes before the sun goes down. Either way, Requiem comes out ahead.

"Step back, gentlemen," the judge says to us. He turns to his court reporter. "I have good news. Mr. Winer and Mr. Daley have agreed to a confidential settlement of this case. Have a nice weekend, everybody."

# # #

"Nice work," Rosie says to me.

"Requiem was very appreciative," I reply.

"I'll bet." Rosie's cobalt eyes twinkle as we're standing in Judge Chandler's empty courtroom. "You just made the world a safer place for consumers of sex toys."

"It will be my lasting legacy to the justice system—and mankind."

Her right eyebrow shoots up in a manner I still find irresistible. "Did you tinker with the switch to make sure it wouldn't turn off?"

"That would have been dishonest."

"I'll take your word for it. I trust you appreciate the irony of an ex-priest representing a client named Requiem in a case involving a sex toy?"

"I wasn't planning to tell the Archbishop." Enough gloating. "Is Grace going out with Bobby again tonight?"

"Yes."

Our sixteen-year-old daughter was one of the few positives to emerge from our marriage. "They've been spending a lot of time together," I observe.

"Yes, they have."

Bobby Fairchild isn't Grace's first boyfriend. He is, however, her most serious. They met at a high school science fair last October. As far as we can tell, their relationship has been reasonably tame. He's the sort of kid that I'd like Grace to marry—in another twenty years. He graduated last week from the prestigious and very private University High School in Pacific Heights. He's on his way to Columbia in the fall. His father is a Superior Court judge who is on the fast track to the federal bench. His mother is a neurosurgeon at UCSF.

"You need to start dealing with it like an adult," Rosie says.

"I'm trying. Is your mother staying with Tommy tonight?"

"Yes."

Our energetic four-year-old son was an unplanned surprise long after Rosie and I split up. Around the same time, we decided to move forward as a permanent—albeit unmarried—couple. Life is full of compromises.

"Does that mean we have time for an early dinner to celebrate my great victory?" I ask.

"Absolutely."

The door swings open and San Francisco's newly elected Public Defender strides forcefully down the center aisle. After three decades of toiling in the trenches, Robert Kidd finally got his chance to fill the top spot of the office he's served capably for so long.

"What brings you to the civil courthouse?" I ask him.

"Slumming."

"Us, too."

In a modest accommodation to the realities of modern political campaigning, our former mentor has ditched his Men's Wearhouse suits for a more polished Wilkes Bashford look. Nevertheless, the charismatic sixty-year-old still embodies the working-class values of his upbringing in the Mission District. His hair is thinner and his jowls are larger, but his clear blue eyes still radiate the same intensity I first saw when he was promoted to the head of the felony division. At six-two and a lean two hundred pounds, he starts every morning with a six-mile run across town to the functional new building a half-block south of the Hall of Justice that houses the PD's Office.

"I just saw Putty Chandler heading to his car," he says.

"Did he have his golf clubs?" I ask.

"As a matter of fact, he did. He said you're developing a new specialty in the law of sex toys."

"It was a cameo appearance on a *pro bono* case. On Monday, we'll be back in the trenches fighting the good fight on behalf of drug dealers, pimps, and other small-time crooks."

"Glad to hear it."

My ever-practical ex-wife interjects. "You didn't come looking for us on a Friday afternoon just to give us a hard time for taking a civil case," Rosie says.

"I wanted to see if you've had a chance to consider my very attractive offer."

He'd asked us to take over his old job as head of the felony division at the PD's Office.

"We're still thinking about it," I say. "We've been busy."

"Working on *civil* cases." It's the ultimate put-down to a defense lawyer.

"We take a few *pro bono* referrals from the Bar Association. Ninety-nine percent of our work is criminal."

"*One hundred* percent of our work is criminal. You aren't a civil lawyer."

"I'm a very civil lawyer. We just don't handle many civil cases."

"We don't handle any."

"We like to pick our clients," Rosie says.

"Most of whom are flaky or deadbeats—or both," he says. "Not to mention the long hours, the little thanks, and the lousy pay."

"That's no different from the PD's Office," Rosie says.

"True enough, except you'd be working for me—that should count for something." He turns serious. "I'm trying to upgrade the quality and reputation of our office. I need competent people like you to train the next generation."

"We're flattered," I say, "but we're trial lawyers. We don't want to spend the next ten years shuffling paper."

"I'll get you help with the admin stuff. I'll let you pick some cases to try. We have decent health benefits and a good retirement plan. You aren't going to get rich, but you won't starve. It's a pretty good deal when you have one kid heading to college soon and another who's starting grammar school. I might even be able to offer you some flex- ibility in your hours." He flashes the recently developed politician's smile that's still a work in progress. "What's it going to take to get your answer today?"

"You sound like a used car salesman, Robert."

"Cars. Lawyers. It's all the same."

"We understand the urgency. We'll get back to you as soon as we can."

The Public Defender of the City and County of San Francisco nods and heads toward the door.

"What do you think?" Rosie asks me as soon as he's out of earshot.

"It may be a chance to work on some interesting cases for a good guy. We'd get to train some talented young lawyers. It would be a regular paycheck and decent benefits. He's even willing to let us work part-time."

"But?"

"I'm not sure I'm ready to cash in our chips to go back to a job that we left fifteen years ago. It's a step backward."

Rosie gives me a thoughtful look. "Maybe it's a step forward," she says.

# # #

I'm lying in bed, thinking about Robert Kidd's offer, when my phone rings. I can tell immediately from the tone of Rosie's voice that something is terribly wrong. "I need you to come over right away," she says.

"Are Tommy and Grace okay?"

"They're fine."

"What about your mother?"

"She's fine, too."

I flip on the lamp in the bedroom of the tiny fifties-era apartment where I've lived since Rosie and I split up. There's just enough room for a sagging double bed, a worn oak dresser, and a couple of mismatched nightstands. My eyes struggle to adjust to the light as I squint at the watch my grandfather acquired for a sack of potatoes in Galway City over a hundred years ago—or so our family legend goes. Gramps was also an accomplished pickpocket. Either way, I know for a fact my father wore the same watch as he walked the beat in San Francisco's toughest neighborhoods when I was born fifty-four years ago.

"It's two o'clock in the morning," I say to Rosie.

"If you wanted to work regular hours, you shouldn't have become a defense lawyer."

It would be a serious tactical error to elevate this discussion into a full-blown argument. "What is it?" I ask.

"Bobby called. It's his father."

"Is Judge Fairchild sick?"

"No," Rosie says. "He's dead."

Saturday, June 18, 2:04 a.m.

"Did he have a heart attack?" I ask Rosie.

"No," she whispers. "He was beaten to death. Bobby found the body when he got home. It may have been a botched robbery."

Dear God. "What else did Bobby tell you?"

"I didn't talk to him. He called Grace on her cell. I tried to call him back, but he didn't answer."

"Does this have anything to do with the Savage case?"

"I don't know."

Judge Fairchild recently presided over the highly charged racketeering trial of the owner of San Francisco's most notorious towing company. George Savage is a warm and fuzzy guy who cut a sweetheart deal with the City to rid our overcrowded streets of illegally parked cars. In performing this valuable public service, his highly trained professionals developed a propensity for cruising upscale neighborhoods and towing vehicles seemingly at random, with a particular affinity for high-end sports cars. When Savage's people took your car hostage, you had to find a cabbie who was willing to risk his life to drive you down to the massive impound lot in the most dangerous corner of the Bayview, where you had to pony up three big bills plus a highly recommended gratuity in cold, hard cash to liberate your vehicle. If you were lucky, your car was missing only its side mirrors and hubcaps. If you were unlucky, it was stripped clean. If you were *really* unlucky, you never saw it again.

A zealous investigative reporter at the *Chronicle* (with the assistance of a couple of our City's erstwhile auditors) determined that Big George had also developed a proclivity for lining his pockets with millions of dollars that rightfully belonged to the hardworking taxpayers of the City and County of San Francisco. Our media-savvy DA filed charges and our well-trained prosecutors spent six months going toe-to-toe in a bloody war of attrition against Savage's well-paid army of defense lawyers. During the trial, Savage made no secret of his contempt for the prosecutors, the jury, and especially Judge Fairchild. Rumors of intimidation and jury tampering were rampant. After three long weeks of deliberations, the jury convicted Savage of a single count of failing to pay his local business taxes and levied a million dollar fine. Most people considered it a slap on the wrist. His well-oiled operation never missed a beat.

"Is Bobby still at his father's house?" I ask.

"As far as I know."

Bobby's mother and father separated acrimoniously about six months ago. Their respective barracudas have been trying to divvy up the spoils and work out support and custody arrangements ever since. At Bobby's graduation last week, his parents sat in separate corners and didn't say a word to each other. His mother, Julie, still lives in what used to be the family home in Cole Valley, a quiet neighborhood wedged between the UCSF Medical Center, Golden Gate Park, and the Haight. His father rented a remodeled Victorian a few blocks away. Bobby and his younger brother, Sean, have been shuttling between the two houses.

"Were you able to reach Julie?" I ask.

"Not yet. I paged her and left a message. The hospital said she was in surgery."

Damn it. "What about Sean?"

Bobby's brother just finished his freshman year at the exclusive Urban High School in the Haight. He's a shy, sensitive kid who has borne the brunt of his parents' separation.

"He didn't answer his cell," Rosie says. "Grace said he was spending the night at a friend's house. I would assume the cops—and Julie—are looking for him."

No doubt. "Where did Grace and Bobby go last night?"

"To dinner and a movie." She waits a beat before she adds, "In the City."

"I thought we agreed that they would stay closer to home."

"Yesterday was Bobby's eighteenth birthday. Grace politely asked for permission."

"Which you granted?"

"You don't get to second-guess my parental decisions if you aren't available for a consultation."

That's never stopped me. "What time did they get home?"

"One o'clock."

"That's way too late, Rosie. She's only sixteen."

"I'm well aware of that, Mike. I made my feelings known to them."

So will I. "The cops are going to want to talk to him," I say. "And to Grace."

"I know."

"Am I the only person who sees a potential problem here?"

Rosie invokes the sanctimonious tone I've always found infuriating. "Bobby graduated third in his class at University High. He was an all-conference baseball player and the editor of the school newspaper. He got early admission to Columbia."

"To the cops, he's also a person of interest."

"It doesn't make him a suspect."

"I didn't say he was. It's also no secret that he and his father weren't getting along."

"It isn't uncommon for teenagers to have strained relationships with their parents—especially during a divorce."

Tell me about it. "How strained was theirs?"

"Bobby wouldn't hurt anyone, Mike. Besides, he has a perfect alibi."

Our daughter.

# # #

"Come in, Michael," my ex-mother-in-law whispers.

Sylvia Fernandez is standing inside the front doorway to Rosie's house. Except for her gray hair and crow's feet, she could pass for Rosie's older sister. She celebrated her seventy-ninth birthday last month by having her left hip replaced so she could keep up with Grace and Tommy. At times, I think she can outrun them. She recently instructed her doctors to accelerate her rehabilitation program. If they're smart, they'll do exactly as she says.

"Is Tommy asleep?" I ask.

She gives me the knowing smile of a grandmother. "Not anymore."

I see my four-year-old son's wide brown eyes peeking out from behind his grandmother. Tommy's round, cherub-like face breaks into an enthusiastic smile. Sporting his trademark San Francisco Giants pajamas, he gives my right leg a tight bear hug. "Hi, Daddy," he shrieks with glee.

It's been a while since I got a similarly warm welcome from his sister. "Hi, Tom. What are you doing up so late?"

"I heard Mommy talking to Grace."

He's a happy kid, but he's also a worrier—a trait he inherited from me. "It's no big deal," I say. "Everything is going to be fine."

"No worries?" he asks. I'm not sure if he picked up the line from me or Barney the Dinosaur.

"No worries," I reply.

I take off my jacket and look around at the cluttered space serving as Rosie's living room, home office, and playroom. Rosie, Grace, and Tommy live in a post-earthquake era cottage in Larkspur, a quiet burg about ten miles north of the Golden Gate Bridge where the neighborhood is safe and the schools are good. Their house is three blocks from my apartment behind the fire station. From time to time, we talk about trying to cohabitate under one roof. Invariably, we find the buffer zone allows us to diffuse our occasional differences of opinion. It also means Rosie takes the brunt of living with a teenage daughter. When Grace directs her angst my way, I try to remind myself she's an honor student and the starting shortstop on the Redwood High School varsity softball team. She's also a mercurial soul who inherited my propensity for stubbornness and Rosie's independent streak—traits that are not always becoming in a teenager.

"Why are you here so late?" Tommy asks.

"Lawyer stuff," I say. It's my standard answer. Tommy has no real comprehension of what Rosie and I do. He understands our work frequently requires us to go downtown in the middle of the night to help people who get into trouble.

"Do you have to go to work?" he asks.

"Maybe for a while. We'll be home soon."

"Can we go to the park tomorrow?"

"You bet."

This elicits a smile. If it were only so easy with Grace. "Is Grandma going to stay with me?" he asks.

"Of course." I take his small hand and squeeze it. "You go back to bed, Tommy. I'll come in and say goodbye before we leave."

"Okay, Daddy." He squeezes my leg again before he sprints down the narrow hallway toward his bedroom. Four-year-olds move at only one speed—fast.

I turn to Sylvia. "Where's Rosie?"

"Talking to your daughter."

Translation: they're arguing. I can hear the muffled sounds of a heated debate through the thin walls. I'll get a blow-by-blow from Rosie later. "What are they fighting about?" I ask.

"Whether Grace is going to go with you to see Bobby."

"Is there any doubt?"

"No. *Your* daughter is as stubborn as *my* daughter."

# # #

"Talk to us, Grace," I say.

No answer.

Rosie is behind the wheel of her Toyota Prius—a recent upgrade over her ancient Honda Civic. We're barreling down the 101 Freeway toward the Golden Gate Bridge. I'm riding shotgun. Grace is in the back seat. Her lips form a pronounced scowl as she stares out the window.

"Grace?" I say.

"What, Dad?"

Until last year, I was still Daddy. When Bobby arrived on the scene, I became Dad. "What did Bobby tell you?" I ask.

"This isn't a cross-exam."

Every question is a personal affront. "We're just trying to help, honey."

"You're going about it the wrong way."

Nowadays, we go about *everything* the wrong way. "What did Bobby tell you?"

"That his father's dead."

"Was he able to reach his mother?"

"I don't know."

"What about Sean?"

"I don't know that, either."

"Did Bobby call the police?"

"Of course. They were on their way to his house."

They're undoubtedly already there. "They're going to want to know what he was doing tonight."

"He was with me."

"They'll want details." So do I.

"Can you stop talking like a lawyer?"

"I'm talking like a parent."

Rosie cuts in using her best maternal tone—though she would readily admit it isn't nearly as effective as it used to be. "Where did you and Bobby go last night?" she asks Grace.

"I already told you."

"Tell me again. Please, Grace."

Our daughter responds with a sigh that would make Putty Chandler proud. "We went out for dinner at Zazie."

It's a homey neighborhood bistro on Cole Street, around the corner from Judge Fairchild's house. "Where did you park?" I ask.

"On Grattan Street next to Bobby's father's house."

"Was the judge at home?"

"No."

"Did you go inside?"

"No. There wasn't enough time."

"Where did you go after dinner?"

"To see *Waiting for Guffman* at the Red Vic."

The Red Vic Movie House is San Francisco's Anti-Multiplex. It was opened by a group of film buffs in 1980 in a funky red Victorian at the corner of Belvedere and Haight. A few years later, it moved down the street to its current location between Cole and Shrader. The new auditorium is larger and equipped with Dolby sound. It's still furnished with comfy old couches. Instead of serving stale popcorn with fake butter, they offer organic treats.

"What time did the movie start?" Rosie asks.

"Nine o'clock. It ended at eleven. We went for a walk down Haight Street."

The Haight has gentrified substantially since the days when my high school buddies and I used to go there to see real live hippies during the Summer of Love—much to the chagrin of my parents and my teachers at St. Ignatius. There are still a few head shops and incense stores interspersed among the upscale boutiques, but the neighborhood is largely unrecognizable from the flower-child days. The corner of Haight and Ashbury is now home to a Ben & Jerry's ice cream store. There is still a modest drug and counter-culture presence as well as a significant homeless population that spills over from nearby Golden Gate Park. It's perfectly safe in the daylight, but things get dicier after dark. It isn't a place where an eighteen-year-old boy should be hanging out with his sixteen-year-old girlfriend late at night—especially when she's my daughter.

"Did you stop anywhere?" I ask.

"We looked at CDs at Amoeba Music."

I'm tempted to ask her if she knows a clerk named Requiem who plays with a band called Death March, but I let it go. "Did you buy anything?"

"Nope."

"What time did you go back and pick up the car?" Rosie asks.

"Around twelve fifteen."

"Was Judge Fairchild at home?"

"I don't know."

"Did you go inside the house?"

"No."

Rosie pushes a little harder. "Not even for a minute?"

"No, Mother. Bobby and his father weren't getting along. Things get tense when people are getting divorced."

Grace's pronounced sigh indicates that this discussion is coming to an end. At the moment, Rosie and I are more interested in our daughter's welfare than in recriminations. After things calm down, I will have a fatherly chat with Grace and Bobby about the advisability of hanging out in the Haight after the sun goes down.

# # #

The fresh-faced young cop looks like he's fourteen years old. "I'm sorry, sir," he says to me. "You'll have to remain outside the restricted area."

"We're friends of the Fairchild family," I tell him.

"This is a crime scene, sir."

No kidding. "I'm aware of that, Officer."

Police lights flash off the trees in front of Judge Fairchild's remodeled blue Victorian on the southwest corner of Belvedere and Grattan. It's three a.m. The neighbors are huddled in small groups outside the yellow tape. Despite its proximity to the Haight, Cole Valley has a low-key character of its own. The closely knit community of refurbished houses and low-rise apartment buildings is bisected by the N-Judah street car line. The businesses along the three-block shopping district on Cole Street are of the mom-and-pop variety. The neighborhood's southern boundary is Tank Hill, named for a 500,000-gallon water tower that survived the 1906 earthquake. A ring of eucalyptus trees was planted around it after Pearl Harbor in an ill-conceived effort to camouflage it from enemy bombers. The tank was removed in the fifties, but the trees and the cement base remain. The rarely used public space has some of the best views in the City.

"Officer," I say, "Bobby Fairchild has asked to see us."

"I'm not authorized to let anybody in, sir. It isn't my decision."

"It is now." I pull out my trump card. "My name is Michael Daley. This is my law partner, Ms. Fernandez. We're Bobby Fairchild's attorneys."

"I'm afraid I can't help you, sir."

"I'm afraid you're going to have to. We need to see our client immediately."

"I'm not authorized."

"Then I need to talk to your sergeant."

"He can't help you, either. Mr. Fairchild isn't here."

"Where is he?"

"At the Hall of Justice."

What? "They didn't need to take him downtown to get his statement."

"They took him downtown because he's been arrested for murdering his father."

Saturday, June 18, 3:10 a.m.

"When did they leave?" I ask the cop.

"Ten minutes ago."

A difficult situation has transformed into a full-blown disaster. Rosie struggles to keep Grace calm while I start pumping the cop for information. "Who made the arrest?" I ask.

"Roosevelt Johnson."

The dean of San Francisco homicide inspectors has handled every high-profile murder investigation in the City for forty years. A half-century ago, he and my father formed the SFPD's first integrated team. The good news is he'll proceed with competence and professionalism. The bad news is he doesn't arrest anybody unless he has the goods.

"Is Inspector Johnson still here?" I ask.

"No, sir. He accompanied Mr. Fairchild downtown."

"Was he able to reach my client's mother?"

"I don't know, sir."

Damn it.

Grace breaks free of Rosie's grasp. "We have to do something, Dad!" she shouts.

"Stay calm," I hiss, immediately regretting the harshness in my tone. Rosie and I quickly escort her out of the young cop's earshot. "I know this is hard," I say to her, "but you have to keep your composure."

Tears are welling up in her eyes. "I'm trying, Dad."

"I'm sorry I snapped at you." TV news vans are beginning to assemble down the street. I turn to Rosie. "We need to start damage control."

She hands me her car keys. "Go down to the Hall of Justice and tell Bobby to keep his mouth shut. Grace and I will find his mother and his brother. We'll meet you as soon as we can."

"I want to come with you," Grace says to me.

"They won't let you inside," I tell her.

"Then I'll wait outside."

"No, you won't," Rosie says. She invokes the unequivocal Don't-Even-Think-About-Arguing-With-Me tone I've heard countless times in court, at the office, and in bed. "You'll end up sitting by yourself in the corridor for hours. I need your help."

In addition to Rosie's independent streak, Grace is also imbued with her mother's sense of cold, hard reality. She surrenders without another word.

# # #

"What do you need, Mick?" the raspy voice asks. My younger brother, Pete, became a cop to prove he was just as tough as our father. He spent ten years walking a beat out of Mission Station before he was forced to resign after he and his partner allegedly broke up a gang fight with a little too much enthusiasm. He's still legitimately angry the City hung him out to dry when the so-called victims threatened litigation. Nowadays, he earns his keep by tailing unfaithful husbands.

Driving Rosie's car down Oak Street through a heavy fog at three-thirty on Saturday morning, I wedge the cell phone between my right shoulder and ear. "Are you working?"

"Margaret has to eat."

My five-year-old niece is a charmer. I'm convinced she and Tommy compare notes about new ways to drive their respective parents insane. "Where are you?"

"St. Francis Wood."

He's working upscale tonight. "Cheating husband?"

"Cheating wife."

"Can you break away for a few minutes?"

"Anything for my big brother. Does this have anything to do with Judge Fairchild?"

"How did you know?"

"I just heard it on the police band. What the hell happened?"

"That's what I need you to find out."

"Is Grace okay?"

"She's fine. Her boyfriend isn't."

"Bobby's a nice kid."

"He's been arrested for killing his father."

"Jesus. Is Roosevelt handling the investigation?"

"Yes."

His silence confirms what I already know—Bobby is in serious trouble.

"How soon can you get to Cole Valley to start asking questions?" I ask.

"Ten minutes."

# # #

"I need to see my client," I say.

Inspector Roosevelt Johnson eyes me through wire-rimmed, aviator-style bifocals. The former college tight end has dropped some weight since he underwent radiation treatments for throat cancer last year. Nevertheless, the seventy-five-year-old legend still carries over two hundred pounds on his imposing six-foot-four-inch frame. The warhorse has fought the cancer to a standstill, but his lyrical baritone has developed a gravelly edge. He's tried to retire three times, but he keeps getting drawn back to work.

"Since when did you become Bobby Fairchild's lawyer?" he asks.

"Since now."

Four o'clock on Saturday morning is not the Hall of Justice's busy hour. We're standing in the new jail wing's high-tech intake center. Known to the cops as the "Glamour Slammer," the Plexiglas edifice was unceremoniously shoe-horned between the Stalinesque old Hall and the I-80 Freeway in a heavy-handed response to a court order to relieve overcrowding in the San Francisco jails. It isn't much to look at, but the utilitarian facility is cleaner and more user-friendly than the original Hall, a maze-like structure combining the architectural elements of a medieval dungeon with a third-world street bazaar.

"How's Rosie?" he asks.

He's genuinely interested in my law partner's well-being. He also never asks a question without a purpose. He wants to see if he can get me to let my guard down.

"She's fine," I say. "I need to talk to Bobby."

"He's still in processing. I'll bring him up as soon as he's done."

"You have a legal obligation to let me see my client."

"As soon as he's done," he repeats.

I up the ante. "If you try to introduce anything he's said to you, I'll get it excluded."

"Dial it down, Mike. For the record, I conducted all of my conversations with your client within the letter of the law."

It's undoubtedly true. He's also holding the face cards, so I soften my tone. "As a matter of professional courtesy, I would appreciate it if you would expedite booking."

"He's been arrested for a serious crime. He'll be processed like everybody else."

Which means Bobby is being subjected to an unpleasant search, showered with cold disinfectant, given a perfunctory medical exam, and issued a freshly pressed orange jumpsuit.

I try again. "As a personal favor, I would be grateful if you would arrange for Bobby to be housed in his own cell until we can straighten out this misunderstanding."

"There's no misunderstanding. We take the killing of a judge very seriously."

"Come on, Roosevelt. He just graduated with honors from University High."

"He told me his father got precisely what he deserved."

"Teenagers say a lot of things. That doesn't mean he killed him."

"We'll have to agree to disagree on that point. The investigation is ongoing. I can't talk about it, Mike."

"You mean you *won't* talk about it." I lower my voice. "Please, Roosevelt. He's Grace's boyfriend."

He looks around the cold intake area as he ponders how much he's willing to tell me. "Judge Fairchild was bludgeoned to death in the laundry room adjacent to the garage of his house. Your client was holding a bloody hammer when the first officer arrived."

"That proves he picked up a hammer," I say. "It doesn't mean he used it."

"There was blood on his hands."

"Obviously, he tried to help his father. Or the hammer was bloody when he picked it up."

"He was angry. His behavior was erratic. He showed no signs of remorse."

"He had just found his father's body. He was in shock."

"I guess we'll have to agree to disagree on that point, too."

"Did you consider the possibility this is related to the Savage case?"

"There's no evidence."

"Savage made no secret of his disdain for the judge."

"I have no more love for Savage than you do. On the other hand, he's smart enough not to pop a sitting judge."

"Maybe he paid somebody to do it."

"We will conduct a full investigation."

"I understand the house was vandalized. It could have been a botched robbery."

"A couple of pieces of furniture were knocked over. There were no signs of forced entry."

"Maybe the killer had a key. Maybe somebody left a door open."

"I don't think so."

"Are you suggesting Bobby trashed his father's house to make it look like a break-in?"

"There were no signs of a struggle or defensive wounds. That suggests Judge Fairchild was killed by somebody he knew."

"Maybe the killer sneaked up on him."

"It's a tight laundry room, Mike."

"Maybe the killer hit the judge as he was coming in the door."

"I'll let you make that argument when the time comes."

"Have you come up with a motive?"

"Too soon to tell. Maybe your client was angry about his parents' divorce. Maybe they got into a fight because he came home so late. Maybe the judge wasn't happy his son was going out with your daughter. Any way you cut it, Judge Fairchild is dead—and your client was holding the murder weapon when we arrived."

"Alleged murder weapon," I say.

"Have it your way."

"Bobby called 911," I say. "He would have tried to get away if he was guilty."

"Not necessarily. He's a smart kid. He knew it would have looked suspicious if he ran. It sounded more plausible to say he found the body."

I probe for additional details, but he isn't forthcoming. Finally, I look into the eyes of the man my father always described as the best cop he ever knew. "Did he mention he was with Grace last night?"

"Yes. That's something else we need to discuss. I expect her full cooperation—immediately."

"You'll get it. They didn't get back to Rosie's house until one o'clock."

"That's consistent with his story. If I were in your shoes, I wouldn't be thrilled my sixteen-year-old daughter was out so late."

"I'm not. We've already talked to her about it. It also means Bobby didn't get back to his father's house until sometime after two."

"That information will help me establish a timeline."

"Bobby couldn't have killed his father if the autopsy puts the time of death before two."

His mouth turns down. He knows I'm trying to back him into a corner while eliminating any suspicion of Grace. "I am not in a position to rule out the possibility he killed his father sometime earlier in the evening."

"That's impossible," I tell him. "Bobby wasn't there earlier in the evening."

"That isn't what he told me."

Saturday, June 18, 4:12 a.m.

"What exactly did Bobby tell you?" I ask Roosevelt.

"He parked on Grattan Street, on the side of his father's house, before he and Grace went out for dinner. They came back to get the car after they went to a movie at the Red Vic."

This is consistent with Grace's story. "So what?"

"It places him at his father's house."

Along with my daughter. "It doesn't place him *inside*."

"Not yet." He invokes the fatherly tone I heard countless times in our back yard when I was a kid. "Let me give you some advice—off the record—friend to friend."

"I'm listening."

"First, you should find somebody else to represent this kid. You're too close to him and your daughter was with him last night."

It's good advice. "Anything else?"

"You'd better get the full story from Grace—and convey it to me ASAP. I love her like she's my own daughter, but if she lies or withholds information, her boyfriend isn't the only one who is going to be in serious trouble."

# # #

Bobby's desperation manifests itself in the form of a plaintive wail. "I didn't kill anybody," he pleads. "You have to believe me, Mike."

"I do." For now.

It's jarring to see Grace's boyfriend so far outside the usual context. Three hours ago, he was just another good-looking, athletic high school graduate with trendy clothes and a future with limitless potential. Now, clad in an orange prison jumpsuit, he's sitting with his arms at his sides in a claustrophobic consultation room in the bowels of the Glamour Slammer, where the heavy air smells of cleaning solvent. He looks as if he's aged ten years under the harsh glare of the unforgiving fluorescent light. His puffy red eyes stare blankly at the dull green wall—almost as if the life has been sucked out of him.

My first instinct is parental. "Are you hurt?" I ask.

He struggles to maintain his composure. "No," he whispers.

The initial meeting with a new client frequently evokes many of the same dynamics as a first date. It takes on magnified importance because it establishes the direction and tone of the relationship. Conventional wisdom says you shouldn't represent somebody you know because your lawyer's judgment may be impaired. At the moment, I can't tell Grace that we won't help her boyfriend because conventional wisdom says it's a bad idea.

I go to my priest voice. "I'm so sorry about your father, Bobby. We'll do everything we can to help you."

"Thanks, Mike. Is Grace okay?"

"Yes." I'm appreciative of his concern for my daughter. However, it's a rather abrupt shift in the topic. "She's having a long night, too."

"I don't want to get her involved in this mess," he says.

"She already is."

"When can I see her?"

"Not for a while." We have more important issues at the moment. "They'll only let you see your lawyers and immediate family."

"Where is she?"

"With Rosie. They're looking for your mother."

"She's probably up at the hospital. I tried to page her. She was on call."

"What about Sean?"

"He was staying with one of his classmates."

"What's his name?"

"Kerry Mullins."

I'll call Rosie in a moment to pass along the information. First, I need to cover some essentials. "I know this is the worst night of your life, but we need to talk about some lawyer stuff for a minute."

"Does that mean you're my lawyer?"

"For the moment. I wanted you to have somebody to talk to right away." More important, I wanted to make sure he didn't talk to anybody before I arrived. "It would probably be a good idea for you to hire somebody who doesn't have an existing personal relationship with you."

"I trust you, Mike. I want you to be my lawyer."

"I appreciate that, but it may not be the best thing for you." It may not be the best thing for Grace, either. "It would be better if you brought in somebody with more professional detachment."

"Does that mean you don't want to be my lawyer?"

"I didn't say that."

"Then I want you to be my lawyer."

"You're absolutely sure?"

"I'm absolutely sure."

"Then it's settled—at least for now. I may reconsider after I talk to Rosie." And he may reconsider when he realizes he'll have to reveal some deep, dark secrets to his girlfriend's father. His mother may reconsider when she finds out her son wants to hire a lawyer who works in a walk-up building across the street from the Transbay bus terminal.

"I need to talk to my mother about paying you," he says. "She's been a little hard up for cash. You know—the divorce."

"We'll worry about that later."

We'll get paid. I'm more concerned about having access to some quick cash to post bail—assuming I can persuade a judge to allow it. Julie's assets may be tied up. From what I've gathered, she's burning through her spare cash to subsidize the lifestyle of her divorce lawyer. If all else fails, we can call Rosie's cousin Sal, a bail bondsman who plies his trade in dingy quarters across Bryant Street. He's one of our best sources of referrals.

"Now that I'm your lawyer," I say, "I need to explain a few ground rules. First, everything you tell Rosie and me is absolutely confidential. We won't repeat anything you say to us—not even to your mother and Grace—unless you give us permission. Understood?"

He nods.

"Second, I don't want you to say a word to anybody in this building. Not the cops. Not the guards. Especially not the other prisoners. Nobody here is your friend. You only talk to Rosie and me. Got it?"

"Got it."

"Third, you have to be absolutely straight with us. We can't represent you effectively unless you tell us the truth. Rosie and I have been doing this for a long time. It's our only hard-and-fast rule. I know this sounds harsh, but if you lie to us or you withhold anything, we'll withdraw."

His voice is barely audible. "Understood."

Now for the hardest one. "You and Grace were together last night. That makes her your alibi—and a person of interest to the police. It is essential that your stories match up."

There's an almost imperceptible hesitation. "They will."

I hope so. "Grace may be called as a witness. It is also possible—albeit unlikely—that they may bring charges against her."

"For what?"

Aiding and abetting—or worse. "It doesn't matter. For now, you just need to know that if her interests conflict with yours, we're going to represent her."

"I understand."

"Any questions?"

"How soon can you get me out of here?"

That's always at the top of the list, and the answer is always unsatisfying. "I can't tell you for sure. Maybe a few hours. Maybe a few days. Maybe longer. If they charge you with murder, bail will be more difficult."

He takes a moment to process the first mention of the word murder. "How difficult?"

"It depends." *Almost* impossible if they go for first degree. *Absolutely* impossible if they ask for the death penalty—which is unlikely for someone with no criminal record who is as young as Bobby. Then again, our DA may view this as an opportunity to get some easy TV time and political traction on a high-profile case. "Let me worry about it," I tell him.

"You aren't in a cell with rapists and drug dealers."

"I've asked them to keep you separated. I need to call Rosie to tell her where she can find your mother and your brother. When I get back, you're going to tell me everything that happened last night—minute by minute—from the time you picked up Grace until the cops arrived at your father's house. Don't embellish and don't sugarcoat. Every single detail could be important."

Saturday, June 18, 4:22 a.m.

"I picked up Grace at six o'clock last night," Bobby says. "We drove to Cole Valley and had dinner at Zazie."

I'm studying his body language intently and listening for any hints of equivocation in his voice. "There are restaurants in Marin County closer to Grace's house."

"Rosie said it was okay."

And I was asleep at the switch. "Where did you park?" I ask, already knowing the answer. It's an opportunity to see how the details of his story will match up with Grace's version.

"On Grattan Street, next to my father's house," he says.

Good answer. "You couldn't find anything closer to the restaurant?"

"It's only a couple of blocks away. Parking is tight in Cole Valley."

"Why didn't you leave it in your father's garage?"

"There's only room for one car. That's where he keeps his Jag."

You mean that's where he *kept* it. "What about the driveway?"

"He would have given me hell if I blocked the garage."

It's one of the few perks of being the parent of a teenager: we trump their parking privileges. "Did you go inside your father's house before dinner?"

"No." He's a little too adamant when he adds, "We were running late. We went straight to the restaurant."

"Was your father home?"

"No. He went to the Bohemian Club for dinner."

The Bohemian Club was formed in the 1870s as a gathering place for newspaper reporters and men of the arts and literature. Nowadays, it's an all-male bastion of the powerful and the famous. Many of its two thousand members are directors of Fortune 1000 companies, corporate CEOs, and top-ranking government appointees. Admission is highly selective and priority is given to artists, authors, musicians, and people with boatloads of cash. Its social activities revolve around member-produced musical and variety shows performed at the Club's historic headquarters on Taylor Street, near Union Square.

The Club derives much of its notoriety from its annual encampment in a grove of old redwoods along the Russian River about seventy-five miles north of San Francisco, near the hamlet of Monte Rio. Spanning three weekends in August, the epic event has evolved into a summer camp for aging white Republican elites, who jockey for cots in the most prestigious "camps" based on their wealth, power, and status. Every spring, many of the Bay Area's second-tier social climbers try to pull strings to score a guest invitation for a weekend of elbow-rubbing with the first-tier social climbers up at "The Grove."

The supposedly hush-hush rituals are some of the worst-kept secrets in the Bay Area. The festivities begin with a ceremony known as the "Cremation of Care," a pageant in which hooded members conduct a mock sacrifice complete with music and fireworks. Other highlights include an elaborate play called the "High Jinx," and musical comedies known as the "Low Jinx," where the female roles are, of necessity, played by men in drag. The campers spend the rest of their time listening to political lectures (dubbed "lakeside chats"), working out the details of multi-billion-dollar mergers, and consuming copious amounts of food and alcohol. At night, the frivolity includes singing light-hearted camp songs around the fire with cheery guys like Dick Cheney, Don Rumsfeld, and Henry Kissinger, and talking about uplifting subjects like the end of Western Civilization.

"Was your father coming straight home from the Club?"

"No. He had a date."

This is news. Rosie and I met Jack Fairchild only twice. While he was cordial enough to us, you could tell he was intensely driven. We've carefully avoided asking Bobby personal questions about his parents. "I didn't know your father was seeing somebody."

"He didn't talk about it."

"What's her name?"

"Christina Evans. She's a law clerk at the court." His tone turns acerbic when he adds, "He's old enough to be her father."

It clearly violated the court's anti-fraternization rules. It also exemplified profoundly bad judgment. "Did your father tell you about this relationship?"

"Nope. My mother did."

"How did she find out?"

His tone remains even. "She hired a private investigator to help with the divorce case."

All's fair in love, war, and divorce. "How long had they been seeing each other?"

"About six months."

"Did your father know that you knew about his relationship with Ms. Evans?"

"Yes. He was unhappy my mother told me about it."

He was undoubtedly angrier that his relationship was discovered in the first place. "Was Ms. Evans your father's only girlfriend?"

"I doubt it."

"Did she ever go to the Club with your father?"

"Nope. Except for the Christmas show, the only women allowed inside the Club are the ones who serve food in the dining room."

I should have known.

"Besides," he adds, "they never went out together in public. That was part of their deal."

Lovely. "What was the rest of their deal?"

"He spent every Friday night at her place."

"Even the Fridays when you and Sean were staying at his house?"

"Most of the time."

It sent a clear message to Bobby and Sean about their father's priorities. "Was he planning to stay at her house last night?"

"He told me not to wait up for him."

"Evidently, he decided to come home early."

"I think they were having problems."

"What kind?"

"I'm not sure."

"Is she married?"

"Not anymore."

We'll talk to her. "Where did you and Grace go after dinner?"

"We walked over to the Red Vic to see *Waiting for Guffman*."

"What part did you like the best?" I'm not interested in a review. I want to confirm they did, in fact, go to the movie.

"The song, 'Nothing Ever Happens on Mars.'"

It's a good bet he saw the movie. "Any chance you have your ticket stub?"

"Don't you believe me?"

"Yes, I do. It would also be helpful if we can prove you weren't anywhere near your father's house before two o'clock. If the Medical Examiner says the time of death was earlier, their case will fall apart and you can go home."

"I don't have the ticket, Mike. I'm really sorry."

"No worries." I'll ask Grace. "Would anybody remember seeing you at the theater?"

"I doubt it."

"I understand you went for a walk after the movie."

"We did." He reads my look of displeasure. "It probably wasn't a great idea to be hanging out on Haight Street that late."

"No, it wasn't." My fatherly instinct to read him the riot act is trumped by my lawyerly training to remain calm. "Where did you go?"

"We walked over to Amoeba to look at CDs. It's a big place. We lost track of time."

"Did you buy anything?"

"No."

"How long were you there?"

"Until they closed at midnight."

"Did you go straight back to your car?"

"Yes." He says it was about a fifteen-minute walk.

"So you got back to the car around twelve fifteen?"

"Yes."

"Did you go inside your father's house when you got back to the car?"

"No."

"Was he home?"

"I don't know."

"Did you see his car?"

"No, but it could have been inside the garage."

"Did you drive straight back to Rosie's house?"

"Yes." He says they arrived a few minutes before one.

"Did you spend any time in the car after you got there?" It's my unsubtle way of asking whether they spent any time making out.

"Just a minute," he says quickly. "We knew we were in trouble."

Yes, you were. "Did you see Rosie?"

"Yes. She wasn't happy we got back so late."

Neither am I. I ask if he drove straight back to his father's house.

"Yes. I got there a few minutes after two. I parked around the corner, on Clayton."

"Grace tells me you and your father haven't been getting along so well."

He shifts uneasily. "What did she say?"

I get to ask the questions. "Not much. We don't gossip as much as we used to. She's been spending a lot of time with her boyfriend."

The corner of his mouth goes up slightly, but he doesn't respond.

"Is it fair to say you and your father have had your share of disagreements lately?"

He flashes the first sign of anger. "I didn't kill him, Mike."

I'd rather hear a vehement denial than a mealy mouthed explanation. Guilty people try to massage their story to fit the circumstances. Innocent people get mad. "You promised to be straight with me," I say.

He swallows. "We were barely talking."

"Why?"

"For starters, I didn't like the way he cheated on my mother."

"I take it you blame him for their divorce?"

"There was plenty of blame to go around, but the answer is yes. I wasn't crazy about the way he treated me, either. I'm a straight-A student. I'm an all-city baseball player. I'm the editor of the student paper. I got into Columbia. I look out for Sean. That wasn't good enough for him. *Nothing* was good enough for him."

Grace undoubtedly feels the same way about me sometimes.

Bobby's words start to flow faster as he becomes more agitated. "My father believed there were two sets of rules. The first applied to him. The second was for everybody else. It was bad enough when he was a lawyer. It got worse when he became a judge. Everybody kissed his butt. He expected the same at home."

"Did he ever hit you?"

"No."

"What about Sean?"

"No, but he was very hard on him. Sean likes to push the limits. He grew out his hair. He wears grungy clothes. He got his ears pierced. He hangs out on Haight Street with the goth kids from Urban High."

I can understand why Judge Fairchild may have been somewhat less than enthusiastic about his fifteen-year-old son wearing black clothes and sporting Satanist tattoos while loitering with his pals in the Haight. My parents expressed similar sentiments when I grew my hair to my shoulders and wore tattered jeans and psychedelic shirts in the sixties. "How far did Sean push the limits?"

His voice fills with brotherly affection. "Just far enough to tweak my father."

Certain elements of the parent-teenager relationship never change. "Drinking?"

"A little. Everybody does it."

So did we. My teachers at St. Ignatius must have known what was going on behind the bleachers at our football games. "What about drugs?"

"He might smoke a little weed, but he isn't into anything serious. Sean looks like an anarchist, but he's pretty careful. He gets good grades. He's never gotten into trouble."

"Did you talk to him last night?"

"No. Like I said, he was staying at Kerry's house. He lives down the street from the old Grateful Dead House. He looks like a freak, but he's a nice kid."

We'll talk to him. "How are things with your mother?"

"Okay." He thinks about it and adds, "She's already been through a lot with the divorce. This is going to be hard on her, too."

His concern seems genuine enough. "How were you and your mother getting along?"

"Better than I got along with my father. She's just as intense, but she's a little nicer about it. Things got better after my father moved out and they started communicating through their lawyers."

"Was he abusive to her?"

"He never hit her, but he gave her a lot of grief. They tried counseling, but that didn't work. Things got progressively worse until my mother decided she'd had enough."

I probe for additional details, but his relationship with his parents is clearly a difficult subject for him. "What happened when you got to your father's house?"

"I knew something was wrong right away. The front door was open."

"Did he have a security system?"

"Yes, but it wasn't turned on. Sean was the last one at the house. He doesn't always remember to turn it on. It drove my father nuts."

Teenagers. "What did you do after you went inside?"

"I flipped on the light. A small table and a coat rack were knocked over in the front hall."

"Was anything else vandalized?"

"I don't think so."

"Was anything missing?"

"I don't know. I called out to my father, but he didn't answer. I found him in the laundry room. He must have been coming in from the garage when somebody hit him in the head with a hammer. There was blood everywhere."

"Was it your hammer?"

"What difference does it make?"

"Just wondering." A professional killer probably would have brought his own equipment.

"Yes, it was ours," he says.

"Did you touch it?"

"I moved it when I tried to help my father. I picked it up and tried to give it to the cops when they arrived. They told me to put it down on the floor."

Which means his prints are probably on the murder weapon. "When did you call 911?"

"As soon as I found him." His eyes turn down. "The cops and the paramedics came right away, but my father was already gone. I tried to reach my mother, but she didn't answer her cell or her pager, so I left a message. She may have been in surgery. I tried Sean's cell, but he didn't answer, either. Then I called Grace."

"Inspector Johnson said you were uncooperative."

"I was upset."

"He also said there was blood on your hands."

"I told you I tried to help my father."

"What else did you tell him?"

"The same thing that I just told you."

"He said you told him your father got what he deserved."

"I don't remember."

"Did anybody have a grudge against your father?"

"He got death threats from people he'd put away. Things got bad during the Savage case. They put a police car in front of our house during the trial."

"Any threats in the past couple of weeks?"

"I don't know. He didn't always tell us."

"Did you notice anything different in his behavior?"

"Not really."

"What else can you tell me, Bobby? Any detail may be very important."

"During the Savage case, my father got a permit to carry a gun."

"Are you serious?"

"A lot of judges pack."

Given the number of recent attacks on judges, I guess it shouldn't surprise me. "Did he know how to use it?"

"Of course."

"Did he have it with him last night?"

"Yes."

"Loaded?"

"They're generally more effective that way."

I'll say. "He took a loaded gun to the Bohemian Club?"

"Do you think they were going to strip-search a judge?"

"Nope. And he took it to his girlfriend's house?"

"He took it everywhere."

I can see the headline in tomorrow's *Chronicle*: Murdered Judge Was Packing Heat. "Did he have the gun when you found him?"

He nods. "It was still in the shoulder harness. The police took it as evidence."

"Had he fired it?"

"Nope."

"Why didn't he use it?"

"Maybe he didn't have a chance."

Or maybe he was killed by somebody he knew. "Is it possible the killer sneaked up on him?"

"Maybe. The laundry room is pretty tight, but somebody could have hidden behind the door."

There's a knock. A clean-cut deputy lets himself inside. "Mr. Daley," he says, "your law partner and your client's mother are here. They'd like to see you right away."

Saturday, June 18, 4:38 a.m.

D r. Julie Fairchild's voice fills with maternal desperation. "Where's my son?"

"I'll take you inside to see him in a minute," I say. "We need you to stay calm."

"How can you expect me to stay calm?"

"I know you're upset, Julie. But if you lose it, he will, too."

The neurosurgeon wills herself to be composed. "Understood," she says.

We're standing in the vestibule outside the intake center of the Glamour Slammer. Julie is wearing a black Nike windbreaker over her surgical scrubs. From her short, highlighted blonde hair to her chiseled facial features, she's a study in intense precision. She attacks every aspect of her life with the same intensity that she approaches complex microsurgeries.

"How is he?" she asks.

"Okay," I say. Except he's in jail and he's been charged with murdering his father. "Did you find Sean?"

"Yes. We took him over to my house. My sister is staying with him. Grace is there, too." She quickly returns to the matter at hand. "How soon can you get the charges dropped?"

"It may take a while."

"How long is a while?"

"Anywhere from a couple of hours to a couple of days." Or maybe not at all.

Her voice gets louder. "You have to get my son out of here, Mike."

"We're doing everything we can."

"Do it faster."

I hold up a hand. "You may want to consider bringing in another attorney who doesn't have a personal relationship with Bobby."

"I want you to handle Bobby's case."

I quickly describe the possible conflicts of interest that may arise because of Grace's potential involvement in the case.

"Bobby trusts you," she says. "That's all that matters to me."

"We'll talk about it again later."

"That's fine." She moves full speed ahead. "It may take some time to get you a retainer. Money's been a little tight since we started the divorce proceedings."

"We'll worry about that later. It would help if you could put your hands on some funds for bail."

"Does that mean they've agreed to bail?"

"It means we're going to start looking for a judge."

Her eyes fill with disappointment. "Let me know how much you need," she says. "Whatever it takes."

"Bobby said he tried to call you."

"He did. I was up at the hospital handling an emergency surgery. I tried to call him as soon as I was finished, but he didn't answer."

"He was probably already on his way over here. What time did you go to the hospital?"

"Eleven o'clock. The surgery started at one fifteen."

"Were you there the entire time?"

This elicits an icy glare. "What are you suggesting?"

"You've watched enough cop shows to know they always start with the victim's spouse."

"I was at the hospital the entire time. Satisfied?"

"Yes." We'll double-check. "Bobby told me things were pretty tense between you and Jack."

"We hadn't spoken in months. We were handling our communications through our lawyers." She doesn't elaborate.

"Is there life insurance?"

"Yes."

"How much?"

"A lot."

"Did Jack change the beneficiaries after you filed divorce papers?"

"Not as far as I know."

Rosie and I exchange a quick glance. The cops are going to want to talk to her, too.

"Bobby told me Jack was carrying a gun last night," I say.

"Do you see why I was trying to get custody of the boys? Jack was getting more paranoid every day."

"Why didn't he use it?"

"Maybe he didn't have the chance."

"The police are going to say it was because he knew the killer."

"Let me make this very easy for you," Julie says. "You can rule out Bobby, Sean, and me. I want to see my son right now."

I turn to Rosie. "I'm going to take Julie inside. Why don't you start looking for a judge."

"I will." As I'm about to escort Julie toward the intake center, Rosie pulls me aside and whispers, "Meet me in the lobby as soon as you can. Julie didn't tell you everything."

Saturday, June 18, 5:06 a.m.

Rosie is waiting for me in the cavernous lobby of the Hall after I return from an emotional meeting between Bobby and his mother. During the daytime, this area is crowded with police, attorneys, judges, jurors, witnesses, and other hangers-on. At the moment, it's eerily silent. "Where's Julie?" she asks.

"On her way to see Sean," I say. "There's nothing she can do here."

"How did it go with Bobby?"

"They didn't say much. It's hard to have a meaningful discussion through a Plexiglas divider with a guard breathing down your neck. Did you find a judge?"

"Yes. Betsy McDaniel was on call."

This is reasonably positive news. Judge Elizabeth McDaniel is a conscientious and good-natured Superior Court veteran who attends yoga classes with Rosie. "Is she willing to consider bail?" I ask.

"She said we can talk about it at the arraignment. It's set for ten o'clock this morning."

"That's quick."

"Nicole smells blood—and TV time."

Nicole Ward is a strident publicity hound and photogenic law-and-order zealot who doubles as the District Attorney of the City and

County of San Francisco. Nowadays, our resident media darling is devoting much of her energy to a divisive and mean-spirited re-election campaign. The latest polls show her running neck-and-neck against a former subordinate whom she unceremoniously canned after he committed the unforgivable political sin of endorsing her opponent in her last divisive, mean-spirited—and ultimately successful—run for DA. For those of us who view San Francisco politics as a spectator sport combining the most entertaining elements of roller derby, pro wrestling, and reality TV, it doesn't get any better.

"Did you talk to her?" I ask.

"Get real, Mike. Media stars like Nicole don't talk to peons like us. She's called a press briefing in a little while. She'll be the lead on the morning news shows."

Ward has a knack for finding media time. "Did you get anything from Betsy?"

"They're going to charge Bobby as an adult. We can fight it, but we'll lose."

She's right. Bobby picked an inconvenient time to celebrate his eighteenth birthday. "Did Betsy know the charge?"

"First degree murder."

"It's a bluff." Prosecutors frequently overcharge as a negotiating ploy to extract a plea bargain for something less. "Nicole will never be able to prove premeditation. She'll go down to manslaughter."

"Not for killing a judge in an election year."

"Maybe Betsy is trying to push us to cut a deal."

"Betsy McDaniel isn't Putty Chandler. She isn't going to play games or pimp Nicole's case just to get a quick resolution or lighten her workload."

Rosie's instincts are usually right. "Bobby told me Julie hired a PI who found out Jack was rolling around with his law clerk."

"That's true. Among his many qualities, Jack was a highly accomplished and insatiable philanderer. Julie has dropped almost a half million bucks in legal fees on the divorce—and they aren't any closer to a settlement than they were six months ago."

In hindsight, Rosie and I handled our separation with greater finesse than I originally realized. We weren't being magnanimous; we didn't have more than a handful of assets worth fighting about.

"In some respects," Rosie continues, "Jack and Julie were mirror images of each other. Jack was a hardass who became a high-powered lawyer and then an even higher-powered judge. Julie's a super-achiever who became a heavy-hitter at UCSF. They're used to having things their own way. The divorce has turned into a clash of egos exacerbated by serial adultery."

Not a pretty combination. "Julie can afford any defense lawyer in the Bay Area," I say. "Why is she so adamant about hiring us?"

"Because we're good."

"Come on, Rosie. Hotshot surgeons don't hire defense attorneys who practice law in an office above a Mexican restaurant."

"For one, she knows us. For two, we're available immediately. For three, Bobby trusts us. For four, we come highly recommended."

"By whom?"

The corner of her mouth turns up slightly. "Jack."

"You're kidding."

"I'm not. He told Julie that he wouldn't invite us for a drink at the Bohemian Club, but he'd call us first if he ever got into serious trouble."

You never know.

"There's more," she says. "Guess where Julie was before she went to the hospital last night."

"I would assume she was at home."

"Then you would be wrong. She was at her boyfriend's house. Evidently, Jack wasn't the only one getting a little action on the side."

"How long has this been going on?"

"A couple of months. I'm guessing it wasn't her first extra-marital relationship, either."

Jack and Julie were more alike than I realized. "Bobby didn't mention it."

"He doesn't know about it. Neither does Sean. Julie figured it would come out now. It's another reason she wants us to handle it. We'll be discreet."

"We can't be *that* discreet. They're going to find out. It would be better if Bobby and Sean heard about it from her."

"I promised I wouldn't say anything until she had a chance to talk to them."

"When is she planning to do that?"

"Soon."

"It had better be *very* soon. Does the boyfriend have a name?"

"Dr. Derek Newsom. He's doing a fellowship in neurosurgery at UCSF."

"He's one of Julie's students?"

"Yes. Before you ask, he's a lot younger than Julie." Rosie flashes a knowing smile. "It's very fashionable for mature women to date younger men."

"Don't get any ideas."

"I'm perfectly happy with my current boy toy."

"Was this some sort of twisted tit-for-tat thing to get back at Jack for doing his clerk?"

"Probably."

"Is he married?"

"Divorced. No kids. He lives on Willard, down the hill from UCSF."

"Did he go up to the hospital with her?"

"No. Julie said he'd just gotten home from a long shift. He was exhausted."

"Evidently, he still had enough energy to have a roll with her. Can anybody corroborate his whereabouts after she left?"

"Probably not. He lives by himself."

Except when he's busy with Bobby's mother. "I presume there could be consequences up at UCSF for Julie and young Dr. Newsom if this becomes a matter of public record?"

"That's not our problem, Mike. It's our job to represent Bobby— even if his mother has decided to turn her life into an episode of *Grey's Anatomy*."

"We need to check out her Dr. McDreamy. Did you get the name of her PI?"

She can't contain a smile. "Kaela Joy."

Kaela Joy Gullion is a statuesque former model and ex-Niners cheerleader who used to be married to an offensive lineman. We've worked with her on a couple of cases. It has never been dull. Her career as a PI got off to an auspicious start when she caught her husband in bed with another woman in a French Quarter brothel the night before a Niners-Saints game. She knocked him unconscious with a single punch in the middle of Bourbon Street. A tourist caught it on video. "The Punch" is still one of the most widely viewed items on YouTube.

"Any chance she was watching Jack last night?" I ask.

"We'll find out. I left her a message."

My mind races as I try to sort out this new information. I measure my words carefully. "Are you sure you want to do this?"

"Bobby wants us," she says. "So does Julie."

"We barely know them."

"Grace wants us to help him. She was a basket case when we drove over to get Sean."

"She was also with Bobby last night. There could be a conflict of interest."

Rosie turns defensive. "Are you saying she was involved?"

"She was there. That makes her a person of interest and a potential alibi witness."

"That doesn't create a legal conflict."

"That doesn't make it a good idea. This could get ugly if we represent Bobby and things go sideways."

Rosie's full lips turn down. "Do you really think it's possible Bobby killed his father?"

"We wouldn't be doing our jobs if we didn't consider the possibility. We can't ignore the fact that Grace is going to be involved in this investigation in some capacity. That's where our primary loyalties lie."

"I agree. That doesn't mean we can't take the case."

"I have a gut feeling we're looking for trouble."

"That's what lawyers do. Bobby wants us to represent him. Grace was begging me to help him. How can we say no?"

"Because it may be the right thing to do."

The managing partner of Fernandez and Daley takes a deep breath as she considers our options. "We'll withdraw if there's a conflict of interest."

"You know that's easier said than done. I still think it's better to have Bobby hire somebody else."

"We'll pull out if things start to go off the rails."

"You're sure?"

"I'm sure."

I'm not. "Okay," I say. "I'm in." For now.

The door to the nearby stairwell swings open and Roosevelt Johnson's commanding presence appears. "I thought I might find you here," he says. "Our District Attorney would like to have a word with you."

Saturday, June 18, 5:28 a.m.

Our mediagenic District Attorney flashes the slightly worn but still radiant Julia Roberts smile that's served her admirably for more years than she would care to admit. Nicole Ward is a capable prosecutor. She's a truly gifted politician. "Thank you for coming in on such short notice," she purrs.

"Inspector Johnson said you wanted to see us."

"I did." She tosses her long auburn locks over her right shoulder and places her hands together as she sits behind her inlaid rosewood desk in her sterile office in the southwest corner of the third floor of the Hall. Her Calvin Klein ensemble is always perfectly accessorized. Rosie says Ward can leap into designer pumps faster than Superman can put on his cape. "I've heard rumors you're going back to the PD's Office."

There are no secrets in the Hall. "That one's been making the rounds for years," I say.

"Any chance it's true this time?"

"We're here to talk about Bobby Fairchild."

"That doesn't sound like a denial." Her voice oozes pure cane sugar. "It would be a good move for you and a great addition to the PD's Office."

"That's very flattering." It would be even more so if I thought she meant it. "From what I've read in the papers, it looks like you're going to win another term."

"That's the hope," she coos. The fake smile broadens. "I trust I can count on your vote."

"Sorry. We're registered in Marin."

"Tell your friends who live on this side of the Golden Gate that I would appreciate their support."

I think I'm going to puke.

"So," Ward continues, "given your potential career change, will you have time to deal with the Fairchild case?"

"Absolutely. Given the demands of your campaign, will you?"

"Of course. I've already assigned Bill McNulty to take the lead. I believe you've worked with him several times."

"We have." This news comes as no surprise. McNulty is the combative and highly effective head of the felony division who has earned the moniker "McNasty" from the defense bar. What he lacks in charisma he makes up for in tenacity and thoroughness. He'd bang his head against a brick wall a thousand times if Ward asked him to do it.

Ward glances at her watch. "I can't chat for long," she says. "I've promised to do a media briefing."

You wouldn't want to keep your public waiting. "Mind giving us a few hints on what you plan to tell them?"

The fake smile transforms into an expression of feigned empathy. "This is a great tragedy," she says. "I knew Jack Fairchild. I tried several cases before him. He was a thoughtful and conscientious judge. His son has committed a very serious crime. Regrettably, we'll have to file first-degree murder charges."

I can tell you're heartbroken. "You can't be serious," I say. "He's a kid."

"I'm afraid I am. We have more than enough evidence to move forward to trial."

"Could you be a bit more specific?"

"You'll get everything in due course."

This tap dance is one of the least-satisfying elements of my job. "You have a legal obligation to provide us with evidence that might exonerate our client," I say.

"In due course," she repeats. She arches an eyebrow. "There is one piece of information I wanted to pass along right away. We've found a witness who heard your client and his father arguing quite heatedly yesterday morning."

"Does the witness have a name?"

"For purposes of this discussion, no. As a matter of professional courtesy, however, I feel obligated to inform you they were fighting about your daughter. Evidently, Judge Fairchild thought your client and your daughter were spending too much time together."

So do I. "Are you suggesting Grace is involved in Judge Fairchild's death?"

"I'm not suggesting anything. I'm simply pointing out she may be involved in this case. You may wish to consider whether it would be advisable to bring in another attorney who doesn't have a personal relationship with any of the participants."

She's trying to squeeze us. "Thanks for bringing it to our attention," I say.

"You're welcome. Our witness also told us your client threatened his father."

"What did he say?"

She makes little quotation signs with her fingers. "That he was going to make him pay."

"Teenagers argue with their parents all the time. Judge Fairchild had a lot of enemies. He got death threats during the Savage trial. He was so concerned that he got a permit to carry a gun."

"He wasn't the only judge in town who carried a weapon."

"The others are still walking around."

"Judge Fairchild would be, too, if your client hadn't killed him. The gun was still in its holster when the police arrived."

"The killer obviously took him by surprise."

"Or he knew the killer—his own son."

"It could have been a robbery," I say. "The house was vandalized."

"There was no evidence of forced entry."

"The killer could have stolen the key or jimmied the lock."

"Look at the evidence, Mike. Your client was holding the murder weapon when the police arrived. His hands were covered with blood. He was uncooperative."

"He tried to help his father. He was upset."

"I'll let you try that story on the jury."

"Did you consider the possibility this might be related to the Savage case?"

"We have no evidence pointing in that direction at this time."

Rosie finally decides to make her presence felt. "You didn't call us down here to argue about the evidence," she says. "Why did you really want to see us?"

"I have a proposition for you."

I figured this was coming.

Ward's kitten voice reappears. "I'm prepared to go down to second-degree murder. Given your client's youth and lack of a criminal record, I'll recommend a light sentence."

"How light?"

"You know I can't go for less than fifteen years."

It's the minimum for second-degree murder. "Not a chance," I say. "I'll never be able to sell it to him."

"You mean you won't *try* to sell it. It's an open-and-shut case."

In my experience, when a prosecutor says a case is open-and-shut, it isn't. "No deal," I tell her.

"It's in everybody's best interests—including your client's and your daughter's—to resolve this matter quickly. It will serve no useful purpose to put your client and his family through the ordeal of a long trial. Not to mention the fact that it will save the taxpayers a lot of money."

"And it's good politics," I say.

"This has nothing to do with the election. Maybe your client got angry and panicked. Maybe it happened so fast he didn't realize what he was doing. He's still a young man. If he pleads, he'll be out when he's in his early thirties. It's a good deal, Mike."

"We may have something to talk about if you're willing to go down to manslaughter," I say. It's a bluff.

"Not for killing a judge. That's *bad* politics."

"The victim's job title has nothing to do with the appropriateness of the charge. What you just laid out was classic manslaughter. Give us something to work with."

"I can't go below second degree. You have a legal obligation to take it back to your client. This offer will stay open only until the arraignment. After that, all bets are off."

Saturday, June 18, 5:42 a.m.

"**N**o deal," Bobby whispers. "I'm not going to plead guilty to a crime I didn't commit."

The consultation room's drab green walls haven't seen a fresh coat of paint since the Carter Administration. "We might be able to persuade the DA to reduce the charges to manslaughter," I say, looking for a reaction.

"I don't care if they drop it to jaywalking. I didn't do it."

It's the type of response I was hoping for. "Did they give you your own cell?" I ask.

"Not yet."

Damn it. A clean-cut kid like Bobby will be an easy target among the career felons, drug dealers, and pimps in the lockup at the Glamour Slammer. "I'll talk to them as soon as we're done."

"You have to get me out of here, Mike."

"I will."

He takes a deep breath in an attempt to calm himself. "Is Sean all right?"

"He's okay," I lie. I have no idea. "He's at your mother's house."

"How's Grace?"

"She's okay, too. She's with Sean."

He swallows. "Tell her I say hi."

I'm impressed by his concern for his brother and his girlfriend. "I will."

"What happens next?"

"They've scheduled an arraignment at ten o'clock." I explain the perfunctory proceeding that starts the legal process. "I want you to look the judge right in the eye and plead not guilty in a clear and respectful voice."

"Can you get the charges dropped?"

"We'll try, but it's unlikely."

"What about bail?"

"It depends." I put a hand on his shoulder. "If the DA charges you with first-degree murder, bail will be more difficult."

His voice starts to rise. "Then what?"

"They have to schedule a preliminary hearing within ten days."

"Can you ask for bail again?"

"Yes." The chances won't be much better at the prelim.

He starts drumming the tabletop with his fingers. "Can you get the charges dropped at the prelim?" he asks, his tone turning more agitated.

"Maybe, but it will be a battle. The DA just has to show there's a reasonable basis to suggest you committed a crime. We'll try to show there isn't. The judge will give the prosecutors the benefit of the doubt."

"Do you think we're going to trial?"

"It's too soon to tell. We have to be prepared for the possibility."

"How soon would that happen?"

"We can ask for a trial within sixty days. It's usually better to waive that requirement to have more time to prepare." And to stall.

"So if we don't get bail, I could be here for months?"

Welcome to the criminal justice system. "Hopefully not."

"I can't be in here for months, Mike. I'll never make it to trial. If you don't get me out of here, they're going to kill me."

#

The sun is coming up, but Rosie and I are glum as we hustle down the front steps of the Hall at twenty after six. We just sat through Ward's beautifully orchestrated media briefing. Shamelessly pandering to the cameras, she offered easily digestible sound bites about the uncontro-verted evidence proving beyond any shadow of a doubt that Bobby killed his father. Give her credit—she knows how to work the media. Her face will be the lead on every news outlet in the Bay Area for the next couple of days. After the show, Rosie and I tried not to sound too smarmy as we mouthed the usual defense-lawyer platitudes about the unsubstantiated charges and the rush to judgment taking place before our very eyes.

A familiar face is waiting for us when we arrive at Rosie's car. "I thought you held your own at Nicole's briefing," Roosevelt says.

"Defense lawyers always end up on the short end of the battle of the sound bites," I say.

"The cops generally don't fare any better."

The wisdom of experience. "I take it this isn't entirely a social call?"

"I need to talk to your daughter."

"In due course."

"Due course is now."

Rosie gives him the Glare. "We'll bring Grace down at the right time," she says.

"The right time is right now. Don't put us in a position where we have to take legal action to bring her in."

"Don't put us in a position where we have to take legal action to stop the harassment of our daughter."

Roosevelt glances around to make sure nobody is watching us. "I got a call from a patrol car in Cole Valley," he says. "Julie Fairchild returned home a little while ago."

"You had somebody follow her?"

"Honestly, no."

"This is more than a coincidence, Roosevelt."

"She lives a few blocks from her husband. We have people in the vicinity. If my guess is correct, Grace is there with Sean."

There is nothing to be gained by lying. "She is."

"As a matter of professional courtesy, I have instructed our officers not to knock on the door until after I talked to you. As a matter of personal courtesy, I'm prepared to wait until you've spoken to Grace and Sean—as long as you promise to let them talk to me as soon as you're finished."

He's holding the cards. "Fair enough," I say.

"Where are you?" Pete asks.

"On our way to Julie's house," I tell him. The reception on my cell phone fades as Rosie and I drive up Market Street. "Have you been able to get inside Judge Fairchild's house?"

"Not yet. The cops are still working the scene. I talked to a couple of the neighbors. As far as I can tell, the judge kept to himself."

"Did anybody see him come home last night?"

"Nope. Nobody saw a murder, either."

Great. "According to our distinguished District Attorney, somebody heard Bobby fighting with his father yesterday morning."

"Nobody mentioned it to me."

"It also seems Jack and Julie weren't exactly Ozzie and Harriet." He listens intently as I fill him in. "We need to verify that Julie was up at the hospital after eleven o'clock last night. We also need to confirm the whereabouts of her boyfriend."

"I'll take care of it." He shifts gears. "I know a guy who tends bar at the Bohemian Club. He said Judge Fairchild had dinner at the Club and left around ten forty-five."

"By himself?"

"Yes."

"Did he know where the judge went?"

"No."

#

"We're so sorry about your father," Rosie says to Sean.

Bobby's younger brother looks at her through glassy, lifeless eyes. "Thanks," he whispers.

He's a more slender version of Bobby, with softer features, unkempt sideburns, and shoulder-length hair that's a half-shade lighter than his torn black T-shirt and tattered black jeans. He's sitting at the glass table in his mother's high-tech kitchen, which looks out of place in her refurbished Victorian on the corner of Seventeenth and Shrader, four blocks from Judge Fairchild's house. Grace is upstairs watching TV with Julie's sister. Roosevelt is waiting impatiently in an unmarked car on the street.

Rosie starts slowly. "We're here to help," she says. "I know this is difficult, but we need to ask you a few questions."

"Okay."

"Did you see your father last night?"

"Nope."

"Did you talk to him?"

"Nope."

This process will be excruciatingly slow if he insists on responding with one-word answers. "When was the last time you spoke to him?" Rosie asks.

"Yesterday morning. I told him I was going to stay at Kerry's house last night."

"That was okay with him?"

"He didn't care. It isn't as if he spent a lot of time with us."

"What time did you go to Kerry's house?"

"Around eight."

"Did you come from home?"

"Yep."

"Was anybody else at home when you left?"

"Nope." His arms are crossed. Still no eye contact.

"Had you been home all evening?"

"Yep."

Julie has been sitting across from him throughout this discussion, her intense eyes locked onto her son's. He hasn't acknowledged her presence.

"Do you remember if you turned the alarm on when you left?" I ask.

He scowls. "Probably not. Is that a problem?"

"It's okay, Sean. Did you go straight to Kerry's house?"

"Yep."

"Were his parents home?"

"He lives with his mother. She didn't get home until one."

This gets Julie's attention. "You were by yourselves until one o'clock?"

"It's fine, Mother."

In my experience, when a teenager describes something as "fine," it usually isn't.

Julie's tone turns acerbic. "It isn't the first time Kerry's mother has been asleep at the switch."

Sean gives her a look as if to say, *The same could be said about you.* "She's a nurse, Mother. She was at work. It wasn't a big deal."

"Yes, it was."

Rosie tries to keep the discussion on point. "What did you do at Kerry's?" she asks.

"We played video games and listened to music."

"Did anybody else come over?"

"Nope."

"Did you go out?"

"Nope."

"Not even for dinner?"

"Nope. We ordered pizza."

Rosie leans in closer. "Sean," she says softly, "did you and Kerry do any funny stuff?"

"What do you mean?"

"Beer? Wine? Booze?"

Sean darts an almost imperceptible glance at his mother. "Nope."

"What about dope?"

Sean responds with an indignant, "I don't do that stuff."

"Does Kerry?"

"Nope."

Julie's protective instincts kick in. "Is this necessary?"

"The police are going to ask him a lot of questions," Rosie says. "I want to avoid any surprises." She's also looking for a reaction.

Sean shakes his head a little too emphatically. "I don't do that stuff," he repeats. "Neither does Kerry."

Rosie takes his response in stride. "Did you talk to Bobby last night?" she asks.

"I sent him a text that I was at Kerry's."

"He said he tried to call you after he found your father."

"I was asleep. I didn't get the message until after he had been taken downtown."

"Will Kerry confirm everything you just told us?"

"Yep."

"Are we finished?" Julie asks.

"For now," Rosie says.

# # #

"Where did you go after the movie?" Rosie asks Grace.

"How many times do we have to go through this?"

"Once more."

Rosie and I are sitting on the black leather sofa beneath two rows of framed diplomas in Julie's immaculate home office. Grace is sitting on a matching side chair. Sean is hunkered down in his room. Julie is with him. Roosevelt is still outside chomping at the bit.

Grace exhales heavily. "We went for a walk."

"Where?"

"I already told you. We went to Amoeba, then back to the car."

Rosie shoots a glance in my direction, then her eyes lock onto Grace's. "We understand Sean sent Bobby a text about a party at Kerry's house."

This is a decidedly different spin on Sean's story. Rosie is playing a hunch.

Graces shakes her head. "There was no party, Mother. Sean texted Bobby that he was staying at Kerry's house. That's it."

"You didn't mention it earlier."

"What's the big deal?"

"You should have told me about it."

"Nothing was going on, Mother."

"Did you go to Kerry's house?"

"No."

"I'm not going to get mad at you, Grace."

"We didn't go to Kerry's house, Mother."

"If there's anything else that we should know, this would be an excellent time to tell us."

"There's nothing, Mother."

Rosie's stilted nod indicates she isn't satisfied. She looks my way for help.

"Grace," I say, "did you notice anything unusual around Bobby's father's house when you went to get the car?"

"Not really."

"Think hard, honey."

She ponders for a moment. "Some idiot parked his car very close to Bobby's. It was practically touching Bobby's front bumper. It was parked in front of the fire hydrant."

"Was there a ticket on the windshield?"

"Of course not."

"Do you remember what kind of car it was?"

"A big, boxy American car."

"Do you remember what make?"

"I'm not sure. I wasn't paying attention."

Saturday, June 18, 7:22 a.m.

We're sitting at Julie's kitchen table, where Roosevelt is questioning our daughter with the gentleness of a grandfather. He was equally patient with Sean.

"What color was the car?" he asks.

"Gray," Grace says.

"Did you notice anything unusual about it? Was it dented or missing a light?"

"I didn't notice."

"Did you happen to pick up any part of the license plate?"

"I'm sorry."

"That's okay, honey. You're doing fine."

I interject politely. "Any chance it was an unmarked police car?"

"No," Roosevelt says, never taking his eyes off Grace. "What time did you see this car?"

Grace swallows hard. "About twelve fifteen."

"Was anybody in it?"

"No."

"Was Judge Fairchild home?"

"I don't know."

"Were the lights on inside the house?"

"I don't remember."

"Did you see Judge Fairchild's car?"

"No, but it may have been in the garage."

"Did you see anybody inside the house?"

"No."

"Did you see anybody leave the house?"

"No."

Roosevelt sighs. "Gracie," he says, "did you or Bobby go inside Judge Fairchild's house when you got back to the car?"

"No."

"You're sure?"

"I'm sure."

Roosevelt waits an interminable moment. "Anything else you want to tell me, Gracie?"

"I've told you everything, Roosevelt."

He gives her one more chance. "You're absolutely sure?"

"Absolutely sure."

# # #

"What did you make of that?" Rosie asks as soon as Roosevelt leaves.

"Grace was poised. Roosevelt was discreet."

"I agree."

"Is there a but coming?"

"Roosevelt knows more than he's letting on," she says.

"What makes you think so?"

"Lawyer's intuition." Her expression changes to one of concern. She adds, "Grace hasn't told us everything."

"How can you tell?"

"Mother's intuition."

12/ DOES YOUR CLIENT UNDERSTAND THE CHARGES?

Saturday, June 18, 10:01 a.m.

"All rise."

The sweltering utilitarian courtroom on the second floor of the Hall of Justice comes to life as Judge Elizabeth McDaniel walks purposefully to her high-backed leather chair. She's a thoughtful jurist whose maternal nature and soft-spoken drawl complement an intense intellect and an unyielding desire to be fair. She expects the lawyers who appear before her to be prepared and concise—a standard she applies even more rigorously to herself. She doesn't need to bang her gavel to silence her courtroom. All it takes is a raised eyebrow.

"Be seated," she says.

The standing-room-only crowd settles into the five rows of hard-backed seats. The local news outlets are well-represented. The sketch artists in the back row have their pencils poised.

Rosie and I take our seats at the defense table. Bobby is sitting between us. His hair is combed, but his orange jumpsuit makes him look guilty of something. Julie is sitting directly behind us in the gallery. She's surrounded by the always-tactful members of the fourth estate. Grace and Sean are at Julie's house. We decided to minimize the chances of an emotional outburst.

Bobby leans over to me. "You have to get me out of here," he whispers. There is no sense of entitlement in his voice. It's pure desperation.

"We're doing everything we can." I realize my answer isn't especially reassuring.

Judge McDaniel dons her reading glasses and switches on her microphone. She looks at the prosecution table, where a radiant Nicole Ward is sitting next to a grim Bill McNulty. It's hard to find two lawyers with more contrasting—yet effective—styles. The charismatic Ward is a shameless grandstander. The owlish McNulty is a meticulous craftsman. "Is the prosecution prepared to proceed?" the judge asks.

Ward stands. "Yes, Your Honor. I will be addressing the court on behalf of the People."

She never misses a photo op. McNasty will undoubtedly sit first-chair at the trial—if we get that far. Ward wants to stay focused on her campaign and McNulty has both the expertise and the stamina for trial work. More important, she can lob the blame over to him if things go south.

"Mr. Daley," the judge says, "does your client understand the charges?"

"Yes, Your Honor."

"How does he plead?"

"If we might take a moment to discuss a couple of preliminary issues."

Ward is still standing. "Your Honor," she says, "the sole purpose of this proceeding is for the defendant to enter a plea. We can address other issues at the appropriate time."

"Your Honor—" I say.

Judge McDaniel cuts me off. "I need your client's plea, Mr. Daley."

I nudge Bobby. As he stands, I whisper, "Be respectful, but firm."

He clears his throat and musters a barely audible, "Not guilty."

"Excuse me, Mr. Fairchild?"

He's a little too loud the second time. "Not guilty, Your Honor."

"Thank you."

Bobby sits down as the judge recites the standard catechism to record the plea. Several reporters quickly head to the door to file the first news reports—as if the not-guilty plea was any surprise.

"Your Honor," I say, "we would like to take a moment to discuss bail."

Ward pops up again. "The People oppose bail."

"Your Honor," I say, "my client is an exemplary young man with substantial ties to the community. He has lived here his entire life and will stay with his mother. He recently graduated with honors from University High School and will attend Columbia University in the fall. He is prepared to surrender his passport and wear an electronic monitoring device. In the interests of justice and fair play, we respectfully request that bail be set in a reasonable amount."

Ward is still on her feet. "Your Honor," she says, "the defendant stands accused of murdering a sitting judge. Bail is inappropriate in a first-degree murder case."

"The judge always has discretion to set bail," I reply.

Ward isn't giving an inch. "The defendant has the means and the wherewithal to flee. It's also a matter of public safety to keep a murderer off our streets."

"Alleged murderer," I correct her.

"Alleged murderer," she repeats with sarcasm. "Your Honor, it is more than just a bad idea to set bail in this case. It's illegal."

Judge McDaniel raises an eyebrow. "How do you figure, Ms. Ward?"

"Section 1270.5 of the Penal Code prohibits bail in connection with a capital case."

What the hell? "Who said anything about a capital case?" I ask.

"I just did."

I turn to my left and see the panic in Bobby's eyes. I turn back to the judge and say, "May we approach the bench, Your Honor?"

"Yes, Mr. Daley."

We make the pilgrimage to the front of the courtroom, where Judge McDaniel turns off her microphone. "What is it, Mr. Daley?"

"Nobody said anything to us about this being a capital case."

"He killed a judge," Ward says. "He was lying in wait. That's a special circumstance."

It's California's euphemism for a death penalty case. "He's a kid," I say.

"He's no longer a minor," Ward says. "He's therefore eligible for the death penalty."

"He just turned eighteen," I say. "No jury is going to impose the death penalty on a young man with no criminal record."

"It is within our prosecutorial discretion to file a first-degree murder charge with a special circumstance even if a jury elects not to impose the death penalty. We believe Your Honor will see the benefit of sending a clear message that we take the killing of a judge very seriously."

Ward's predecessor was voted out of office after she didn't ask for the death penalty in a cop-killing case. Ward isn't going to make the same mistake—especially in an election year.

I strike an indignant tone. "This is just a grandstand play. It's a blatant attempt to try to squeeze us into a plea bargain."

"It's nothing of the sort," Ward insists.

Judge McDaniel stops us with an upraised hand. "For the purposes of this proceeding, I am required to resolve all ambiguities in favor of the prosecution. For now, the defendant stands charged on a first-degree murder count with a special circumstance. The defense is entitled to file motions in due course to contest the appropriateness of the charges."

"But, Your Honor—"

"I'll look forward to reading your papers, Mr. Daley."

Her signal is clear: she can't do anything about it today, but she isn't happy about Ward's attempt to turn this into a capital case.

"Your Honor," I say, "that still leaves open the possibility of bail."

"Not in a capital case," Ward says. "Section 1270.5 of the Penal Code says a defendant charged with an offense punishable by death cannot be admitted to bail when the proof of his guilt is evident or the presumption thereof is great."

"Your Honor," I say, "this offense is not punishable by death."

"It is until you file your papers, Mr. Daley."

"The proof of his guilt is not evident and the presumption thereof is not great."

Judge McDaniel gives me a sympathetic look. "You're free to make that argument in your papers," she says. "I have no choice, Mr. Daley. For now, bail is denied."

My anger is exacerbated by Ward's smug grin. "Your Honor," I say, "my client's life has been threatened in the San Francisco County Jail. We request that you order the Sheriff's Department to house him in a separate cell."

"Your Honor," Ward says, "I can assure you the Sheriff's Department will take all necessary steps to ensure the defendant's safety."

Judge McDaniel throws us a bone. "That's going to include his own cell, Ms. Ward."

"But, Your Honor—"

"Listen to me carefully, Ms. Ward. I am holding you personally responsible for the defendant's safety. You're going to make arrangements with the Sheriff's Department to ensure that he is detained separately from the rest of the prison population. He will have a guarded escort whenever he leaves his cell for meals and exercise. Understood?"

"Yes, Your Honor."

It's a small victory. "Your Honor," I say, "we further ask you to impose a complete media blackout on all parties involved in this case." It's a blatant attempt to tweak Ward. A gag order in an election year is almost as bad as an acquittal.

Ward can barely contain herself. "Your Honor," she says, "the public has a right to be fully informed of developments in this case."

"They aren't going to hear about it from you."

"But, Your Honor—"

"Let me make this simple for you, Ms. Ward. I am imposing a gag order on everyone involved in this case. If I see either of you talking to the press or appearing on TV, I'm going to fine you and send you to jail. Period."

"But, Your Honor—"

"Don't push me on this issue, Ms. Ward. Anything else, Mr. Daley?"

"We would like to schedule a preliminary hearing as soon as possible."

"I understand the urgency, but I want you to have adequate time to prepare."

"Bobby Fairchild shouldn't be forced to stay in jail on these egregious and unsubstantiated charges. He has a statutory right to a preliminary hearing within ten days. We'd like to schedule it sooner if possible."

The judge takes a moment to study her calendar. "I might be able to squeeze you in at ten o'clock on Wednesday morning."

That's quick. "We'll be ready, Your Honor."

"Your Honor," Ward says, "we've just started our investigation. It will strain the resources of our office to prepare for a preliminary hearing on such short notice."

"It didn't strain your resources when you filed charges and demanded this proceeding on short notice, Ms. Ward."

"A prelim requires more preparation than an arraignment."

"That's why I'm giving you until Wednesday."

# # #

Julie's frustration bubbles to the surface in the empty courtroom after Bobby is led out. "That was a disaster," she says to me.

"We're doing everything we can," I tell her.

"You're doing great so far. You couldn't get the charges dropped. You didn't get bail. You couldn't stop Ward from turning this into a death penalty case."

"She's playing to the press," I say. "She's overreaching to try to get us to consider a plea bargain."

"That's out of the question."

"I agree." I lower my voice. "The prosecutors always have the advantage at this stage. The special circumstance will never stick."

"The murder charge better not stick, either."

"It won't."

"You'd better be right."

"You have to trust us, Julie."

"Then get your asses in gear and get Bobby out of jail."

Enough. "We've already told you it might be a good idea to hire another lawyer. For what it's worth, this would be a good time to do it. Bobby won't be back in court until Wednesday."

"Bobby and I want you to handle this case," she says. Her anger is replaced by the steely eyed calm of a surgeon. "What do we do next?"

I'm beginning to tire of the whole passive-aggressive thing. "We have until Wednesday morning to gather as much information as we can for the prelim. I want you to go back to our office with Rosie and tell her everything you can about your husband. We need a list of his friends, neighbors, colleagues, co-workers, lovers, and, most important, enemies—especially anybody who may have had a grudge. We'll feed the information to Pete, who is already talking to people in Cole Valley. We should also consider the possibility of bringing in a psychiatrist to do some testing."

"You think Bobby is crazy?"

"No, but we may want to consider one or more psychological defenses."

"My son isn't going to plead insanity."

"But, Julie—"

"It's out of the question. It would ruin his future. What else?"

"We need to talk to your boyfriend and your private investigator."

"I'll tell them to cooperate. Where are you going now?"

"To talk to the Chief Medical Examiner."

13/ THAT CHANGES EVERYTHING

The Chief Medical Examiner of the City and County of San Francisco strokes his trim gray beard. "Nice to see you again, Mr. Daley," he lies politely.

"Same here, Dr. Beckert," I reply with comparable feigned sincerity.

Dr. Roderick Beckert has been examining corpses in a cluttered, windowless office in the basement of the Hall of Justice for almost forty years. The dean of big-city coroners is also an emeritus professor of pathology at UCSF. He wrote a widely used treatise on forensic science and is called upon frequently as an expert witness in other jurisdictions. He's announced his retirement effective at the end of the year.

I look around at the rows of test tubes and the bookcases lined with heavily used medical texts. Framed snapshots of his grandchildren sit atop medical journals stacked neatly on his overburdened credenza. A life-sized model skeleton smiles at me from under a Giants baseball cap.

Good manners are always essential in dealing with Beckert. "Thank you for taking the time to see me."

"You're welcome." He absentmindedly adjusts the sleeves of his starched white lab coat. "I was afraid I wasn't going to have an opportunity to work with you on another case."

I sense your profound disappointment. "Are you really going to retire?"

"Yes." He looks at the photos of his grandkids. "I've spent a lot of time with dead bodies over the years. I'd like to spend more time with the living."

"They grow up fast," I say.

"Yes, they do. Are you really going back to the PD's Office, Mike?"

We've been on opposite sides of a dozen cases over the years. It's the first time he's ever addressed me by my first name. "I don't know," I tell him honestly. "My career plans seem to be a hot topic around here."

His brown eyes twinkle. "Most of the people in this building are horrendously overworked and ridiculously underpaid. Gossip is the only thing they can't take away from us." The sincerity in his voice is genuine when he adds, "You were a good PD."

"Thanks."

"I mean it. I haven't always agreed with your tactics, but the system needs people like you and Rosie. You keep Nicole honest."

Now I know he's serious about retiring. "Thanks, Dr. Beckert."

He gives me a grandfatherly smile. "From now on, it's Rod."

Go figure. "Thanks, Rod."

"Now, what can I do for you?"

"I understand you've completed the Fairchild autopsy."

"I'm still waiting on some lab results, but I don't think they will alter my conclusions."

"And?"

"You know I'm supposed to tell you to read my report."

Some things never change. "For old times' sake, I thought you might be willing to share the highlights, Rod."

"Judge Fairchild died of a single blow to the side of his skull by a heavy blunt object."

"Such as a hammer?"

"Such as the one your client was holding when the police arrived. The judge died in the laundry room just inside the door leading to his garage. There were no defensive wounds. He didn't draw his weapon. This indicates he was attacked by somebody he knew—such as his son."

"Or the killer was able to sneak up on him," I suggest.

"That would have been very difficult, Mike. It's a tight space."

"But not impossible."

"I'm going to miss dealing with defense lawyers."

"What about time of death?" I ask.

"I was called to Judge Fairchild's house quickly enough to take very detailed measurements of body temperature, lividity, rigor mortis, and the state of digestion of the food in his stomach. This allowed me to make a very precise estimate."

"Which is?"

"Between eleven forty-five p.m. and twelve thirty a.m."

Bingo.

"Why are you smiling?" he asks.

"That changes everything," I say. "Bobby wasn't there."

"You might want to talk to Inspector Johnson again before you jump to any hasty conclusions."

"Dr. Beckert put the time of death between eleven forty-five and twelve thirty," I say to Roosevelt. "That changes everything."

He's sitting at his desk with his arms folded. "No, it doesn't," he replies.

I'm seated in a cracked swivel chair in the cluttered bullpen area on the fourth floor of the Hall that houses San Francisco's sixteen homicide cops. The aroma of stale coffee wafts through the thirty-by-thirty-foot space that's slightly roomier than their old digs downstairs. The metal desks are arranged in pairs and buried in stacks of papers and black binders. There are no dividers or cubicles. Homicide cops like to talk to each other.

"This case is over, Roosevelt."

"No, it isn't."

"How do you figure?"

"I can't talk about it."

Either he knows more than he's letting on or he's bluffing. It's more likely to be the former, so I push harder. "Are you saying Beckert is wrong?"

"He hasn't been wrong in forty years."

"Bobby didn't get home until two o'clock. He couldn't have done it. End of story."

He wipes his wire-rimmed bifocals with a small cloth, even though his glasses were spotless. I've seen this gesture countless times. He's taking an extra moment to choose his words. "You need to talk to your client," he says.

"About what?"

"Telling the truth. There's more evidence—a lot more."

"Come on, Roosevelt."

He lowers his voice. "You aren't doing him any favors by letting him lie. I can assure you that there is no way the charges will be dropped between now and the prelim."

"Can you place Bobby at the scene before two o'clock?"

"I can't talk about it now. You need to sit down with your client and find out what really happened. It's in his best interests—and your daughter's."

#

Pete calls my cell as I'm walking down Bryant Street toward Rosie's car. "I heard things didn't go so well at the arraignment," he says.

"You got that right. No bail. They're trying to turn this into a death penalty case."

"That's crap, Mick. Ward is playing to the media."

"And doing it very well. Not to mention the fact that our client's mother is profoundly pissed off at us."

"Comes with the territory, Mick. You got any good news?"

"Maybe. Beckert put the time of death between eleven forty-five and twelve thirty."

"That's great," he says. "Bobby wasn't there. We can go home."

"Roosevelt said they have other evidence."

"Did he happen to mention what it is?"

"He isn't talking."

"Do we have any reason to disbelieve our client?"

"Not yet."

"If Bobby is lying, so is Grace."

"I'm well aware of that, Pete."

"I take it you want to continue the investigation?"

"Absolutely."

"In that case, how soon can you get over here?"

"Twenty minutes. Why?"

"I've persuaded the cops to let us take a look inside Judge Fairchild's house."

Saturday, June 18, 1:27 p.m.

Officer Philip Dito is an imposing veteran patrolman who has worked out of Park Station for almost three decades. He's standing ramrod straight just inside the front door of Judge Fairchild's remodeled Victorian. "Roosevelt said I could show you around," he says in clipped police dialect. "If you touch anything, I will kill you instantly."

I believe him. I played football with Phil at St. Ignatius. I was a back-up running back and he was an undersized linebacker who made All-Conference on tenacity and guts. Those qualities came in handy dealing with his six older brothers. They were even more helpful during his two tours of duty in Vietnam. The leather-faced vet is the living embodiment of a competent, professional cop. Then again, he was trained by one of the best—my father.

"Were you the first officer here?" I ask.

"Yes."

Pete and I put on the obligatory shoe coverings and rubber gloves, then Phil ushers us through the narrow foyer and down the path carefully laid out by the evidence techs, who are still at work. Judge Fairchild recently moved in and may not have been planning to stay here for long, judging by the utilitarian furnishings. Unpacked boxes are piled on the dining room table. The bare walls are freshly painted. The window coverings are more functional than decorative. There are no family photos.

We walk carefully around an overturned table and coat rack that block our path. "I take it these items were already knocked over when you arrived?" I say.

"Yes. For the record, our evidence techs found your client's prints on both of them."

"Those prints could be months old."

"I know."

"Did you find anybody else's prints?" I ask.

"Too soon to tell."

"Is anything missing?"

"Not as far as we can tell."

"Was anything else vandalized?"

"Nope. No signs of forced entry."

"The perp could have stolen a key or jimmied the lock."

"I'll let you lawyers argue about that."

"What about the security alarm?"

"Judge Fairchild's younger son told us he turned it off when he got home at six o'clock last night. He said he forgot to turn it on when he left to go to a friend's house at eight. We confirmed the timing with the security company."

That much of Sean's story checks out. It also explains why the intruder—if there was one—didn't set off the alarm. "It means somebody could have broken into the house any time after eight o'clock without triggering the alarm."

"We're well aware of that, Mike."

"Did you talk to Sean's friend?"

"Yes. A young man named Kerry Mullins confirmed that Sean arrived at his house at eight fifteen last night. He was there until Judge Fairchild's wife came over to pick him up at three o'clock this morning."

"Any chance he may have been covering for Sean?"

"I don't know. I didn't talk to him."

I will. "Would you mind showing us where you found the body?"

He walks us around the coat rack and stops at the doorway to a small laundry room wedged between the stairway and the garage. There is barely enough space for a blood-spattered washer and dryer, a sink, and a built-in shelving unit jammed with laundry supplies and small tools. He points at the chalk outline on the gray linoleum floor that's covered in dried blood. "Right there."

Pete leans across the yellow crime scene tape. "Mind if I take a closer look?" he asks.

"Sorry. That's as close as you can get."

Pete takes it in stride. "Was the garage door open or closed when you got here?" he asks.

"Closed."

"What about the door leading from the garage into the laundry room?"

"The body was propped up against the door. It kept it from closing." Dito says the judge parked his Jag and probably closed the garage door using the remote. "It looks like he was attacked as he entered this laundry room."

Pete takes another long look around cramped, blood-stained room. "Pretty tight space," he observes.

Dito nods. "No place to hide."

Pete looks at the corner of the room. "The perp could have hidden behind the door."

"That would have been really tight," Dito observes.

"But not impossible," Pete says. "The perp could have nailed the judge as he was coming in from the garage."

Dito shakes his head. "The judge would have seen it coming"

"Not if the lights were off. He probably never knew what hit him.

That would also explain the lack of defensive wounds."

It's always helpful to have an ex-cop at the scene.

Dito isn't convinced. "I'll let the lawyers argue about that, too. We found your client's bloody fingerprints on the washer. We found his shoe prints in the blood on the floor."

"He admitted that he tried to help his father," Pete says. He scans the scene again. "There's something missing. If Bobby attacked his father, you would have found blood on his clothes."

"We did," Dito says. "I thought Roosevelt told you."

Uh oh. "Told us what?" I ask.

He points at the washer. "We found your client's clothes in there. He had run them through the wash cycle, but we were still able to determine that they were soaked in blood."

16/ DO YOU HAVE ANY IDEA HOW BAD THIS LOOKS?

Saturday, June 18, 2:18 p.m.

"Do you have any idea how bad this looks?" I say. Bobby is hunkered down in an uncomfortable chair in the consultation room. His voice fills with contrition. "I'm sorry, Mike. I wasn't thinking."

Evidently not. "They're going to say you were trying to destroy evidence when you put your clothes into the washer."

"I wasn't."

"It still looks terrible."

"I know."

"Then why did you do it?"

He tries to collect himself. "I got blood on my clothes when I tried to help my father. I put everything in the washer while I was waiting for the cops."

"Your father was on the floor bleeding and you were washing your clothes?"

"It was making me sick."

"I've been doing this for a long time, Bobby."

"It's the truth, Mike."

"You aren't making things any easier."

"I'm really sorry, Mike." The remorse in his voice sounds genuine.

"Bobby," I say, "the people working on this case are very good. They're using the best homicide cops and the top forensics people. If there's anything else at your father's house, they're going to find it—and use it against us."

"There's nothing else, Mike. I swear to God."

# # #

Rosie makes no attempt to hide her exasperation. "Does Bobby appreciate how serious this is?"

I press my cell phone tightly to my ear. "He gets it."

"I sure as hell hope so. Do you believe him?"

"I think so."

She doesn't sugarcoat her feelings. "If he's lying, we're dead."

"Thanks for bringing that to my attention." I hit the "Off" button and take a moment to get my bearings in the empty hallway in the basement of the Glamour Slammer. My phone vibrates again a moment later.

"How soon can you get back to Cole Valley?" Pete asks.

"Twenty minutes. Why?"

"I found the neighbor who heard Bobby fighting with his father yesterday morning."

17/ HE COULD DO BETTER THAN A GIRL FROM THE BARRIO

Saturday, June 18, 3:17 p.m.

"**T**his is a quiet neighborhood," the retired teacher says. She's tugging absentmindedly at the gold chain that holds her reading glasses. "Nothing like this has ever happened."

Evelyn Osborne taught first grade at nearby Grattan Elementary School for four decades. Her sensible shoes and polka-dot housedress evoke a simpler era long before the Summer of Love.

"Thank you for taking the time to see us, Mrs. Osborne," I tell her. I haven't slept in thirty hours and my head is splitting. "I know it's been a difficult day for you."

"It has, Mr. Daley."

"It's Mike."

There is no reciprocal invitation to address her by her first name.

Pete and I are standing on the sidewalk in front of the neatly tended white bungalow where Mrs. Osborne lives by herself. A warm afternoon sun is shining down on the mature oak trees that form a canopy over the street. Except for the yellow crime scene tape surrounding Judge Fairchild's house next door, a sense of normalcy is returning to Belvedere Street.

"How long have you lived here?" I ask.

"Forty-seven years. We were here before the hippies. Back then, working-

class people could afford houses in Cole Valley. My husband taught at
Lincoln High School." She gets a faraway look in her eyes. "It's a lovely
neighborhood."

"When did your husband pass away?"

"Five years ago."

"I'm so sorry."

"So am I."

I give her a moment to get her bearings. "Mrs. Osborne," I say, "how
well did you know Judge Fairchild?"

"Not that well. He moved in next door a few months ago after he
and his wife separated. He was quiet and he kept to himself. He sent the
boys over to help me from time to time."

"I understand things got pretty tense during the Savage case."

"A police car was parked in front of his house for a while. Things calmed
down after the trial ended. At my age, there isn't much that frightens me
anymore."

"Have you noticed anything unusual in Judge Fairchild's behavior
recently?"

"I didn't see him much. He worked hard. He always had a smile and
a kind word."

He was also packing a gun. "How well do you know the boys?"

"They seem like fine young men. Bobby was very excited when he
got into Columbia. Sean is a little quieter. They play their music a little
too loud sometimes."

"Teenagers."

"I raised three of them."

"Were you home last night?"

"Yes."

"Did you notice anything suspicious?"

"Nothing out of the ordinary."

"Did you happen to see Judge Fairchild come home?"

"No."

"What about Bobby or Sean?"

"I'm sorry, Mike. I go to bed early. I didn't see either of them."

Pete has been watching in silence. He summons his gentlest cop voice. "Mrs. Osborne," he says, "you told me you heard Bobby and his father arguing yesterday morning."

"I did."

"Are you sure it was Bobby and his father?"

"Yes. I was having breakfast. Their kitchen looks right into mine."

"Do you know what they were fighting about?"

She considers how much she wants to reveal. "The judge was angry because Bobby has been staying out late with his girlfriend. He didn't like her."

"Did he say why?"

"He said he could do better than a girl from the barrio."

I can feel my skin starting to burn. Pete keeps his tone soothing. "How did Bobby respond?"

She frowns. "He told his father to go to hell. I couldn't believe he talked that way to his father."

I can't believe his father talked that way about my daughter.

Mrs. Osborne clasps her glasses more tightly. "The judge told Bobby that he would ground him for a month if he didn't break up with his girlfriend. Bobby told his father that he would stop seeing her as soon as the judge stopped seeing *his* girlfriend. The judge went through the roof. I don't blame him."

What a lovely parental moment. "Do you recall if Bobby said anything else?" I ask.

"Yes. Bobby told his father that he was going to make him pay."

"He used those exact words?"

"Yes. I remember it quite specifically."

Swell. "I take it you told the police about this?"

"Yes."

I go to the confessional voice. "Mrs. Osborne, do you really think Bobby would have hurt his father?"

She fumbles with her glasses. "I taught school for forty-two years. I raised three children. I have seven grandchildren. People say things they don't mean when they're angry."

"Do you think this was one of those situations?"

"Bobby wouldn't have hurt anybody."

I hope she's prepared to testify to that effect.

# # #

"She'll be a strong witness," Pete observes. "She's incapable of telling a lie. They'll use her testimony to try to show that Bobby had motive."

He has a good feel for how things will play to a jury. "Her testimony could be very damaging," I say. "Especially when you combine it with the discovery of the bloody clothes in the washer."

"It still doesn't place Bobby at the scene before two a.m.," he says. "Did you know the judge felt that way about Grace?"

"Nope."

"Aren't you pissed off?"

I'd like to scream. "Yep."

"Are you planning to do anything about it?"

"There's nothing I can do now."

His tone turns practical. "Notwithstanding the fact that Jack Fairchild was a philandering, racist pig, we still have Grace to provide an alibi for Bobby."

"It would help if we could find somebody to corroborate their story," I say. "I want you to track down Julie's boyfriend. Then I want you to figure out what George Savage was doing last night."

"Where are you going?" he asks.

"To meet Rosie. We're going to have a little talk with Judge Fairchild's girlfriend."

Saturday, June 18, 4:10 p.m.

"**A**re you sure this is it?" I ask Rosie.

"Yes," she replies.

Judge Fairchild's girlfriend, Christina Evans, lives in a remodeled two-flat down the street from the Palace of Fine Arts, a short hike from the Presidio and the Golden Gate Bridge. The Marina District is a yuppie enclave of stucco houses and low-rise apartment buildings, where spandex-clad single professionals exchange e-mail addresses in the produce aisle at the upscale Safeway. Its shopping area, Chestnut Street, is lined with coffee houses, pick-up bars, and trendy cafes. The last remnant of the neighborhood's working-class roots is an iconic saloon called the Horseshoe Tavern run by an outgoing six-foot-eight-inch giant named Stefan Wever, whose major league career was cut short when he blew out his rotator cuff in his first start with the Yankees.

"Where's Julie?" I ask.

"She's at home with Sean." Rosie pushes out a sigh. "She's also making the funeral arrangements for Jack. Somebody has to do it."

"Does he have any other family?"

"Nope."

How painful. "And Grace?"

"She's at home with my mother."

"Is she okay?"

Rosie scowls. "Given the circumstances, she's holding up pretty well."

"And Tommy?"

"He has no idea what's going on. I'm trying to act normal around him."

It's all we can do. We watch a young mother pushing a thousand-dollar stroller on her way to the Marina Green. "Feeling old?" Rosie asks.

"Yep."

"I have a priest question for you," she says. "What's the appropriate way to express your condolences to a grieving mistress?"

"We're very sorry for your loss."

"I guess all those years in the seminary didn't go to waste."

# # #

"We're very sorry for your loss," I say to Christina Evans.

"Thank you, Mr. Daley."

"It's Mike."

She tosses her flowing blonde hair and smiles. "Christy."

If she's heartbroken about her boyfriend's untimely demise, she isn't showing it. She's wearing a pastel jogging suit and sipping iced tea from a designer tumbler. Judge Fairchild liked them young. And tall. And leggy. And athletic. And stacked. Her clear blue eyes surround a model's prim nose. Her muscles have a personal-trainer tone. We're seated around a redwood table on the rooftop deck of her upscale flat. The leafy enclave smells of jasmine and has an unobstructed view of the Golden Gate. It's a nice setup for a young law clerk.

"We appreciate your cooperation," I say.

"I've already spoken to the police," she says. "I want to find out what happened to Jack just as much as you do."

"How long have you lived here?"

"A couple of years. My ex-husband works for one of the investment banks downtown. I got the condo and the dogs in the divorce. He got the Beemer and the retirement money."

Seems fair. We exchange stilted small talk for a few minutes before we turn to business. "How long were you and Jack seeing each other?" I ask.

"About six months. It was casual." There isn't a hint of remorse in her tone. "Jack's marriage was imploding. I was spinning out of a divorce. We were working late one night. One thing led to another."

"I presume this sort of thing was frowned upon at work?"

"We're adults. We understood the implications."

"You continued to see each other."

"It wasn't as if we were going to get married."

"Did the people at your office know about it?"

"Probably. We tried to be discreet, but San Francisco is a tough place to keep a secret."

"Julie found out."

Her voice fills with contempt. "She hired a private investigator to get dirt on Jack for the divorce case."

"The boys knew about it, too."

"Julie told them. She was doing everything in her power to turn the boys against Jack. It was unfair to put them in the middle. Jack was a terrific father who worshipped his kids. He would have done anything for them."

Bobby and Sean have a slightly different take on that subject. "We understand Jack was supposed to come over to see you last night."

"He was."

"Did it bother you that he left his teenage sons home alone when he came over to see you?"

"We talked about it. Jack said that the boys would be fine. They were his kids, not mine."

Nice. "What time did he get here last night?"

"He didn't."

"What do you mean?"

"I thought you knew."

"Knew what?"

"He was supposed to come over after he left the Bohemian Club. He never showed up."

Saturday, June 18, 4:25 p.m.

"Where did he go?" I ask Christy.

"I presume he went home."

"He didn't call you?"

"Nope."

I'm no expert on the protocols of extra-marital relationships, but it seems to me that basic courtesy would entitle a mistress to a phone call. "Weren't you concerned?"

"Not really. It wasn't the first time. I figured he got stuck at the Club."

"Were you here the rest of the night?"

She pauses. "I went out for a drink around midnight."

Christy gets around. "Where?"

"The Balboa Café."

The hotspot on Fillmore is known as the "Bermuda Triangle," where the City's beautiful young singles congregate to hit on each other. "When did you get home?"

"Eleven o'clock this morning."

Evidently, her relationship with Judge Fairchild was even more casual than I thought.

She gives me a knowing look. "I'd be happy to give you the name of a gentleman who can verify my whereabouts."

"That would be helpful."

Her tone turns indignant. "It isn't as if Jack was the only one cheating on his spouse. Julie's sleeping with one of her students."

"How do you know?"

"She wasn't the only one who hired a PI."

I guess this shouldn't come as any surprise. "We're aware of that relationship," I say.

"Did Julie also mention that her squeeze threatened Jack?"

"What are you talking about?"

"Young Dr. Newsom caught Jack's PI rummaging through his garbage on Tuesday night. He got pissed off and confronted Jack in the parking lot at the Hall of Justice. I saw the whole thing. Newsom told Jack that he would get him if he didn't leave Julie alone. Then he took a swing at Jack. Fortunately, he missed."

Perhaps he connected the second time.

# # #

Rosie shakes her head in frustration as we're walking down Chestnut Street a few minutes later. "Why do bright, talented young women waste their time sleeping around with older married men?" she asks.

"Is that question intended to be a rhetorical one?"

"No, it isn't. What did Christy Evans see in a man old enough to be her father?"

"You mean a man like me?"

"Yes."

"The same things that you see," I tell her. "Maturity. Wisdom. Experience."

"Shut up, Mike."

My cell phone vibrates and I flip it open. "Where have you been?"

I ask Pete.

"UCSF. I talked with a couple of the doctors who were here last night. Julie's story checked out."

"You're unclear on the concept, Pete. The idea is to identify potential suspects, not rule them out."

"It's usually more helpful if I tell you the truth instead of what you want to hear. Besides, I find it hard to believe you'd want to foist the blame for this fiasco on Bobby's mother—especially since she's paying our fees."

"Quite right. Where are you now?"

"Dr. Newsom's house. He just got home."

"We'll be right there."

Saturday, June 18, 5:30 p.m.

S itting at the kitchen table of his rented one-bedroom bungalow adjacent to the green belt separating Cole Valley from the UCSF Medical Center, Dr. Derek Newsom studies a patient's chart. The wooded area behind his house has derived notoriety as the summer home of a flock of wild green parrots who spend most of the year perched on Telegraph Hill. The athletic young surgeon-in-training strokes the trim black goatee that sharpens his chiseled face. His hair is still wet from a shower. He is already well on his way to developing the fearless self-confidence—some might call it arrogance—that is essential for surgeons. His bedside manner is still a work-in-progress.

He finally deigns to look up. "I can't talk for long. I have to get to the hospital."

"We just need a few minutes," I say. "We've been waiting for you to get home."

"I went out for a bike ride," he snaps. "I don't have a lot of free time."

He's certainly taking the death of his girlfriend's husband in stride. "Have you talked to Julie?"

"Briefly. She said I should talk to you."

"Have you been over to see her?"

"That would get complicated. She hasn't told her sons that we're seeing each other."

"They're going to find out now."

He tries to assert control. "I have a few ground rules," he says. "I need to keep this discussion confidential—at least until Julie talks to Bobby and Sean."

"We'll try."

"Not good enough. I need assurances. This situation has ramifications for everybody."

"You mean it might be a career-limiting move if the powers-that-be over at UCSF discover you're romantically involved with your supervisor?"

"It isn't the first time this sort of thing has happened," he says.

"There will also be repercussions for Julie."

"She has more than enough on her plate trying to deal with Jack's death and Bobby's arrest. The fact that we're dating is the least of her problems."

That much is probably true. "How long have you and Julie been seeing each other?"

"A couple of months."

"Are you planning to make your relationship a more permanent one?"

"We haven't talked about it."

"Where were you last night?"

"Here. I got home at seven thirty. Julie came over at eight. We had dinner. She was called up to the hospital at eleven."

So far, this jibes with her version of the story. "Why didn't you go with her?"

"I offered. I'd been on call for thirty-six hours. She insisted I stay home and get some rest."

"Did she go straight up to the hospital?"

"Of course."

"Was she there until my partner found her at three o'clock?"

"Yes. She called me at three fifteen when she was on her way downtown to see Bobby."

"Were you here all night?"

"Of course."

"Can somebody corroborate your whereabouts last night?"

"Are you suggesting I'm a suspect?"

"Actually, we're trying to rule you out." It's a small lie.

He looks around his unadorned house, which has an ambiance similar to my apartment. "I live by myself," he says. "You can talk to my neighbors, but I don't think anybody was snooping around my bedroom window last night."

Fair enough. I take a sip of bitter black coffee. It's a signal to Rosie to take over. "Did you know Judge Fairchild?" she asks.

"Nope."

"You never met him?"

"Nope."

"Ever?"

"Nope."

"What did you think of him?"

"He was a smart asshole who treated Julie and his kids like crap."

That covers it. "Dr. Newsom," Rosie says, "did you know Judge Fairchild hired a private investigator to gather information on Julie for their divorce proceedings?"

There's a hesitation. "Yes."

"How did you find out?"

"Julie told me."

"Didn't you also find him rummaging through your trash recently?"

Another pause. "Yes."

"Did that bother you?"

"Wouldn't it bother you?"

"Yes. Did you do anything about it?"

"No."

"Are you sure about that?"

"Yes."

My turn. "Dr. Newsom," I say, "we talked to some people down at the Hall of Justice who saw you confront Judge Fairchild earlier this week."

No response.

"Look," I say, "I can understand why you would have been pissed off about somebody pawing through your garbage. The cops already know about your little encounter with the judge. You're only going to make things worse if you try to deny it."

"It was nothing," he says. "I went downtown and told Jack to leave Julie and me alone. That was it."

"How did he respond?"

"He said he was going to destroy my career and make my life a living hell."

"Did you believe him?"

"Yes. He said that he would kill me if I didn't stop seeing his wife."

"Sounds like a threat."

"It was."

"Did you call the cops?"

"Of course not. I didn't want to reveal that Julie and I were seeing each other. Besides, it would have been his word against mine."

Now it's his word against Christy's. "What did you do?"

"I told him to go to hell. Then he tried to hit me."

Christy had a different spin on who started the encounter. "Did you hit him back?"

"I defended myself. That was the end of it."

"Did you tell Julie about it?"

"Yes. She said her lawyers would deal with it."

#

"Derek was at home last night," Julie insists.

"How do you know?" Rosie asks.

"Because he told me." Julie glares at us from her seat on the sofa in her living room. She's clearly in no mood to be questioned about the details of her extramarital relationship. "Surely you could be spending your time more productively than harassing Derek."

"Why didn't you tell us Dr. Newsom had words with Jack?"

"It's a non-issue."

"He took a swing at him."

"No, he didn't. Derek was upset when he found Jack's PI rummaging through his trash. I don't blame him. He told Jack to knock it off. I made a similar request through my attorney. End of story."

"We have no way of verifying his whereabouts after you left his house last night," Rosie observes.

"Are you having trouble hearing me? I told you Derek said he was at home all night."

"That isn't good enough."

"It's good enough for me."

Saturday, June 18, 9:45 p.m.

"How long have you been watching Judge Fairchild?" Rosie asks.

Kaela Joy Gullion takes a long draw from her pint of Guinness. Julie's PI is a striking brunette who flashes the polished smile that used to appear regularly in fashion magazines. "On and off for the past year," she says. "Julie hired me to find out if Jack was cheating."

"Was he?"

"Absolutely."

Pete joins us at the small table in the back of Dunleavy's, a blue-collar saloon on Judah Street that looks exactly the same as it did when my great-uncle opened it sixty years ago. We used to live around the corner at Twenty-third and Kirkham. My father helped build the long bar that's still in working order. The current proprietor is my uncle, Big John Dunleavy, a gregarious soul who was married to my mother's sister for almost a half-century, until she died a few years ago. Big John used to throw darts with my dad in the back room every night to help him unwind after his long days on the beat. He still lives a few blocks from here.

"Why did Julie wait so long to file divorce papers?" Rosie asks.

"Human nature," Kaela Joy says. "She tried to keep things together for the boys. She tried counseling. Eventually, she ran out of patience."

"We understand things got quite acrimonious."

"It was a nightmare."

"How well do you know her?"

"Pretty well. She isn't easy to deal with, but she's a straight shooter. She's also smart enough to understand the cops will consider her a suspect until they can rule her out. I told her to lawyer up and be cooperative. She's given her statement to Roosevelt Johnson."

I ask about Julie's relationship with Derek Newsom.

Kaela Joy takes another sip of her beer. "I think Julie would acknowledge it wasn't an inspired choice on her part. Then again, it isn't the first time this sort of thing has happened."

"She's very protective of him."

"She likes him."

So it seems. "What do you know about him?"

"He's a promising surgeon. He's also clean. No arrests. No bad habits. Nothing."

"We understand he had words with Jack last week."

"So I've heard. I wasn't there."

"Dr. Newsom told us he was at home last night."

"I have no reason to disbelieve him. He doesn't get out much."

"We haven't been able to find anybody who can corroborate his story."

"You probably won't. He lives by himself."

"What about Jack's PI?"

"Jack fired him after Newsom caught him snooping around in his trash."

"You realize we can't rule Newsom out as a potential suspect."

Kaela Joy downs the rest of her beer in a single gulp. "Look, I know that it's your job to try to deflect the blame away from your client. If necessary, you'll point a finger at Julie's boyfriend."

"Only if we have evidence." Or we're desperate.

"You might even try to implicate Julie."

Only if we're even *more* desperate. "We have no desire to try to prove our client's innocence by blaming his mother," I say. "We've talked to several people at the hospital who have confirmed that Julie was there from eleven o'clock last night until three o'clock this morning. That appears to rule her out."

The worldly PI gives me a knowing look. "Let's be honest, Mike. You wouldn't hesitate to throw Julie or her boyfriend under a bus if you had to."

True enough. "I hope it won't be necessary. Any chance you were watching Jack last night?"

"As a matter of fact, I was."

This is good news. "We've verified that he left the Bohemian Club at ten forty-five. We believe he was supposed to see his mistress, Christy Evans. She told us he never got there."

"He didn't."

"Do you know where he went?"

"This gets a little weird."

"How?"

"In addition to seeing Christy, it seems that Judge Fairchild was into some, uh, more exotic forms of recreation. After he left the Club, he went to the Sunshine Massage Spa in the Tenderloin."

This is more than weird. It's bizarre. The Tenderloin is a seedy twenty-block enclave west of Union Square where drugs, prostitution, and homelessness are rampant. "Is the Sunshine an AAMP?" I ask.

"Yes."

AAMP is the acronym for an Asian Apartment Massage Parlor. Such upstanding establishments are frequently run by sex traffickers. From the outside, they look like run-down apartment buildings. On the inside, they're staffed by sex workers from Asia—many of them underage. The girls speak limited English and are heavily indebted to their pimps. Their lives are highly regulated, and they're too scared to admit they're being held against their will. In a surrealistic twist, many of the AAMPs are licensed by the city. The cops tend to look the other way unless somebody complains—which doesn't happen very often.

"He was a judge," I say. "He had a family. He had a mistress. He had plenty of money. Couldn't he have found a more upscale brothel?"

Kaela Joy shrugs. "Evidently, he had a thing for young Asian girls. He was willing to pay a substantial premium."

This is beyond weird—it's sick. "How long has this been going on?"

"At least a couple of months."

"How often did he go to the Sunshine?"

"A couple of times a week."

"Does Christy know about it?"

"Probably not."

"What about Julie?"

"Of course." She arches an eyebrow. "The next phase in the divorce proceeding was going to be very interesting."

I'll bet. I'm reluctant to ask the next question, but I need to know the answer. "Do the boys know about it?"

"As far as I know, Julie hasn't told them about it—yet."

Which means, in addition to everything else, they're about to find out that their father—a hard-line, law-and-order judge—frequented a massage parlor that provided underage girls who were probably brought here illegally. And with the tacit approval of our local government, no less. "How did he pick the Sunshine?" I ask.

Kaela Joy's tone is business-like. "There are dozens of AAMPs in the City. He probably got a referral from somebody he knew. Or maybe he checked it out on myredbook.com."

"What the hell is that?"

"A website dedicated to reviewing and ranking sex workers on a one to ten scale. It lets first-time customers—including judges—comparison shop from the comfort of their own homes before they venture out to their local sex parlor. It's very popular."

Turns out there's more to the Bay Area technology industry than Google and Craigslist. "What time did Jack get to the Sunshine?" I ask.

"A few minutes after eleven. He took care of business quickly. He left at a quarter to twelve."

"I take it you didn't follow him inside?"

"That's correct."

"Do you know the name of his masseuse?"

"I'm afraid not."

"Any chance somebody at the Sunshine was angry at the judge?"

"I wouldn't know. It seems unlikely he owed them money. It's strictly a pay-as-you-go operation."

No doubt. "Where did he go from there?"

"Straight home."

"Did you follow him?"

"Yes. He got home at midnight." She says he drove into his garage and closed the garage door behind him with his remote.

"Did you stick around to keep his house under surveillance?"

"Nope. I had everything I needed."

So it would seem. "Did you see Bobby?"

"Nope."

"Did you see anybody else?"

"You mean like somebody with a bloody shirt who looked guilty as hell?"

"Preferably."

"I'm afraid not."

"Did you notice anything out of the ordinary?"

"There was a gray Crown Vic parked illegally in front of the fire hydrant on the corner of Grattan and Belvedere. I hadn't seen it before."

"Was anybody inside?"

"No."

"Did you happen to pick up a license plate number?"

"There weren't any plates."

"Any chance it was an unmarked police car?"

"I don't think so. There was also a truck from Bayview Towing double-parked on Grattan down near Cole. I could barely squeeze around it when I was driving home."

"Was anybody inside?"

"No."

"Have you talked to the cops about this?"

"Of course. I gave them a statement. I have a policy of cooperating with the police."

The good news is Judge Fairchild was still very much alive at midnight—which means we can cut off the first fifteen minutes of the window of opportunity determined by Rod Beckert. The bad news is we still don't know what happened at the judge's house after Kaela Joy left.

# # #

"More coffee, lad?" Big John Dunleavy was born and raised in the Mission, but he can summon a lilting Irish brogue at will.

"No thanks, Big John," I say.

My uncle has been known as Big John since he was a kid. He topped off at six four and two hundred and forty pounds in the eighth grade. He developed his massive hands by lugging beer kegs up from the basement of his father's bar. He would have played college football if he hadn't blown out a knee in the all-city championship game as a senior at St. Ignatius.

"You're looking pretty grim," he observes.

"Rough day," I reply.

"I'll bet. I saw you on TV. You seem to have your hands full."

"Yep."

"That Kaela Joy Gullion is still quite a looker," he says.

"Yes, she is."

Big John turns to Rosie and lays on the charm. "Not as beautiful as you, darlin.'"

He gets the smile he was hoping for. "Thanks, Big John."

"Why the long faces?"

"Well," Rosie says, "we just found out that our client's father—a distinguished judge—had a fetish for underage Asian sex slaves."

"Nice. That would be the father of the boy who has been accused of murder?"

"Yes. Given the fact that his father was a pervert, he seems pretty well adjusted."

"That's the same boy who's been dating my beautiful great-niece?"

"Yes.

"I trust she hasn't been seeing a boy who has a proclivity for killing people."

"That's what we're trying to prove, Big John. He says he's innocent."

"Do you believe him?"

"I think so. It's our job to be skeptical."

"I understand." Big John's blue eyes twinkle. "Would Grace be interested in meeting some other boys?"

"Possibly."

"Let me see what I can do."

I glance at the framed photo of Willie Mays that's hung on the wall behind the bar since the Giants moved to San Francisco in 1958. "Let me ask you something," I say to my uncle. "If somebody parks in your loading zone, who do you call?"

"The same people everybody uses: Bayview Towing. They're very efficient."

It's George Savage's operation. "Who handles Cole Valley?"

"The same guy who takes care of us: Brian Hannah. They call him Thunder."

"Why?"

"He was quite a football player in high school."

"Is he a nice guy?"

"No, but he's very good at his job."

"Does he have a criminal record?"

"A mile long."

"Has he ever killed anybody?"

"He's never been convicted."

"You're okay calling this guy when you need him?"

"I call him to tow cars out of my loading zone, Mikey. I don't invite him inside for a beer."

Got it. "Any idea where we might find him?"

"He could be anywhere in the neighborhood. When he isn't towing, he usually parks in the lot of the McDonald's on Stanyan and works out in the weight room in the basement of Kezar Pavilion."

"You got a phone number?"

He smiles. "If you run a bar in San Francisco, you memorize two phone numbers: your beer distributor and your towing company."

I lay two twenties on the table and stand up. "Thanks, Big John."

He pushes the bills back toward me. "You know your money is no good in here."

"It isn't for the drinks," I say. "I'm paying for information."

"Forget it, lad. You can buy the next round."

He hasn't let me buy a round in thirty years. "Thanks, Big John."

"Where are you lads off to?"

"To find Thunder."

There is a look of genuine alarm on his face. "He isn't a guy you want to mess with."

"We'll be careful."

Rosie shakes her head. "You aren't going off to play cops-and-robbers tonight, are you?"

"Nope."

"Then you shouldn't have a problem if I tag along with you."

It's Pete who responds. "I think it might be better if Mike and I did this alone."

Saturday, June 18, 10:38 p.m.

"Nice place you have here," Pete says, his tongue planted firmly in cheek.

The muscular young man's sleeveless black T-shirt is drenched in sweat. He places two ten-pound dumbbells on the home-made wooden rack in front of him. "Yeah," he grunts.

"How did you get access to such a fine health club?"

"I have friends."

We're standing in a makeshift weight room in the musty basement of Kezar Pavilion, a crumbling barn-like arena that was once the home of the USF Dons basketball team. Over the decades, it's hosted everything from pro wrestling to the Bay Area Bombers roller derby team. It's across the parking lot from Kezar Stadium, where the Niners played before they moved to Candlestick in 1970. The old football stadium was torn down in 1989 and replaced by a smaller high school field. The pavilion, however, looks exactly the same as it did fifty years ago.

"Are you Thunder?" Pete asks.

"Maybe. Who's asking?"

"Pete. This is Mike."

Brian "Thunder" Hannah doesn't extend a hand. "Why should I care?"

I sense hostility.

"We might be able to help each other out," Pete says.

If he doesn't kill us first.

Thunder wipes his brow with a tattoo-covered arm larger than my thigh. "I don't need your help," he says.

"I think you might."

Thunder's cell phone blasts the earsplitting sound of Jay-Z, interrupting our cheery conversation. He presses the talk button and holds it up to his ear. "Yeah," he says. "Ashbury and Frederick. Blue Miata. Ten minutes." He hits the disconnect button. "I gotta run."

"We need just a second," Pete says. "I hear you work for George Savage."

"A lot of people do."

"I hear you're one of his best employees."

"George doesn't give out awards for employee of the month. Who the hell are you?"

"We represent Judge Fairchild's son."

"The kid who popped his dad?"

"He's a kid, but he didn't pop his father."

"Says who?"

"Says me."

Hannah grabs one of his dumbbells from the rack. He does a rapid-fire set of curls, causing his massive biceps to flex. "What the hell does this have to do with me?"

"Your boss didn't like Judge Fairchild."

"My boss doesn't like a lot of people." He puts the weight down and starts to walk away.

Pete calls out to his back. "The cops have a witness who saw your truck parked down the street from Judge Fairchild's house last night."

Hannah stops but doesn't turn around. "I work in the neighborhood," he says.

"What were you doing over on Grattan?"

"Towing a car."

"What kind?"

Hannah finally turns to face us. "A Mercedes."

"Where was it?"

"Blocking the loading zone of Finnegan's Wake."

It's a bar on Cole. "You're sure it was a Mercedes?"

"I think so. I tow a lot of cars."

"Did you go down near Judge Fairchild's house?"

"Nope."

"Did you see anybody go into the judge's house?"

"Nope."

Pete folds his arms. "I have a friend over at Verizon," he says. "I had him check the calls to your cell phone last night."

"That's illegal."

"Sue me."

Hannah takes a drink of water from a plastic bottle. He studies Pete to discern if he's bluffing—which he isn't. Pete has sources at every phone company in the Bay Area. "I get a lot of calls," he says.

"We're only interested in one: from Savage's cell phone."

"He's my boss. He calls me all the time."

"Why'd he call you last night?"

"To tell me to pick up a package this morning."

"From whom?"

"One of our customers."

"Which one?"

"Cole Valley Auto Body."

"What kind of package?"

"An envelope."

"What was inside?"

"Beats me." Hannah's eyes narrow. "I get paid to tow cars, make deliveries, and keep my mouth shut. If you want to know what was inside the package, you'll have to talk to George."

# # #

We're sitting in Pete's car a few minutes later. He's parked in the McDonald's parking lot across the street from Kezar Pavilion. I say goodbye to Roosevelt and flip my cell phone shut.

"Is Roosevelt going to talk to Hannah?" Pete asks.

"Yes."

"Did you tell him Hannah admitted he was parked down the street from the judge's house last night?"

"Of course. But it doesn't place him *inside.*"

"Hannah's rap sheet is a mile long."

"Roosevelt is going to talk to him."

"Not good enough."

"What else do you expect him to do?"

"Lean on him. Hannah was in the vicinity. He got a call from a man who threatened the judge."

"It isn't enough to arrest him, Pete."

"Hannah knows more than he told us."

"Maybe. Do you think it was a good idea to hassle him?"

"I wasn't hassling him. I was interviewing a potential suspect."

"He's going to tell Savage he's on our radar."

"Savage is a smart guy. He already knows."

"He'll deny any involvement."

"Then we should watch him," he says. "Maybe he'll make a mistake."

"Maybe. Otherwise, this exercise was probably a waste of time."

"Not entirely." He opens his jacket and pulls out one of the weights that Thunder was holding when we first arrived. "We should be able to lift some prints off this," he says, "along with some DNA."

"You stole it?"

"I borrowed it."

He isn't planning to give it back. "You realize stealing is illegal."

"So I've heard."

"We'll never be able to use it in court."

"I understand. We need to find out if the cops lifted any prints from inside the judge's house. If we can match them to the prints on this dumbbell, we'll know Hannah was inside. Then it just becomes a matter of proving it—legally."

"We still can't use any prints lifted from the dumbbell."

"You're a smart lawyer. You'll find a way to work around it—and nobody will ever need to know about my little petty theft."

"I don't like it."

"Grow up, Mick."

"I'll have to deny that this conversation ever took place."

"Your moral indignation is duly noted. Where are we going next?"

"It's been a stressful day. It's only fifteen minutes to the Tenderloin. I think I could use a massage."

23/ WE'RE A FULLY LICENSED FACILITY

Saturday, June 18, 11:47 p.m.

"This is a bad idea, Mick."

"I'll be fine, Pete."

My brother's modified police-issue Chrysler is parked at the corner of Eddy and Leavenworth, halfway between the elegant shops of Union Square and the majestic rotunda of City Hall. The Tenderloin is one of the few areas in San Francisco that somehow continues to elude gentrification. Its low-rise residential hotels, teeming streets, and narrow alleys are home to the destitute and the disenfranchised. The neighborhood takes its name from an infamous district in Manhattan where the cops used to supplement their meager earnings with extortion money. They spent their spoils on the choicest cuts of meat. The sidewalks here smell of urine and the streets are populated by drug dealers and sex workers. The Sunshine Massage Spa operates on the top two floors of a crumbling three-story building. The ground-floor space next to the garage is home to a peep show and a locksmith shop.

"Let me handle it, Mick."

"I want to see what's inside."

"It's too dangerous."

"They sell sex, not guns."

"Then let's go together. We'll get a group rate."

"It'll be less conspicuous if just one of us goes inside."

"They'll know you don't belong."

"They cater to judges and lawyers."

"I can look upscale," he says.

"I can act upscale."

My brother isn't convinced. "Ever been inside a whorehouse?"

"A couple of times."

He can't contain a smile. "I had no idea, Mick. When you were a priest?"

"No. When I was a lawyer. And it was official business."

"Sure, Mick."

"Rosie and I have represented a few madams and hookers." We draw the line at pimps.

"Did they pay their bills?"

"Always."

"Did anybody ever offer you a tip?"

"Knock it off, Pete."

He turns serious. "What are you planning to do inside?"

"I want to look around."

"This isn't Nordstrom's. You aren't allowed to window shop."

"I want to identify Judge Fairchild's girl."

"You should let *me* identify Judge Fairchild's girl."

"You can track her down later."

"What are you going to do if you find her?"

"Ask her a few questions."

"You don't get to ask questions inside a brothel, Mick."

"According to my former clients, you can do whatever you want as long as you're willing to pay for it."

We argue about it for a couple of minutes before he finally relents. "Keep your cell phone on," he says. "I'll be outside if you need me."

#

"Who sent you?" A stern voice barks from the intercom.

"The judge," I say. I'm standing in front of the iron gate at the entrance of the Sunshine Massage Spa at midnight, a thick fog settling over the city.

"Cash only," the voice says.

"I understand."

"I'll be right down."

A moment later, an imposing young Asian man with slick black hair and arms covered with dragon tattoos appears on the other side of the gate. The Sunshine's first line of defense wasn't hired for his exemplary customer service skills. "What do you want?" he snaps.

"A massage," I say.

"You a cop?"

Give him points for directness. "No. I'm a lawyer."

"Let me see your driver's license."

I hold it up to the gate.

"Pass it through," he says.

"When we get upstairs," I say.

"Two hundred in cash," he says. "Up front."

"Upstairs."

"Now."

I push a wad of twenties through the metal bars.

"Wait here."

#

The elegant Asian woman of indeterminate middle age with dyed black hair and a flowing red dress smiles seductively as she checks me out in the small foyer at the top of the rickety stairway. "I am Miss Amanda," she says in lightly accented English. She's been through this ritual count-less times and is undoubtedly fluent in several languages—the most important being the language of money. "Welcome to the Sunshine."

"Thank you," I say.

The ten-by-ten room is furnished with an L-shaped leather sofa and two small side chairs. The cracked gray walls are covered with cheaply framed travel posters of downtown Seoul. The aroma of lav-ender candles wafts through the heavy air in an effort to blunt the smell of cleaning solvent.

"Louis tells me it's your first time here," she says.

"It is." Louis is the muscle-bound guy with the tattoos who answered the buzzer and escorted me upstairs. My new pal is probably a member of Miss Amanda's extended family—the side that hits people with tire irons. He's retreated to an adjacent office where he's watching a Korean soap opera on a small black-and white TV. I have no doubt he'll reap-pear in an instant if Miss Amanda needs assistance.

"How did you find us?" the madam asks.

"The judge recommended your services very highly," I say.

"How nice. Which judge?"

I wonder how many judges have passed through these hallowed halls. "Judge Fairchild."

"Judge Fairchild," she repeats. A phony frown replaces her phony smile. "It is very sad."

"Yes, it is."

"Are you also a judge?" she asks.

"A lawyer," I say.

"A lawyer," she repeats. The smile reappears. Premium rates. "How can we help you?"

"Judge Fairchild told me you offer a variety of services."

"We're a fully licensed facility."

I'll bet. "The judge said your girls give wonderful massages."

Her gracious tone can't mask the suspicion in her eyes. "They do."

"How do we start?"

"We require a deposit of three hundred dollars from new customers."

High rent in a low-rent district. "I already gave two hundred dollars to Louis."

"That was the entrance fee for first-time guests. This is an additional deposit."

And a test of my creditworthiness. I'm reasonably sure there are no refunds. "That's fine," I say. I pull out my wallet and hand her the money.

"I'll need another two hundred dollars for the initial services," she says.

This is getting expensive. I quickly hand her more twenties.

"Please wait here for a moment," she says. "I'll bring some of our girls for you to meet."

"Thank you."

She glides through the torn velvet curtain leading to the private rooms in the back. Louis eyes me warily as I wait by myself. Miss Amanda returns a moment later with a half-dozen waif-thin Asian girls wearing identical white dresses. They take their places on the sofa. The oldest looks sixteen. She's slightly more adept at faking a smile than her younger counterparts, who look uncomfortable as they stare across the room.

"Very lovely," I say.

"Thank you," Miss Amanda says. "Is there anybody you would like to meet?"

"Judge Fairchild's favorite."

Miss Amanda frowns. "I'm afraid Jasmine isn't working tonight."

I feign disappointment. I'm also surprised Miss Amanda doesn't call Jasmine on a pager. "I would really like to meet her," I say. "Will she be available tomorrow?"

"Yes. She's one of our most requested girls."

"I'll come back."

Miss Amanda doesn't bother making a token gesture of returning my so-called deposit.

# # #

My brother is genuinely interested when I get back to the car. "Did you get lucky, Mick?"

"Of course not."

"You just looked?"

"More or less."

Pete's disappointed. "Did you see a guy with tattoos?"

"Yes. His name is Louis. He's the muscle guy."

"Did you get a last name?"

"No."

"Did he say anything to you?"

"Not much. He has a limited vocabulary."

"He was watching you from the window when you left."

"I need you to find a girl named Jasmine," I say. "It's probably not her real name."

"Did you get a last name?"

"Nope."

"What does she look like?"

"Young, Asian, and petite."

"That's helpful, Mick. Can you be more specific?"

"I'm afraid not. She wasn't working tonight."

"How much cash do you have left?"

"About five hundred bucks."

"You've already dropped almost a thousand bucks?"

"Justice is expensive, Pete."

"I'm in the wrong line of work. I hope you can bill this to the client."

"I can."

"Gimme the money, Mick."

I hand him a roll of twenties. "Are you planning to sample the goods?"

"I'm a married man. Donna would kill me."

"You aren't tempted?"

"That would involve unpleasant ramifications for some of my favorite body parts."

"Got it. So what are you going to do?"

"I'm going to find Jasmine."

"Right now?"

"Later. I want to show you something first."

Sunday, June 19, 1:18 a.m.

"W"hy are we here?" I ask Pete.

"Keep your voice and your head down. You're going to ruin my day if you get our asses killed."

Over the years, I've learned it's good for my health to do as he says. We're parked at Third and Oakdale—known to the locals as the corner of Heroin and Crack. It's the scariest spot in San Francisco's most dangerous neighborhood. The Bayview once housed thousands of people who worked at the adjacent Hunters Point Naval Shipyard, a massive base shut down in the seventies. It's been a decaying toxic swamp ever since. The Bayview now has the highest poverty, unemployment, teen pregnancy, and homicide rates in San Francisco. An attempt to redevelop the old Naval base finally gained traction during the boom times in the nineties. There are signs of economic life in the depressed community. Real estate prices are starting to edge upward, and a new light rail line connects the southeast corner of the City to downtown. Whether there will be sufficient economic momentum to replace the numerous liquor stores and currency exchanges dotting almost every corner remains to be seen.

I try again. "Why did you drag me down here?"

"To show you where George Savage works."

The expansive impound lot is encircled by an electrified chain link fence topped with razor wire. Hundreds of towed cars are parked haphazardly inside. There's a small tollbooth-like structure at the gate where you go to retrieve your car from the helpful attendants who work behind bulletproof Plexiglas.

"I would have taken your word for it without a tour," I say. I point toward a two-story brick building on the corner of the lot surrounded by yet another barbed-wire fence. Savage values his personal safety as much as his inventory. The lights are on, and there is activity inside. "What's in there?"

"That's the warehouse for Savage's auto parts business," he says. "He's one of the biggest distributors on the West Coast."

"I didn't realize the auto parts business was a round-the-clock operation," I say.

"It isn't—except here. At night it's a chop shop."

It's the euphemism for an operation that resells stolen auto parts. "Why don't they shut him down?" I ask.

"He's the biggest employer in the Bayview. He paid for a couple of new baseball fields. He gives money to the schools and hires kids from the area."

"The DA filed criminal charges against him for skimming money."

"Savage paid his fine and picked up where he left off."

"What does this have to do with us?"

"Maybe nothing." He gestures toward another small building adjacent to the warehouse. "That's where they crush the junkers."

"So what?"

"I've had somebody watching them tonight. Among other things, they crushed a gray Crown Victoria."

"You think it was the Crown Vic that was parked in front of Judge Fairchild's house last night?"

"I don't know. It could be just a coincidence."

25/ I'M GETTING TOO OLD FOR ALL-NIGHTERS

Sunday, June 19, 1:40 a.m.

"Inspector Johnson," the voice says.

"Roosevelt, it's Mike." The fog hanging over the bay makes it hard to see as I drive across the Golden Gate Bridge. "I'm sorry for waking you."

"I was still up."

He'll never admit he's tired.

He quickly adds, "This better be good if you're calling at this hour."

"Pete and I spent some time with George Savage's operator in Cole Valley."

"We've already talked to Brian Hannah."

He's moving quickly. "Did he mention that his truck was parked down the block from Judge Fairchild's house at midnight last night?"

"He said he was looking for cars in the vicinity."

"Wouldn't it have been easier for him to have cruised the neighborhood in his truck?"

"Possibly."

"Did he tell you he got a call from Savage at eleven o'clock last night?"

"Yes, he did."

Roosevelt and Hannah are playing it straight. "Did you consider the possibility he may have been looking for Judge Fairchild?"

"The thought crossed my mind. There's still the small matter of proving he was inside the judge's house."

"Did you check for his prints?"

"Of course. We had his prints on file from his prior arrests. So far, no matches inside the house."

So much for Pete's stolen dumbbell. "He could have worn gloves," I say.

"Thanks for bringing it to my attention, Mike."

"Did you find any other prints in the house?"

"Your client's. His father. His brother."

"What about unidentifiable prints?"

"A few."

It's a more cryptic answer than I expected. We'll follow up. "Did you talk to Kaela Joy Gullion?"

"We took her statement."

"Did she mention Judge Fairchild didn't get home until midnight?"

"Yes. We find her story credible. We're operating on the assumption that the judge was killed after midnight. It still doesn't exonerate your client."

"Kaela Joy saw a gray Crown Vic parked illegally in front of the judge's house."

"She told me the same thing. So what?"

"Pete and I just got back from Savage's lot in the Bayview. A gray Crown Vic was brought in and crushed a couple of hours ago. It could be the same car."

"You got any proof?"

"Not yet."

"We'll look into it. There are a lot of Crown Vics in the Bay Area, Mike."

#

"So," Rosie says, "did you and Pete have a good time at the whorehouse?"

"Lovely," I say.

We're sitting in her living room at two o'clock on Sunday morning. My head screams as I fill her in on our visits with Brian Hannah and Miss Amanda. She's legitimately appalled when I describe Judge Fairchild's proclivity for purchasing the services of young Asian girls. Her interest is piqued, however, when I tell her we can place Hannah's tow truck a short distance from Judge Fairchild's house.

"Do you have any evidence that he went inside?" she asks.

"Not yet." I explain that Roosevelt has already confirmed he hasn't found Hannah's prints inside the judge's house.

"He could have worn gloves," she says. "Did they find any other unidentifiable prints?"

"Some."

"It's worth pursuing. Anything else?"

"Pete and I went down to the Bayview to see Savage's facility."

"Are you insane?"

"We were careful, Rosie."

"Anything we can use?"

I tell her about the crushed Crown Vic.

"Can you prove it's the car that was parked in front of Judge Fairchild's house last night?" she asks.

"Probably not."

"Leaving aside the profound stupidity of your decision to go down to the Bayview in the middle of the night, it sounds like a very tenuous connection to me."

She may be right. I glance at the fireplace and change the subject. "How's Grace?"

"Scared." Rosie takes a deep breath. "Trying to put up a good front.

At least her story hasn't changed."

"That much is good. And Tommy?"

"Worried. He has no idea what's really going on, but he knows Grace is nervous."

"We need to keep things low key around him."

"I agree."

I reach over and touch her hand. "And how are you holding up?"

Her professional cool can't mask the tension in her voice. "I'll be all right."

It's a more equivocal answer than I expected. "What is it, Rosie?"

"I'm worried about Grace."

"So am I."

"I mean it, Mike. She could be implicated. She can't go to jail."

"She won't. We'll make sure."

"If this thing goes south, there will be big problems for all of us."

"I know."

"Maybe it was a mistake to represent Bobby."

"Maybe. Is there something else?"

"I'm exhausted, Mike. I'm getting too old for all-nighters."

"Me, too. Did you hear anything from Julie?"

"She called to ask us when we're going to get Bobby out of jail."

"We need to manage her expectations."

"The lockup is no place for a kid like Bobby. He has a target on his back because he's young, smart, and affluent."

"We may not be able to get him out of there anytime soon, Rosie."

"I know. Julie also reiterated her displeasure that we're harassing her boyfriend."

"Sometimes she seems more concerned about her squeeze than her son. You'd think she has more important issues on her plate."

"She's under a lot of stress, Mike."

"So are we."

The voice of practicality makes its presence felt. "We're going to need more than Grace," she says.

"I know."

"Where do you want to start in the morning?"

"Why don't you go down to the office to work on witness lists and subpoenas. You should probably start talking to Grace about her testimony."

She nods. "What about you?"

"I'm going back to the Bayview with Pete. We're going to try to get an audience with Savage."

Sunday, June 19, 9:30 a.m.

The Towing Czar of San Francisco exudes nervous energy as he leans back in a cracked leather chair and looks out a small window protected by iron bars and razor wire. At barely five feet tall, the wiry sixty-year-old with the denim work shirt and slick gray hair is hardly an imposing physical specimen. Despite his diminutive stature, George Savage runs his business with an iron hand from behind a metal desk in a cluttered office in the heavily fortified building on the edge of the impound lot that Pete and I admired from the outside early this morning. The operation is equally intimidating in the daylight. The interior has the ambiance of a run-down truck stop. I guess you don't hire a decorator when you share space with a car crusher. Framed photos of his children and grandchildren are interspersed between the auto magazines piled high on his file credenza.

"Thanks for seeing us," I tell him.

"You're welcome."

I'm somewhat surprised he hasn't called out his army of lawyers. Then again, he strikes me as someone who can take care of himself. There is also the slim possibility he has nothing to hide.

"Judge Fairchild's death is a great tragedy," he says with feigned sincerity. "I feel bad for his family."

Sure you do. "How's business?"

"There's never a recession for towing cars in San Francisco."

True enough. As far as I can tell, his recent legal troubles have had no adverse impact on the operations of Bayview Towing. The lot is full, and the crusher is running at full steam. "What's the going rate to liberate your car nowadays?" I ask.

He responds with a smirk. "Depends on how much your vehicle cost and how badly you want it back."

Never underestimate the arrogance of a man who can tow your car with impunity. "Isn't that how you got into trouble in the first place?"

He holds up his hand. "Nah," he says. "It was an accounting issue. The City said we owed them money. We fired our bookkeeper and straightened everything out. The whole thing was blown out of proportion."

"That's not the way it played in the press."

"They've been out to get us for years. We run a legitimate business. We're regulated by the City. They watch us like hawks."

"You made some rather pointed comments about Judge Fairchild during the trial."

"I was upset. I got a wife and four kids. We had to pay an outrageous fine. It was a shakedown."

"People might interpret some of your comments as threats," I say.

"Do you really think I would have been stupid enough to pop a sitting judge?"

"Nope." I wouldn't rule out the possibility that you might have set it up.

"I have a business to run," he says, "Why'd you come down here?"

I tap my finger on the metal desk. It's a signal to Pete to take over.

"We talked to Brian Hannah last night," he says.

"He's one of my best employees."

"So we understand. His truck was parked down the block from

Judge Fairchild's house at midnight on Friday. The judge was killed around the same time."

"Are you accusing me of something?"

"Nope. We just want to know what Hannah was doing."

"He works in the neighborhood."

"It's still quite a coincidence. We have a witness who said Hannah wasn't inside his truck at midnight. Hannah didn't give us a very satisfying answer when we asked him about it. We were hoping you could fill in some of the details."

"He was probably looking for illegally parked cars. That's his job."

"He said you called him at eleven o'clock on Friday night."

"I talk to him a lot. So what?"

"What did you guys talk about?"

"I asked him to pick up a package from one of our customers."

"Which one?"

"Cole Valley Auto Body."

His story is matching up with Hannah's so far. "You called him at eleven o'clock at night to remind him about a pick-up?"

"He works nights."

"What was in the package?"

"Money."

"Are you serious?"

"Of course. Our customers pay us to keep their loading zones clear. It's no secret this is a cash business. That's why I entrust certain delicate tasks to certain employees. Brian is one of them."

"I trust the people at Cole Valley Auto Body will confirm your story?"

"You can talk to the owner. Anything else?"

Either he's a world-class liar or he's telling the truth. "The police told us that there was a gray Crown Vic parked illegally in front of Judge Fairchild's house on Friday night. Do you know whose it was?"

"Nope."

"Did you guys happen to pick up a Crown Vic in Cole Valley on Friday night?"

"Do you have any idea how many cars we tow on a given night?"

"We're just asking about one."

"Hang on." He picks up the phone and punches in a four-digit extension. He asks if they picked up a Crown Vic on Friday night. He says uh-huh a couple of times, and then he hangs up. "We picked up a gray Crown Vic in the Excelsior on Friday night," he says, "but we have no record of a Crown Vic in Cole Valley. The car from the Excelsior wasn't drivable and the police had reported it as abandoned." He writes down the name of the owner and the license number on a slip of paper and hands it to me. "Anything else?"

"Can we see it?" I ask.

"Nope. We crushed it."

#

Robert Kidd intercepts me as I walk out the door of the Glamour Slammer at eleven thirty on Sunday morning. The Public Defender of the City and County of San Francisco smiles broadly. "Got a minute?" he asks.

"This isn't a great time, Robert."

"It's never a great time, Mike." We continue to talk as he follows me into the lobby of the old Hall. "Are you going to be able to get Bobby Fairchild out of here anytime soon?"

"Let's just say the odds aren't looking so good. The prelim starts Wednesday. We're still piecing together what happened. We're short-handed and we have very little time."

"I understand your daughter was with him on Friday night."

"She was."

"Does that mean she's his alibi?"

"So far."

"I would think that might complicate matters for you."

"It does. My client's mother expects us to get the charges dropped at the prelim."

"That's unrealistic," he understates.

"We know that, but she doesn't. She'll probably fire us if we can't get Bobby out of jail by the end of the prelim."

"That might put you in a bind strategically. On the other hand, it might be good news for me. I figured you'd be tied up with this case for months. Now you might be finished this week."

After the past few days, it's nice to feel loved.

"Anything I can do to make your life easier?" he asks.

"You can start by finding the guy who killed Judge Fairchild."

"That might be difficult. What else can I do to get your answer within the week?"

"Rosie and I want you to buy us new office furniture if we accept."

"You can pick out anything you want at Ikea."

"Deal."

"What are you doing here on a Sunday?" he asks.

I stop in front of the elevators and push the Up button. "McNulty wants to see us," I say.

Sunday, June 19, 12:30 p.m.

"Thank you for coming in to see me," McNulty says with exaggerated politeness. He's a small man with a large round head and a wisp of hair that he tries to strategically comb over his dome. "I know you're busy."

"We are," I reply. A half hour ago, Rosie and I received a cryptic phone message summoning us to McNulty's workman-like office. The sparse furnishings include a standard-issue oak desk, two wooden chairs, and a couple of metal cabinets. Manila folders are stacked neatly on the floor. There are no personal photos. A clear reflection of the humorless career prosecutor. "Why did you want to see us, Bill?"

"Professional courtesy."

Don't react. Let him talk.

"This could get very unpleasant in the next few days," he says. "I know you think I'm just a mouthpiece for Nicole, but in reality, I take no pleasure in prosecuting a young man for killing his father."

I believe him. Despite being a terminal curmudgeon, McNasty is a competent lifer who takes his responsibilities seriously. Two decades ago, he coveted Ward's job. Unfortunately, he lacks style and charisma— essential elements of running for office in my hometown. Nowadays, he seems content to put the bad guys away and train the next generation of hard line prosecutors.

"Nicole and I thought there might be a way to minimize the damage to everybody," he continues. "I've persuaded her to let me convey a final offer."

Ward will attempt to portray any deal as a victory for justice. "We're listening," I say.

He speaks as if he's reading from a script. "Based upon the evidence I've seen so far, I believe your client may have acted without premeditation. Nicole is therefore willing to go down to voluntary manslaughter." He quickly adds, "It's a fair deal, Mike."

It's a lot more reasonable than a capital murder charge. "It would be fair if he had killed his father," I say.

"He did."

"No, he didn't."

He feels no obligation to engage in a lengthy discourse on the merits of his case. "You aren't going to get a better offer, Mike," he says. "Take it or leave it."

"We're very appreciative, Bill, but it isn't going to fly."

"You mean you won't make it fly."

"Nothing has changed since we last talked."

"Yes, it has." He clears his throat. "A witness has placed your client at the scene."

Out of the corner of my eye, I catch a glimpse of Rosie's concerned expression. I ask, "Did this witness see Bobby inside Judge Fairchild's house?"

"Just outside," McNulty says. "Running west on Grattan."

"Which means he would have been running *away* from his father's house—if it was Bobby."

"Correct."

"Either way, he wasn't *inside* the house."

"I realize that."

"So he wasn't *at* the scene."

"Close enough."

"Not for me. What time did your witness allegedly see Bobby?"

"Twelve ten a.m."

"Was he by himself?"

"Yes."

My mind races into overdrive analyzing the potential scenarios. Bobby and Grace both said they left Amoeba at midnight and got back to Bobby's car around twelve fifteen. The car was parked on Grattan, which runs next to the judge's house. They've steadfastly insisted they were together the entire time. If they're telling the truth, there is no way Bobby could have been running *away* from his father's house by himself.

"Your witness is mistaken," I say.

"Your client is lying."

"No, he isn't."

"Yes, he is."

We snipe at each other for a couple of minutes with no satisfactory resolution. "Either way," I finally say, "we want to talk to your witness. We'll need his name and address."

"We will provide that information in due course."

"You have a legal obligation to give us his name if you plan to put him on your witness list."

McNulty takes a deep breath. "It's Keith Treadwell," he says.

"You can't be serious. You can't base your case on the testimony of one of your own guys."

"He isn't one of our guys."

"He's an ADA."

"He's retired."

"Doesn't matter."

"Sure it does."

Treadwell is a respected former prosecutor who spent his career putting drug dealers away. He worked his way up to the head of the felony division and mentored some of the best attorneys in the office—including McNulty. Now in his seventies, he stays busy teaching criminal procedure at Hastings Law School and doing continuing education seminars for judges.

"There's a conflict of interest," I say. "We'll get his testimony excluded."

"Judge McDaniel has no grounds. You can try to impeach his credibility on cross."

"You're going to look bad, Bill. We have a witness who's prepared to testify that Bobby never went inside his father's house."

"With all due respect, your daughter's testimony is inherently unreliable."

Rosie can no longer contain herself. "Are you calling our daughter a liar?"

McNasty keeps his tone maddeningly even. "She's the defendant's girlfriend and defense counsel's daughter."

"She's telling the truth."

"She's trying to protect her boyfriend."

Rosie glares at him for a long moment. "You're going to embarrass yourself and your office if you base your case on the testimony of one of your own guys."

"He isn't one of our guys anymore. And he's very reliable."

"Eyewitness testimony is inherently unreliable—especially late at night on a dark street."

"Not in this case."

"No deal," Rosie says.

"Have it your way."

Rosie and I are about to leave when McNulty stops us. "There's a lot more," he says.

"What aren't you telling us?" I ask.

"In due course."

"Come on, Bill. If you want us to play ball, give us something to work with."

"I've already given you more than I should have. Against my better judgment, I've made a generous offer. If you don't cut a deal now, things are going to get very unpleasant for your client—and your daughter."

Sunday, June 19, 1:45 p.m.

"Thank you for seeing us on short notice," I say, mustering as much sincerity as I can.

Retired Assistant District Attorney Keith Treadwell takes a bite of his sausage-and-mushroom crêpe at one forty-five on Sunday afternoon. "I figured I'd hear from you sooner or later," he says.

"I guess this means it's sooner."

Treadwell is a lanky man with angular features and a pronounced widow's peak that makes him resemble Bela Lugosi. A pair of horn-rimmed Coke-bottle glasses rest on his hawk nose. He was on the front line in San Francisco's drug wars for three decades. His heavy-handed tactics, blunt manner, and single-minded determination led to numerous commendations and more than a few complaints from the defense bar. He generously passed down the secrets of his combative streak to McNulty, one of his most enthusiastic disciples.

"You realize I have no legal obligation to talk to you," he observes.

"Yes, we do."

Rosie, Treadwell, and I are seated in the back corner of Crepes on Cole, an airy breakfast and lunch spot at the corner of Cole and Carl that once housed the Other Café, a legendary comedy club where Robin Williams and Dana Carvey learned their craft. If you look closely, you can still see the faded Other Café sign hanging above the door.

"Helluva thing about Jack Fairchild," I say.

"Now they're killing judges," he says.

"We understand you were neighbors." Treadwell lives at the corner of Belvedere and Rivoli, about two blocks south of the judge's house.

"We were also friends. I watched his kids grow up."

"We were surprised to see your name on Bill McNulty's witness list."

He points toward an athletic black Lab sitting at attention, tethered to the parking meter outside the restaurant. "I took my dog out for a walk on Friday night."

"Bill said you walked by Judge Fairchild's house shortly after midnight."

"I did. That's where I saw your client."

"What time was that?"

"Twelve ten."

"Where were you when you saw him?"

"Walking north on Belvedere. Bobby was running west on Grattan."

"You're sure it was Bobby?"

"I've known him since he was a kid."

"Any chance it could have been somebody else?"

"Nope."

I nod to Rosie.

"Keith," she says softly, "did you say Bobby was running *away* from his father's house when you saw him?"

"Yes."

"So he was running away from you?"

"Yes."

"Which means you saw him from behind?"

"Yes."

"Then how could you have seen his face?"

He lowers his voice. "It was Bobby."

"Did he see you?"

"I don't think so."

"Did you say anything to him?"

"No. He was too far away. He was also clearly in a hurry."

Rosie responds with a skeptical expression. "You didn't feel compelled to talk to your neighbor's son when he was running down the street after midnight?"

"I didn't think anything of it."

"Did you consider the possibility that he might have been in trouble?"

"Nobody else was around."

"Did you see him leave his father's house?"

"No."

"So you don't know if he was inside his father's house on Friday night, do you?"

"No."

"Did you see anybody else inside Judge Fairchild's house?"

"No."

Rosie keeps pushing. "Where was he going?"

"I don't know."

"Did you notice a Crown Vic parked in front of the fire hydrant on Grattan?"

"I'm afraid not."

"Did you see a truck from Bayview Towing double-parked farther down Grattan?"

"I didn't notice."

Rosie takes a sip of cold coffee and pauses to gather her thoughts. "George Savage made some rather pointed comments about Judge Fairchild recently."

"I know."

"Some people interpreted those remarks as a threat."

Treadwell nods. "That's a reasonable interpretation."

"One of Savage's employees was parked down the street from the judge's house on Friday night. A convicted felon named Brian Hannah."

"I know him. I prosecuted him for armed robbery a few years ago."

"Savage placed a call to Hannah's cell phone at eleven o'clock on Friday night."

"That's interesting."

"Any chance you saw Hannah running down Grattan on Friday night?"

Treadwell shakes his head emphatically. "I'm afraid not."

"Any chance Hannah might have been involved in Judge Fairchild's death?"

"I have no idea." Treadwell takes a final swallow of his coffee and wipes his lips with his paper napkin. "Look," he says, "I take no pleasure in any of this. I've known Bobby since Jack and Julie were pushing him around in a stroller. He's a nice kid who's never been in trouble. I know things were tense between Jack and Bobby for the past few months. I'd love to foist this disaster off on Savage and his people just as much as you would—probably more. Frankly, I was disappointed my former colleagues couldn't bring him down when they had a chance. On the other hand, I know what I saw. I can't provide any connection between Savage or Hannah and Jack's death."

Which means Treadwell is mistaken or Grace and Bobby are lying.

Sunday, June 19, 3:30 p.m.

"Something has come up," I say to Bobby.

His body tenses. He's sitting in one of the uncomfortable plastic chairs in the consultation room in the Glamour Slammer. Rosie is sitting across from him, her arms folded, her expression stoic.

"What is it?" he asks.

"A witness says he saw you running down Grattan at twelve ten on Saturday morning."

"It wasn't me."

"He was sure."

"He made a mistake. He must have seen somebody else."

Rosie holds up a hand and takes over. "It's Keith Treadwell," she says. "He says he knows you."

"He does. He's been our neighbor forever, but he's still wrong." There's a slight hesitation. "I swear to God."

"I need you to tell us what happened one more time," Rosie says.

"Fine." He taps the table impatiently and lays it out again. "Grace and I went to the movie. Then we went to Amoeba. Then we went back to the car. We drove straight to your house. That's it."

Either he's telling the truth or he's internalized his story to the point where he truly believes it himself.

"You and Grace were together the entire time?" I ask.

"Yes."

"You weren't by yourself even for a minute?"

"No."

"You didn't go inside your father's house?"

"No."

"Is there any reason Treadwell would be out to get you?"

"Not as far as I know. He's a nice guy. He knew my father for years."

# # #

The battle resumes in Rosie's living room at ten thirty on Sunday night. Grace is standing with her arms folded. An oversized Cal sweatshirt hangs loosely on her shoulders. Rosie is sitting on the sofa. I'm standing next to the doorway to the kitchen. Sylvia is knitting in the armchair near the windows.

"Where did you and Bobby go after the movie?" I ask Grace.

"We've been through this, Dad."

"We need to go through it again, honey."

"Come on, Dad." We've moved beyond anxiety into open hostility.

"Please, honey."

Rosie takes off the reading glasses that replaced her contacts. She addresses our daughter in a soft tone. "We need to know exactly what happened on Friday night, honey."

Sylvia comes to her granddaughter's defense. "What's this about, Rosita?"

"No offense, Mama, but it would be better if we talked to Grace in private."

"She's my granddaughter."

"Technically, you could be called to testify about anything she tells us. There is no grandmother-granddaughter privilege."

"Don't give me lawyer talk. I'll rot in jail before I testify against my granddaughter."

"Please, Mama."

Sylvia is savvy enough to pick her fights carefully. "I'm going to check on Tommy."

"Thank you, Mama."

Sylvia has the last word. "I *will* find out what this is all about, Rosita." My ex-mother-in-law makes a melodramatic display of strutting down the hall toward Tommy's room.

Rosie moves in closer to Grace. "So?"

"How many more times do we have to go through this?"

"Just once."

"What's this about?"

Rosie struggles to find the right words and inflection. "One of Judge Fairchild's neighbors says he saw Bobby running down Grattan at twelve ten—alone."

Our daughter frowns.

"Grace?"

"It wasn't Bobby," she says. She bites down on her lower lip, but there is no equivocation when she adds, "He was with me."

"The entire time?"

"The entire time."

"You went straight from Amoeba to Bobby's car?"

"Yes. Then we came straight home."

"You didn't go inside Judge Fairchild's house?"

"No."

"You didn't see anybody on the street?"

"No."

"You're absolutely sure?"

"I'm absolutely sure."

#

"Do you believe her?" I whisper to Rosie after Grace has gone to her room.

My ex-wife is staring intently at the fireplace in her living room. "I think so."

It's the first hint of doubt. "But?"

She recovers quickly. "No buts. I know my daughter better than anybody else on the face of the earth. I believe her."

Or she's choosing to believe her. My cell phone rings. The display shows Pete's number. "Where are you?" I ask him.

"In the Tenderloin. I need you to get down here right away. I found Judge Fairchild's girl from the Sunshine Spa."

Monday, June 20, 12:37 a.m.

"This is Jasmine," Pete says.

The tiny Asian girl with the pale complexion and the plain white dress nods demurely, but doesn't speak. Her delicate features suggest she's younger than sixteen, but her hollow eyes look much older. I pick up the scent of the lavender candles that I smelled when I visited Miss Amanda at the Sunshine on Saturday night.

"I'm Mike," I say.

Another nod.

I glance at Rosie, who is sitting next to me. "This is Rosita," I say. "She's my law partner."

Jasmine's eyes open slightly as Rosie extends a gentle hand.

"Nice to meet you, Jasmine," Rosie says softly. "I think we might be able to help you."

We're sitting in the back of the Grubstake Restaurant, an unlikely landmark inside an old railcar that somehow found its way to the middle of the block on Pine Street between Polk and Van Ness, just north of the Tenderloin. The burgers are terrific and they stay open until four a.m. Harvey Milk held court here until the wee hours as he built his political organization at a table near the front door. Oddly enough, the funky diner with the mismatched chairs and sloping floor offers a full selection of Portuguese dishes. The aroma of cheeseburgers mixes easily with the house specialty, Bacalhau a Tomes de Sa, a codfish platter with potatoes, onions, hardboiled eggs, parsley, and olives. It's an unusual—albeit reasonably private—setting for a meeting among two defense lawyers, a tough PI, and an underage sex worker who is probably in this country illegally.

"We need to hurry," Pete says. "Jasmine has to be back by one."

I will find out later precisely how Pete managed to extricate her from the Sunshine—if only for a few minutes.

"How long have you worked at the Sunshine?" Rosie asks.

Jasmine is staring down at the floor. "Nine months. I owe them money."

"For what?"

Her English becomes more stilted. "Bring me here from Korea. Tell me I make lots of money. Now I have to pay travel costs. They charge rent. They charge for food."

It will take years to work off her debt. "Can you leave?" Rosie asks.

"No. They keep my passport. They will harm my family."

"How much do you owe them?"

"Twenty-five thousand."

Rosie pushes out a sigh. "How old are you?"

There's a pause. "Twenty," Jasmine decides.

Rosie isn't buying it. "How old are you really?"

Another hesitation. "Seventeen."

A year older than Grace.

"Are you allowed any contact with your parents?" Rosie asks.

"No. They think I work at a restaurant. They would be ashamed of me."

"You mustn't blame yourself, Jasmine."

"I have dishonored my family."

"We can help you if you're willing to help us."

Jasmine finally looks up. "How?"

"We're lawyers," Rosie says. "We can get you a visa to stay here legally."

"I don't want to stay," she says. "I want to go home."

"We can help you there, too."

"Still need twenty-five thousand."

"Are you willing to talk to the authorities?"

"No. I will get in trouble."

Yes, she will.

"We'll get you protection," Rosie says.

"You can't protect me. Another girl went to the police. She disappeared."

"Are you saying the people at the Sunshine made her disappear?"

"I don't know."

"You have to trust us, Jasmine."

She ponders her situation for a long moment. "Maybe," she says.

Rosie shows her a photo of Judge Fairchild. "Do you recognize this man?"

"The judge."

"What can you tell me about him?"

"Good tipper."

Rosie touches her hand. "The judge was killed on Friday night."

"I know. Miss Amanda told me. Very sad. He was one of my best customers."

"For how long?"

"Three months."

"How often did he come to see you?"

"Twice a week."

"For what?"

"A massage."

"What else?"

Her eyes turn down. "You know."

Rosie nods. "Yes, I do. Did he always ask for you?"

"Yes. He liked young girls."

I'm not interested in the details of the precise nature of their relationship.

Rosie keeps pushing. "Did you see the judge on Friday night?"

"Yes."

"What time did he arrive?"

"Eleven." She says he left at a quarter to twelve.

"Do you know anybody who may have been angry at the judge?"

She swallows hard, but doesn't respond.

"Jasmine?"

"My boss."

"Miss Amanda?"

"Yes."

"Why?"

"He owed money."

"For what?"

"For me."

I believe her.

"How much did he owe Miss Amanda?" Rosie asks.

"Five thousand. Miss Amanda was going to take it out of my wages if he didn't pay."

It comes as no surprise that Miss Amanda is quite the hard-nosed businesswoman. "Did Miss Amanda threaten the judge?" I ask.

"She told the judge she wouldn't let him see me again if he didn't pay. The judge said he would put Miss Amanda out of business."

# # #

Rosie is biting on her right fist as we drive across the Golden Gate Bridge at one o'clock on Monday morning. "Jasmine must be desperate," she says.

"Can we get her out?"

"For twenty-five grand. There must be hundreds of girls like her in San Francisco."

"No doubt."

Rosie's tone turns practical. "Even if we can liberate her and convince her to testify, it doesn't help our case. She was with the judge until eleven-forty-five on Friday night. It proves he was a creep who liked Asian girls. It doesn't tell us anything about what happened after he got home."

"What about Miss Amanda's argument with the judge?"

"She'll never admit it. It would be her word against Jasmine's. It seems unlikely Miss Amanda drove out to Cole Valley to bludgeon the judge to death."

"Maybe she set it up."

"You can bet she'll have an ironclad alibi. Besides, we still have no evidence placing her—or anybody else—at the scene."

"Then we'll have to find some."

"Fine. Call Pete and tell him to have somebody keep an eye on the Sunshine."

We drive the rest of the way to Marin in silence.

Monday, June 20, 11:00 a.m.

Sean Fairchild's best friend slouches on the tired camelback sofa in the living room of his mother's fixer-upper on Ashbury, just above Haight, a five-minute walk from Judge Fairchild's house. It's the first day of summer vacation and Kerry Mullins looks like he just woke up. "Is Sean in trouble?" he asks.

"No," I reply.

I'm flying solo. Rosie is at the office piecing together our presentation for a prelim that's less than forty-eight hours away. Pete is out on the street looking for anybody who might have seen something on Friday night. We have two days to find a needle in a haystack. So far, the haystack is ahead.

"I'll do what I can to help," Kerry says.

"You can start by telling me where you were Friday night."

"Right here," he says. "So was Sean."

For someone who looks like the antichrist, he's a surprisingly engaging young man. His cherubic face is camouflaged by two gold nose rings, a cobra tattoo, and dyed jet-black hair that cascades down his shoulders. His youthful features evoke images of a young Leonardo DiCaprio—although it seems unlikely that Leo ever wore army fatigues and ankle-length black leather boots to high school.

"Where's your mother" I ask.

"At work. She's a nurse at UCSF. She's worked there since my father split."

I glance around the disheveled living room littered with empty pizza boxes and soda cans. The large color TV is tuned to Comedy Central. Dishes are piled up on a chair next to the small kitchen. Kerry probably spends most of his time without adult supervision. "How long ago was that?" I ask.

"When I was a baby. I don't know him."

Tough stuff. "I'm sorry."

"So am I."

"Do you have any brothers or sisters?"

"Nope."

"How long have you lived here?"

"My whole life. This house belonged to my grandparents. They died when I was a baby."

That might explain how Kerry and his mother can afford to live in a house worth more than a million bucks in San Francisco's insane real estate market. I give his mother credit. She is making ends meet and sending her son to an excellent private school. Putting aside his quirky appearance, he seems to be reasonably well-adjusted. "Why did you decide to go to Urban?" I ask.

"I like the focus on technology and the environment."

It's a more thoughtful answer than I expected. "What do you do in your spare time?"

"I work at a juice bar on Haight. I hang out with Sean."

"Doing what?"

"Drinking coffee. Surfing the Net. Checking out the scene."

"Is that what you and Sean were doing Friday night?"

"Nope. We stayed here. We ordered a pizza and played video games."

"What time did he get here?"

"Around eight."

"How well do you know Sean's brother?"

"Not that well. We don't have a lot in common. He's a jock and a brain."

"Is that a problem?"

"Not for me. Good for him."

"How was he getting along with his father?"

"Not great. You know—the divorce."

"What about Sean?"

"He *never* got along with his father. The judge wasn't an easy guy to like. He and Sean didn't talk."

"Did Sean tell you anything about the divorce?"

"He said that his father cheated."

"Did that bother him?"

"Wouldn't it bother you?"

"Yes, it would."

"Sean doesn't say much, but he's a solid guy. He gets good grades, but he couldn't please his father."

"Does he have a temper?"

"Nope."

"Kerry, do you know if Bobby was into any funny stuff?"

He cocks his head to the side. "What do you mean?"

"Alcohol. Drugs. That sort of thing."

"I don't think so."

"What about Sean?"

"Not really."

"A little?"

"This is the Haight. Everybody does a little."

True enough. "Were you guys doing any funny stuff on Friday night?"

"Nope."

"You won't get into trouble, Kerry."

"We weren't doing any funny stuff."

His story is matching up with Sean's. I hand him a business card. "Will you call me if you talk to anybody who saw anything on Friday night?"

"Sure."

#

"Hey, Mike," the familiar monotone says.

"Hey, Requiem," I reply.

My favorite *pro bono* client used some of the proceeds from our victory on Friday for a makeover, including new purple spikes in her hair and a third nose ring. I'm standing at the counter of Amoeba Music at noon on Monday. Hip hop music pulsates through the sound system. An eclectic mix of high school slackers, hip young professionals, left-over hippies, and a few well-mannered street people fill the long aisles of the old bowling alley. The checkout line is where we used to rent bowling shoes. The walls behind the beat-up counter are covered with psychedelic posters from shows at the old Fillmore Auditorium. To my right is one of the largest collections of new and used CDs and vinyl LPs in the Bay Area.

"How are things?" I ask.

"Okay."

This represents chattiness for Requiem. "Got a gig this weekend?"

"Friday at midnight. Private party in the Mission. You want to come?"

"I'll have to take a rain check. We have a new case."

"What kind?"

Requiem isn't much for watching the news. "Murder. A judge got killed. He lived in the neighborhood."

"No shit?"

Such a delicate way with words. "No shit. Were you working Friday night?"

"Yeah." She says she started at five and got off at midnight.

I pull out photos of Bobby and Grace. "Did you see these people?"

She chews her gum forcefully as she studies the pictures. "Maybe," she finally decides. "It was crowded. I don't remember."

"This young man has been accused of killing his father. This young woman is his girlfriend, who happens to be my daughter. They said they were here on Friday night."

"You don't believe your own daughter?"

"We need to check out their story."

"In other words, you want me to provide an alibi."

"If you can. I helped you. Now I need you to help me."

The caustic smirk disappears. She studies the photos intently for another long moment. "I'm sorry, Mike," she says. "It was busy. A lot of people come and go."

"You hesitated," I say.

She shrugs. "They may have been here. I just don't remember."

Which means she can't testify that she did. "Do you have security cameras?"

"The system's been broken for a couple of weeks."

That rules out the possibility we'll find Grace and Bobby in the security videos from Friday night. "Mind if we talk to your co-workers?"

"Be my guest. The cops were here asking questions earlier today about the people in the photo."

"Do you remember their names?"

"A couple of beat cops and a homicide inspector—African American. Old. Deep voice."

"Roosevelt Johnson?"

"Yeah."

"What did you tell him?"

"The same thing that I just told you, which is the same thing that everybody else told him. The store was crowded on Friday night. Your daughter and her boyfriend may have been here—I just didn't see them. As far as I can tell, neither did anybody else." Requiem looks at the line that's forming to my right. "I need to get back to work."

"Did the cops talk to anybody outside?"

She gestures toward a homeless man guarding the entrance to the store. "They spent some time with Lenny," she says.

"Do you know what they were talking about?"

"You'll have to ask him."

# # #

The disheveled man of indeterminate age sits in the doorway between a shopping cart loaded with empty cans and a sleeping German shepherd. His wild gray hair, leathery face, and unkempt beard reflect a lot of nights sleeping outdoors. His soiled military fatigues and worn Giants sweatshirt haven't seen laundry soap in a long time.

He nods toward his dog as I approach him. "Would you be kind enough to spare some change so I can get Fidel something to eat?" he asks. San Francisco has many well-educated street people. Many of them have drug, alcohol, and psychological problems. In Lenny's case, it could be a combination of all three.

I take a whiff of the urine-soaked sidewalk as I hand him a dollar. "What's your name?" I ask.

"Lenny. What's yours?"

"Mike."

"You're representing the judge's son," he says. "I saw you on TV."

"You're right." I wonder how a guy whose worldly belongings are loaded in a shopping cart happened to see me on TV. "Mind if I ask you a few questions?"

He looks down at the dog again. "Fidel's going to need a little more love."

I hand him a ten-dollar bill. "I understand the cops were here earlier today."

"There were."

"Were they asking you about Judge Fairchild's murder?"

"They were."

"Mind telling me what you told them?"

"Maybe I happened to be in the vicinity of Judge Fairchild's house on Friday night."

"Where exactly were you?"

"That information might require a slightly larger donation for Fidel's college fund."

I hand him a twenty. "You got a taste for a burger, Lenny?"

"You bet."

Monday, June 20, 12:30 p.m.

"**A**re you from around here?" I ask Lenny. I've discerned that his full name is Leonard Stone.

"I grew up in the Richmond," he says. "Graduated from Washington High."

"College?"

"Nope. Too expensive. I volunteered for the army after I graduated. Served in the first Gulf War. I was an auto mechanic for a while after I got back, but I had a little trouble readjusting to civilian life."

So it appears. "Where do you sleep?"

"The Muni tunnel over at Clayton and Carl. It's warmer than the park."

Pete has joined us. We're seated at one of the three picnic tables in front of BurgerMeister, a hamburger joint on Carl, just east of Cole, where the Niman Ranch burgers and curly garlic fries are a cut above the pedestrian décor. They make their shakes from scratch with ice cream from Mitchell's in the Mission.

"Where do you hang out during the day?" I ask.

"I spend the mornings in the park." He slips a piece of his burger to Fidel, who is sleeping at his feet. "Fidel needs exercise. I spend the afternoons in front of Amoeba. There's a lot of foot traffic. I usually pick up a few bucks for dinner."

"How long have you been living on the street?" I ask.

"Almost ten years." His tone is business-like. "I lost my last job when my crack habit got a little out of hand. I lost my apartment when it got even worse."

Not an uncommon story. "Do the cops hassle you?"

"A little. They usually leave us alone at the park. It gets dicier on Haight. The shop owners hate us because we're bad for business. It's going to get worse. The mayor wants the cops to clear everybody out."

"Where would you go?" I ask.

He shrugs. "Beats the hell out of me. South City isn't going to roll out the welcome mat for hundreds of homeless people."

True enough. Every administration in my lifetime has tried to address San Francisco's homeless problem with varying degrees of failure. A comprehensive answer is going to be elusive—if not impossible.

"Ever tried a shelter?" I ask.

"Too many rules. No dogs."

"I know some people who can give you a hand."

"No thanks."

If there were a simple solution, thousands of homeless people wouldn't be living on the streets. "So," I say, "why were the cops asking you about Judge Fairchild?"

"We were neighbors."

"What are you talking about?"

"The judge's house is a couple of blocks from where I sleep."

"You know where he lived?"

"Everybody does. His house was surrounded by cop cars during the Savage trial. I stayed away until it was over." He takes another bite of his burger. "I'm in with some of the guys at Park Station. They know I'm connected in the neighborhood. We try to help each other out."

He's a snitch. "Is that why they let you sleep in the Muni tunnel?"

"Let's just say the fine art of mutual back-scratching hasn't completely disappeared in our humble community."

Well said. "What did you tell them about Judge Fairchild?" I ask.

"The truth."

"Which is?"

"Fidel and I went out for our regular walk around midnight on Friday."

"Isn't that a little late?"

"Nobody hassles us at that hour. We were looking for bottles and cans."

"Did you walk by the judge's house?"

"Yes."

Yes! "What time was that?"

"Maybe five after twelve on Saturday morning."

"Was he at home?"

"Beats me."

"Did you see anybody?"

"Nope."

"Did you notice anything unusual?"

"Yeah," he says. He wipes the grease stains from his beard. "There was a gray Crown Vic parked in front of the fire hydrant on the corner."

"There are a lot of Crown Vics in town. How come you noticed this one?"

"It had tinted windows and no plates. It looked like an unmarked cop car." He flicks a fry to Fidel, who gobbles it up in one bite. "Notwithstanding my exemplary relationship with San Francisco's Finest, Fidel and I try to stay away from them."

With good reason. "Was anybody inside the car?"

"Nope."

"Did you notice a truck from Bayview Towing parked down Grattan?"

He gives us a knowing look. "You think Brian Hannah had something to do with this?"

"You know him?"

"Everybody knows him. I call him if I see an illegally parked car. He gives me a few bucks as a tip."

Lenny works every angle. "We understand he isn't the most popular guy in the neighborhood."

"He isn't. He has a job to do."

"His boss didn't like the judge."

"I heard."

"Did you see him on Friday night?"

"Nope."

"You wouldn't lie to protect him, would you, Lenny?"

"Nope."

"Did you notice anything else?"

"The Crown Vic was gone when Fidel and I walked past the judge's house on our way back."

Pete and I exchange a glance. "You passed by the house a second time?" I say.

"Yes. Fidel and I went up to the playground behind the school. I let him run for a few minutes, then we came back. We walked by the judge's house on the Grattan Street side."

"What time was that?"

"Probably around twelve fifteen."

"Are you pretty sure about that time?"

"Pretty sure. Could have been a few minutes either way."

"Did you see anybody on the street?"

"Nope."

He should have seen Grace and Bobby returning from Amoeba. Then again, if his timing was just a little off, they might have already left. He's wearing a dirt-encrusted Casio watch on his left wrist. Whether he checked it as he was walking past Judge Fairchild's house is questionable. "Did you see anybody inside the judge's house?" I ask.

"Nope."

I pull out a photo of Bobby and show it to him. "Any chance you saw this guy?"

He studies it for a moment. "Nope."

"You're sure?"

"The cops showed me a picture of the same kid. I presume it's the judge's son."

"It is."

"I told them the same thing I just told you—I didn't see him. In fact, I didn't see anybody."

It isn't a perfect alibi, but it could help. "Are you prepared to testify if we need you?"

"Maybe."

"What's it going to take?"

"A few more cheeseburgers."

"We can work that out."

"And some cold, hard cash."

I drop a twenty on the table in front of him. "Here's a down payment," I say.

"A couple more of those would be nice."

I slide two more twenties toward him. "Where do we find you?"

"In the daytime, in front of Amoeba. At night, at the Muni tunnel."

"Are you going to be around on Wednesday?"

"I'm not going anywhere."

"We'll be in touch," I say.

# # #

"It still isn't enough," Pete says.

"It's a little more than we had an hour ago," I reply.

We're standing on the sidewalk near the corner of Belvedere and

Grattan where the phantom Crown Vic was illegally parked on Friday night. Except for the crime scene tape still draped across the front door of Judge Fairchild's house, there are no visible signs a judge was killed a few steps from here.

"It doesn't exonerate Bobby," Pete says.

"It helps," I say. "Lenny can testify that Bobby wasn't there when he walked by the judge's house—twice."

"He doesn't know for sure. Bobby could have been inside."

"That's up to the prosecutors to prove."

"It doesn't contradict Treadwell's testimony, either," Pete says. "He claims he saw Bobby running down the street at twelve ten."

"It doesn't hurt," I say.

"If you want to base your case on the testimony of a homeless guy."

"And my daughter."

My brother folds his arms. "If it's all the same to you, I'm going to keep looking."

"Fine with me. Anything else on Savage?"

"I have somebody watching him. Hannah, too."

"And the Sunshine?"

"I'm going back there later tonight."

My cell phone rings and I recognize Roosevelt's number. "You got good news for me?" I ask.

"I need to see you and Rosie in my office right away."

33/ WE FOUND SOME DISTURBING NEW EVIDENCE

Monday, June 20, 2:45 p.m.

Roosevelt places a stack of police reports on his metal desk and slides them over to me. "This is everything we have," he says. "I have fulfilled my legal obligation to provide every shred of evidence that might tend to exonerate your client."

Rosie and I look at the pile. "What about evidence that would tend to show our client is guilty?" I ask.

"I have fulfilled my legal obligation," he repeats.

"You said there was something we needed to talk about."

"There is. We finished our forensic investigation of Judge Fairchild's house. We found some disturbing new evidence."

We wait.

He lowers his voice. "We found Grace's fingerprints in Judge Fairchild's living room, dining room, and kitchen. We also found them on the banister."

"It doesn't mean anything," Rosie says. "Grace has been to Bobby's house several times."

Roosevelt clears his throat. "We also found her prints on the nightstand in Bobby's bedroom."

"That proves she visited Bobby's house," Rosie says. "Nothing more."

"We think it might mean more."

"What are you suggesting?"

"There is more to this case than meets the eye. You'd better figure out what happened on Friday night."

"Anything else?"

Roosevelt glances around the empty room that houses the homicide cops. "In terms of legal advice, no. In terms of parental advice, yes. I have a sixteen-year-old granddaughter. I have explained to her on several occasions why I think it's a bad idea for her to spend time in her boyfriend's bedroom."

34/ HAVE YOU BEEN SLEEPING WITH OUR DAUGHTER?

Monday, June 20, 3:25 p.m.

"What happened?" I ask Bobby. We've taken our usual positions in the attorney consultation room. His right cheek is swollen and he looks at me through puffy red eyes.

"Nothing," he whispers.

In the Glamour Slammer, like every jail, the streetwise thugs prey on the uninitiated. Bobby's youth, intelligence, and good looks are of little practical value in a facility filled with everyone from career felons to small-time shoplifters.

"Come on," I say. "That wasn't an accident."

His voice fills with an unnerving combination of fear and resignation. "I don't want to talk about it. It will only make it worse."

"You need to tell me what happened."

"You have to get me out of here," he says. "They're going to kill me."

"Who?"

"The people in the lockup."

"Can you identify the person who hit you?"

"Only if I want to die. Were you able to talk to the judge again about bail?"

"We won't have another chance until Wednesday," I say.

"Damn it. I'm not going to make it to the prelim."

"You have to hang in there for a few more days."

"Does that mean you can get the charges dropped?"

"That's probably going to be tough."

"You're going to put on a defense, right?"

"Of course, but we may not want to show too many of our cards at the prelim. We don't want to telegraph our defense strategy if we move forward to trial."

"There isn't going to be a trial. They're going to kill me if you can't get the charges dropped."

"I know this is difficult, Bobby."

"No, you don't." The last vestiges of the poised young man disappear into a fury of anger and fear. "It's more than difficult. It's impossible."

"Then give us something to work with."

"Like what?"

"Somebody who can verify that you weren't at your father's house on Friday night."

"Grace."

"Somebody who isn't your girlfriend and my daughter."

"I thought you said you could make this go away if we can prove that the time of death was sometime before I got home."

"Keith Treadwell is going to testify that he saw you running down Grattan at twelve ten."

"He's wrong. You need to find somebody who can refute his testimony."

"We're trying. We found a witness who walked by your father's house at twelve-oh-five and again at twelve fifteen. He said he didn't see anybody."

"That's good."

"He should have seen you and Grace."

"Maybe he got the time wrong."

"The witness may not be terribly credible."

"Who is it?"

"A guy named Lenny Stone."

"You're kidding."

"You know him?"

"Yeah. He's a homeless guy who got some bad drugs. He's delusional."

"Did you see him Friday night?"

"Of course not." He pauses to gather himself. "Does this mean you're going to base my defense on the testimony of a homeless drug addict?"

"It may be part of our case."

"That isn't good enough."

"It's all we have so far, Bobby."

"What about Savage? What about Hannah? What about my mother's boyfriend?"

"We haven't been able to place any of them at your father's house."

Rosie makes her presence felt. "We need to talk about something else," she says.

Bobby tenses. "What now?"

"They found fingerprints in your father's house."

"Whose?"

"You, your father, and your brother." She recites the rest of the list: Julie; the cleaning people; two neighbors; a couple of Bobby's friends. "They also found Grace's prints."

"She's been to my father's house," he says.

"I know. That's why it didn't surprise me when they found her prints in the living room, kitchen, and family room. It did surprise me, however, when they found her prints in your bedroom."

He swallows. "We've spent some time downstairs."

"Doing what?"

"Stuff on the computer."

"That's all?"

"That's all."

Rosie looks my way. I lower my voice and say, "Was Grace in your bedroom on Friday night?"

"No."

"We're going to ask her the same question."

His tone turns more adamant. "She wasn't."

"This conversation is covered by the attorney-client privilege, Bobby. It will be a disaster if we find out in open court that you're lying. So far, the prosecutors have given us no evidence proving you were inside your father's house on Friday night, but they may be holding something back. As your lawyers, we need to know if there's anything else."

"There isn't."

"Good. I need to ask you one more question." I look straight into his eyes. "Have you been sleeping with our daughter?"

"What does that have to do with my defense?"

"Nothing. I'm not asking as your lawyer. I'm asking as Grace's father."

"No," he says simply.

If you're lying, the murder charges will be the least of your problems.

# # #

"They found your fingerprints in Bobby's bedroom," I say to Grace. She's sitting on the gray sofa in Rosie's airless office at four thirty on Monday afternoon.

"He's my boyfriend," she says. "We spend a lot of time together."

"In his bedroom?"

"We've spent some time down there."

"That's a bad idea."

"It wasn't a big deal. Bobby's computer is in his room. You can probably find his fingerprints in my room. It doesn't mean we were doing anything wrong."

"I didn't say you were."

"Your implication was crystal clear."

Yes, it was. It's been a long, difficult day with little to show for it. Sylvia brought Grace downtown so we could start preparing her for her testimony. Sylvia had to bring Tommy along with them. He's busy watching cartoons in our conference room. Murder cases are hard enough without a stressed-out teenager and a four-year-old in your office.

"Were you at Judge Fairchild's house on Friday night?" I ask.

Grace shoots daggers in my direction. "How many times do I have to say this? We weren't there, Dad."

"You're sure?"

"I'm sure. Bobby was with me the entire time. End of story."

"And you're prepared to testify to that effect?"

"Of course. It's the truth."

"The prosecutors on this case are very good," Rosie says. "They're going to try to poke holes in your story."

"I have nothing to hide." Grace takes a moment to gather herself. "Are we done?"

"Not quite," Rosie says. "How serious is your relationship with Bobby?"

"Pretty serious." Grace swallows. "I think I love him, Mother."

"You're only sixteen."

"So what?"

"Let me put it more bluntly: you aren't allowed to have sex."

Grace responds with a stony silence.

"The police are looking at you very suspiciously," Rosie says. "We need to know the entire story."

"I've already told you the entire story."

"Not quite."

"Are you asking me if Bobby and I were sleeping together?"

This time Rosie hesitates. "Yes."

"What does that have to do with Bobby's case?"

"Maybe nothing, but you're Bobby's alibi. We need to know if they're going to be able to attack your credibility because he's your boyfriend."

"I'll do everything I can to protect him," Grace says, "but I won't lie."

"You still haven't answered my question," Rosie says.

"It's none of your business."

"It is now."

"I don't want to talk about this."

"I'd rather talk about it now than ask you about it in open court."

Our daughter's lips shrink to the size of a tiny ball. Her voice fills with a level of indignation similar to the tone Rosie reserves for arrogant prosecutors and incompetent judges. "No, Mother," she says. "Bobby and I have not been sleeping together."

# # #

"Tommy fell asleep," Sylvia says. "I'll wake him up and take him home."

"Thanks, Mama," Rosie replies.

"Are you finished with Grace?"

"For now."

"Then I'll take her home, too."

Sylvia is seated in the spot where Grace was sitting a few minutes earlier. Her expression clearly indicates she's as unhappy as Grace, who stormed down the hall a few minutes ago. "What are you doing?" she asks.

"What do you mean?" Rosie says.

"Why are you going after her?"

"How much of our little discussion did you hear?"

"All of it. Grace has been through hell the past three days. She's scared to death. Why are you making it harder?"

"We have to, Mama. It's our job."

"No, you don't. Her boyfriend is in trouble. She isn't."

"She's his alibi. This case may turn on her testimony. They're going to go after her."

"Then help her."

"We're trying. We need to be sure her story will hold up."

"By browbeating her?"

"By preparing her. We need to know the truth, Mama."

"I'm all for the truth, Rosita. On the other hand, if you keep treating Grace like a criminal, you may end up winning your case and losing your daughter."

35/ WHAT THE HELL DO YOU THINK YOU'RE DOING?

An uninvited visitor arrives shortly after Sylvia has departed with Grace and Tommy. An irate Julie Fairchild storms into Rosie's office and picks up where Sylvia left off. "What the hell do you think you're doing?" she snaps.

"Calm down, Julie," I say.

"No, I won't. I just saw Bobby. Where do you get off calling him a liar?"

"I didn't," I say.

"Yes, you did."

"I asked him what happened on Friday night."

"You asked him whether he's been sleeping with your daughter."

Well, that, too. "Is he?"

"No."

"Good."

"What does that have to do with his defense?"

"The police found Grace's fingerprints in Bobby's room."

"So what?"

"We wanted to know how they got there."

"She's been spending a lot of time there. They'd have found her fingerprints in his bedroom at my house, too. It doesn't mean they were sleeping together."

"I didn't say it did."

"Your implication was quite clear."

Suddenly, everybody is an expert at interpreting my implications.

Rosie joins the discussion. "Julie," she says, "let me ask you something—parent-to-parent, off the record."

Bobby's mother responds with a cold silence.

"Has Bobby been sexually active?"

Julie pauses before she answers in a muted tone. "Maybe," she says. "I don't know for sure."

"Have you asked him about it?"

"He won't discuss it. We haven't talked much since the divorce. He's a little more communicative than Sean, but not much."

"We're familiar with the problem. Will you do me a favor?"

"It depends."

"If you find out Bobby has been sleeping with Grace, will you tell us?"

"Will you do the same for me?"

"Yes."

"Okay."

"What else did Bobby tell you?" Rosie asks.

"He's scared."

"With good reason. The Glamour Slammer is a rough place. We got the judge to issue an order to separate him from the other prisoners. He'll get his meals in his cell. It isn't a perfect solution, but he should be reasonably safe until the prelim."

Julie swallows hard. "Realistically," she says, "what are the chances that you'll be able to get the charges dropped?"

Rosie answers her honestly. "Probably not so good. Preliminary hearings are the prosecutor's show. They just have to show enough evidence to provide a reasonable implication that Bobby may have committed a crime."

"Then you'll have to prove them wrong."

"We'll do everything we can. Strategically, it's usually better to see what the prosecutors have and not telegraph our entire defense for the trial."

"There can't be a trial."

"You have to start preparing yourself—and Bobby—for that possibility."

"He'll be killed in jail."

"No, he won't."

The esteemed surgeon inhales the musty air in Rosie's office. In the operating room, she's in charge. In the judicial system, she's just a spectator. "Maybe Jack was wrong about you. Maybe you're more interested in protecting your daughter than my son."

"That isn't true," Rosie says. "We're doing everything we possibly can to help Bobby."

"Even if it implicates your daughter?"

"We have no evidence she had any involvement in this case."

"Except she was with Bobby on Friday night."

"Which makes her a witness. And Bobby's alibi."

"Which brings me back to my original question: Are you prepared to do whatever it takes to defend my son, even if it implicates your daughter?"

"We've been through this," Rosie says. "If there is a conflict of interest, we'll have to withdraw."

"In other words, your answer is no."

An overwhelming silence envelops Rosie's office.

Julie's voice fills with disdain when she finally speaks again. "I guess it's the answer I should have expected," she says.

"We'll understand if you decide to hire another lawyer," Rosie says.

"I want to think about it."

"That's fine."

"In the meantime, let me be very clear about my expectations for the next few days. I expect you to put on a full defense for my son at the prelim."

"But Julie—"

She cuts her off. "I'm not interested in lawyerly parsing or worthless excuses. My son's life is in danger. You haven't been able to get him out on bail. He's been beaten up in jail. I'm giving you one more chance—because I have no choice. If you can't get the charges against Bobby dropped at the prelim, I'm going to find him another lawyer."

# # #

"Where does that leave us?" I ask Rosie.

"I think Julie has made her position quite clear."

"She's under a lot of stress. She'll calm down."

"Maybe," she replies. "Let's try to keep this in perspective. What's the worst thing that can happen?"

"Bobby is convicted of murder."

"No, that's the second-worst thing. The worst thing is if Grace is somehow implicated."

Ever the voice of practicality. "It won't happen," I say.

"She's Bobby's alibi. The prosecutors are going to put as much heat on her as they possibly can."

"They have no evidence against her."

"They don't need a shred of evidence to make her life—and ours—miserable." Rosie's cobalt eyes turn to cold steel. "There's only one way to make sure this mess comes out the way we'd like. We have one more day to find out what really happened to Judge Fairchild."

Monday, June 20, 11:30 p.m.

"How long have you been sitting here?" I ask Pete. He's parked across the street from the Sunshine. The Tenderloin is quiet at eleven thirty on Monday night. "A couple of hours," he says.

The locksmith shop on the ground floor is dark, but the porn shop is busy. "Were you able to figure out who owns this upstanding establishment?" I ask.

"A privately held California corporation known as Sunshine Investments, Inc."

I ask him how he was able to obtain that information.

"They're licensed by the City. Their filings with the Secretary of State are up to date. If you didn't know any better, it looks like everything is on the up-and-up. They also own the locksmith shop and the sex shop."

"Sounds like it's a fully integrated X-rated conglomerate."

"You might say that, Mick."

"Do you know who owns Sunshine Investments?"

"According to their filings with the City, a husband-and-wife team named Richard and Amanda Kim."

"That would be Miss Amanda?"

"So it would seem."

"They aren't trying to hide their identity." The blinds are drawn on the top two floors of the building, but the lights are on inside the Sunshine. "Any customers tonight?"

"Just a couple," Pete says. "It's been a slow night."

"Anybody I might recognize?"

"Judge Weatherby and a member of the police commission."

"Are you serious?"

"Why would I lie?"

He wouldn't. "Is Jasmine working tonight?"

"Probably."

"Have you talked to her again?"

"Nope. She hardly ever leaves the building."

I shoot another glance across the street. "Do you think this is a dead end?"

"I don't know. This isn't our only possibility. I have people watching Savage and Hannah. I have somebody watching Julie's boyfriend."

"Any proof any of them may have been involved in Judge Fairchild's death?"

"Not yet. As far as I can tell, everybody is going about their business. I don't expect them to confess to murder."

Neither do I. "We need something by Wednesday morning."

"I'm doing everything I can, Mick." He points at the Sunshine. "Looks like a customer is going inside."

A slight, middle-aged man wearing a blue sport jacket and a beige beret walks up to the metal gate and pushes the buzzer. He looks around impatiently as he waits for an answer. A moment later, the muscular young man who showed me inside on Saturday night appears on the other side of the gate. A brief discussion ensues. Money changes hands. The customer waits outside for a few minutes. Then I hear the sound of the buzzer. The customer pushes open the gate and heads upstairs.

"Miss Amanda approved," Pete observes.

We watch in silence for a few more minutes. A couple of tough-looking youths wander into the peep show.

"Do you want me to go inside to see what they're doing?" Pete asks.

"I think we already know."

"Yes, we do." He's about to say something else when he stops. "Look at that. The light just went on inside the locksmith shop. It's the second time it's happened tonight."

"Why would somebody be inside the locksmith shop at this hour?" I ask.

"It can't hurt to find out," he says.

"How do you plan to do that?"

A crooked smile crosses his face. "I guess I'll have to ask Jasmine."

Tuesday, June 21, 3:30 p.m.

R osie looks up over the top of a manila file folder as I enter her office. "Any word from Pete?" she asks.

"He has people watching Savage and Hannah," I say. "He has somebody camped out at UCSF to watch Julie's boyfriend."

"Anything we can use?"

"Nothing yet."

"Damn it." Her hair is pulled back into a tight ponytail. It's been a whirlwind day of serving subpoenas, preparing exhibits, and briefing our witnesses—and we're nowhere near finished. "What about the Sunshine?" she asks.

"He's trying to hook up with Jasmine again."

"What are the chances he'll get something useful?"

"Slim." I shift to the matter at hand. "Did you get a final witness list from McNulty?"

"Yes," she says. "Just what you'd expect. Roosevelt. Beckert. The first officer at the scene. A field evidence technician. A fingerprint expert. Treadwell. Mrs. Osborne."

"That's it?"

"They're playing it by the book. They're going to show just enough to get to trial."

"Is Julie on the list?"

"Nope. She has nothing to add to the prosecution's case. Neither does Dr. Newsom."

"What about Grace?"

"They don't need her, either."

"But we do," I say. "Are we in agreement that we'll build our case around her alibi?"

"Unless Pete finds something in the next eighteen hours, we have no choice."

"It will give McNulty a chance to go after her on cross."

"That's inevitable, Mike."

"We can wait until trial. We'll know more of the facts and she may be in a better emotional state of mind."

"We have no choice," she repeats.

She's right. "We have other witnesses," I observe. "We have Kaela Joy."

"Her testimony will prove the judge liked underage girls."

"It will also prove he was still alive at midnight. That narrows the time frame."

"Not enough."

"We can put on Lenny Stone."

"He can testify he didn't see Bobby when he walked by the judge's house, but a homeless drug addict is inherently unreliable."

"Then we need to give the judge some options," I say. "We'll start with Savage."

"He'll deny everything."

"He threatened the judge."

"That was months ago."

"So what? He called Hannah at eleven o'clock on Friday night."

"Hannah works for him."

"We need to stir the pot. We can call Hannah, too. He's admitted he was down the street from Judge Fairchild's house on Friday night."

"We can't place him inside the house."

"Let's put him on the stand and rough him up a bit. He's unsympathetic. He might turn on Savage. Maybe he'll tell us something we don't already know."

"You're beginning to sound desperate, Mike."

"If we don't come up with something by ten o'clock tomorrow morning, we *will* be desperate."

Tuesday, June 21, 4:30 p.m.

"When do I testify?" Bobby asks.

"You don't," I reply.

Dressed in his orange jumpsuit, he's sitting in the consultation room, hands at his sides. This is likely to be our last chance to talk before the prelim starts tomorrow morning. "Why not?" he asks.

"Too risky. The prosecutors will take you apart."

"I can hold my own."

His bravado is unconvincing. "You've never been in court under cross-exam. Everything happens very fast. A good lawyer like McNulty will tie you in knots."

His shoulders slump. "Am I ever going to get to tell my story?"

"Probably not." Certainly not until we get to the trial, and even then not unless we're desperate.

Bobby responds with a cold stare.

"How are things inside?" I ask.

His lifeless tone matches the vacant look in his eyes. "Bad."

"How bad?"

"Real bad. The guys in the next cell told me they're coming after me."

"Stay in your cell."

"I will."

"The guards are supposed to give you meals in your cell until the prelim is over."

"Then what?"

"We'll deal with it after the prelim if we have to. You have to hang in there."

"I can't do this much longer."

"Everything is going to be fine, Bobby."

"Sure," he says.

# # #

"We need to go through your testimony one more time," I say.

Grace's lips turn down. "Again?" she says.

"Just once more."

"We've been through this twenty times. It's late, Dad."

"Please, honey."

"Fine," she says.

The air is still in Rosie's office at ten thirty on Tuesday night. It's been a long day of planning, strategizing, and rehearsing. The two hours we spent with Lenny Stone were among the most frustrating. Our grim mood is exacerbated by the fact that our efforts to find new witnesses have been futile.

Grace sitting is in one of the uncomfortable swivel chairs. I'm standing next to the open window hoping to find a breath of fresh air. We considered doing this exercise at home. Ultimately, we decided Grace would get a better sense of the pressure and urgency of the situation if we stayed here. Not surprisingly, she's gotten testier as the evening has grown longer.

"So," I say, "what's the first rule of being a good witness?"

Grace's monotone reminds me of learning my catechisms. "Answer only the question that was asked," she recites.

"Good. What's the second rule?"

"Don't volunteer anything."

"And the third?"

"Keep your answers short."

"That's great, honey."

"Right, Dad."

Rosie temples her fingers in front of her face. "Okay," she says, "let's go through your direct testimony one more time. Follow my lead."

Grace nods. Rosie takes her through a moment-by-moment highlight trip of her evening with Bobby: dinner; the movie; the walk to Amoeba; driving home. Grace's delivery is smoother on the third go-around, although her voice is tinged with fatigue.

"That's good, honey," Rosie says.

"Thanks."

"Let's talk about the cross-exam again."

"Do we have to?"

"Yes."

Grace tenses. "Okay," she says.

"Where did you go after the movie?"

"To Amoeba. We stayed there until they closed at midnight. Then we walked back to Bobby's car."

"Did anybody see you?"

"I don't know."

"Where was Bobby's car parked?"

"On Grattan, on the side of his father's house."

"What time did you get back to his car?"

"Twelve fifteen."

"Did you see anybody?"

There's a hesitation. "No."

Rosie's interest is piqued. "Grace?"

"What?"

"Did you see anybody when you got back to Bobby's car?"

"No."

Rosie leans back. "Did you hear anything?"

"No."

"Did you see anything unusual at Judge Fairchild's house?"

"No."

"You're sure?"

"Yes." Grace takes a deep breath. "Damn it, Mother, why are you harassing me?"

"I'm trying to give you an idea of what to expect tomorrow." Rosie takes Grace's hand. "Actually, honey, I've been pretty easy on you. If anything, the prosecutor will be nastier. It's his job to try to trip you up. He's going to look for any conceivable inconsistency in your story. You have to stay focused, Grace."

Grace stares down at the piles of paper on Rosie's desk. "I'm not sure I can do this."

"Yes, you can," Rosie says. "I know this is hard, but we need you to testify. *Bobby* needs you to testify. You're his best chance."

Grace swallows hard. "I'll do the best I can, Mother."

"That's all we can ask, honey."

Grace looks up. "Maybe it would be better if Dad did the direct exam."

"Whatever would make you more comfortable, Grace."

"I think Dad should do it."

"That's fine, honey."

Grace is fighting to hold back tears. "Can we go home now?"

"Sure, honey."

# # #

"There's something she isn't telling us," Rosie whispers as she packs her briefcase a few minutes later. Grace is in the bathroom.

"What makes you think so?" I ask.

"Instinct."

Rosie is the most intuitive person I know—especially when it comes to our daughter. "Did she say something else to you?" I ask.

"It isn't what she said. It's how she said it. I just hope it doesn't explode in open court."

"It's going to be all right," I say.

"It can't get much worse," she replies.

# # #

It gets worse almost immediately. My cell phone rings a few minutes after midnight, as I'm driving mid-span on the Golden Gate Bridge. "It's Roosevelt," the voice says.

"What is it?" I ask.

"I need you to come down to the Hall right away. Your client just tried to kill himself."

"**A**re you okay?" I ask Bobby.

"I'm fine." He says it without conviction. "I don't want you to tell my mother about this."

"I already told her. She's on her way here."

He nods grudgingly. His right wrist is wrapped in bandages. A blanket is draped over his shoulders. He's sitting on an antiquated gurney in the Dickensian infirmary in the basement of the Glamour Slammer. The buzzing fluorescent light emits an eerie glow. The room smells of industrial-strength disinfectant. An irritated deputy is standing guard at the door.

"What happened?" I ask.

"Nothing." His voice is lifeless.

"They said you cut yourself on the bed frame."

"It was an accident."

"No, it wasn't."

"Yes, it was."

We stare at each other for an interminable moment. He doesn't budge. Finally, I tell him they're going to keep him here overnight for observation.

"Fine," he says.

"We'll ask for a delay in your hearing."

"No, you won't."

"Yes, we will. You can't go to court if you aren't a hundred percent."

"I won't make it to court if you don't get me out of here."

"Be reasonable."

"I don't have time."

"We'll talk again later."

"No, we won't. We're moving forward."

# # #

Rosie and I huddle with Julie in the empty lobby of the Hall at two fifteen on Wednesday morning. We're due in court in less than eight hours. The guards let Julie see Bobby for an all-too-brief ten minutes. She's exhausted, and understandably upset.

Rosie's tired voice echoes off the tile floor. "We should ask for a delay."

"The hell you will," Julie snaps. "You have to get Bobby out of here."

"It doesn't work that way."

"Then make it work that way."

Rosie remains unfailingly patient. "We're doing everything we can. The legal system moves slowly."

"My son is going to get killed."

"He's in no shape to sit through a prelim."

"You can't leave him in this hellhole until someone kills him—or he tries to kill himself again. You're the geniuses who know how to make the system work. Start doing your job."

"You're paying us for our judgment on legal issues," I say. "It would be a serious strategic mistake to proceed today."

"I don't care about legal strategies. I'm worried about my son."

"Let's regroup at nine and see how Bobby is doing."

#

Rosie finishes a brief conversation with Grace and snaps her cell phone shut. We're driving across the Golden Gate Bridge at a quarter to three on Wednesday morning.

"How is she?" I ask.

"Putting up a good front."

"Just like her mother."

Rosie frowns. "She isn't going to get any sleep tonight."

"Neither are we."

"What if Bobby really insists on moving forward?"

"He's the client," I say. "We'll do what he says."

"It's a bad idea."

"I know." I try to stay focused. "We'll use the old 'rush to judgment' defense. Then we'll give the judge some options."

"Does that mean you're still planning to try to foist this off on Savage and Hannah?"

"It's our best bet."

"We haven't found a shred of evidence placing Hannah at the scene."

"Savage called Hannah's cell phone on Friday night," I say. "Hannah was around the corner from the judge's house."

"For all we know, he was playing basketball. What's the back-up plan?"

"Kaela Joy and Lenny."

Rosie shakes her head. "Great. We're going to base our defense on the testimony of a former cheerleader and a homeless guy."

"Do you have any better ideas?"

"At the moment, no. And if that doesn't work?"

"Grace will testify that she was with Bobby the entire time and that he didn't go inside his father's house."

#

My cell phone rings again as I'm trudging up the stairs to my apartment at three twenty on Wednesday morning. "We need to talk," Roosevelt says.

I fumble with the key to my apartment and let myself in. I flip on the light and set my briefcase down. "What now?" I ask.

"Meet me in the parking lot of the McDonald's in the Haight right away. Brian Hannah is dead."

40/ ARE YOU PLANNING TO PRESS CHARGES?

Wednesday, June 22, 3:58 a.m.

"Over here, Mike," Roosevelt says.

He's gesturing to me from behind the yellow crime-scene tape strewn across the McDonald's parking lot on the corner of Haight and Stanyan. Ronald McDonald encountered fierce resistance from the neighbors when plans for the fast food emporium were announced thirty years ago. The corporate suits ultimately wore them down. The Golden Arches still appear hopelessly out of place smack-dab in the middle of what was the epicenter of the Summer of Love. Four black-and-whites and a van from Rod Beckert's office are parked near the drive-thru. The blinking red lights from an unneeded ambulance cut through the fog. A handful of FETs are engaged in the meticulous process of taking crime-scene photos and videos.

"He's dead," Roosevelt says to me.

"So I gathered." A rookie assistant medical examiner is hovering over Hannah's motionless body.

"No Rosie tonight?" Roosevelt says.

"It's tough to get a babysitter at this hour."

"What about Pete?"

"He's watching Hannah's boss."

"He picked the wrong guy to follow."

"Evidently. How did it happen?" I ask.

"A single gunshot to the chest about an hour ago."

"I take it this wasn't a suicide?"

"Nope."

"Any suspects?"

"We know who killed him."

What the hell? "Who?"

He gestures toward a black Lincoln Town Car that's parked in the corner of the lot. A tow truck bearing the Bayview Towing logo is parked a few feet away. "The owner of the Lincoln," he says. "He lives in the neighborhood and has a bad habit of parking here overnight. Hannah had a standing order from McDonald's to tow any car parked here after closing. He was setting the hook when the owner arrived to pick up his car for an early airport run."

"So he shot him?"

"Hannah had towed his car a couple of times. They'd had words before. The driver said Hannah came after him with a tire iron. He pulled a .38 and fired in self-defense."

"So he says."

"We have a witness."

"Who?"

"The security guard from McDonald's saw the whole thing." Roosevelt gestures toward a nearby squad car, where a uniformed rent-a-cop is sipping coffee. "You can talk to him after we get his statement."

"We will." I'm not inclined to question his story. Any way you cut it, Hannah will still be dead. "Any other witnesses?" I ask.

"Nope."

Perfect. "You think Savage had anything to do with this?"

"Doubtful."

"Are you planning to press charges against the limo driver?"

"Not at this time." He reads my skeptical look. "We're going to take him downtown and get a statement, but we have a witness."

# # #

"Do you really believe the limo driver killed Hannah in self-defense?" Julie asks.

My cell phone is pressed against my right ear as I'm standing in the doorway of Amoeba at four fifteen on Wednesday morning. Julie was my third call after Rosie and Pete. Haight Street is quiet. "The security guard saw the whole thing," I tell her. "The DA may bring charges against the limo driver for manslaughter, but there's no connection to Savage. We should ask for a continuance while this gets sorted out."

"No, we won't."

"Hannah was our most promising alternative suspect. Now we can't put him on the stand."

"You can still blame him. He isn't around to defend himself."

That much is true. "We don't have any evidence he was inside Jack's house last Friday."

"Then find some."

"The prelim starts in less than six hours."

"You'd better get busy."

"I want to talk to Bobby about it."

"There's nothing to talk about. Bobby didn't kill Jack. You're going to prove it. End of discussion."

Our defense is coming apart. And we're going to war.

Wednesday, June 22, 10:02 a.m.

"**A**ll rise."

The sauna-like courtroom springs to attention as Judge McDaniel takes her seat on the bench. She pretends to ignore the packed gallery as she switches on her computer and dons her reading glasses. "Please be seated," she says.

The bailiff is a dignified Asian woman who has been maintaining decorum in Judge McDaniel's court with understated efficiency for two decades. "The People versus Robert Joseph Fairchild," she recites.

It always sounds serious when they use all three names.

Bobby is sitting silently at the defense table between Rosie and me. We've replaced his orange jumpsuit with a navy sport jacket and a striped tie. For the time being, he looks more like a high school senior than a felon. We've told him to remain attentive and make eye contact with the judge. I lean over and remind him again about the importance of appearances.

Julie and Sean are sitting behind us in the front row of the gallery. In general, potential witnesses are not permitted in court. We were able to persuade Judge McDaniel that motherhood occasionally requires some flexibility in the interpretation of courtroom procedures—even in a murder case. The same courtesy does not extend to the girlfriends of accused murderers. Grace is sequestered in the basement of the Hall under Sylvia's watchful eye. Dr. Derek Newsom is also conspicuously absent. It would send the wrong message if the grieving widow were sitting in the gallery next to her youthful boyfriend.

The DA's Office has also called out the troops. McNulty is studying his notes at the prosecution table. Two glum ADAs from the felony division are unpacking exhibits. Three others fill the first row of the gallery. Roosevelt is sitting at the end of the table. As the SFPD's designated representative on this case, he's allowed to remain in court, even though he's likely to be their star witness.

There is another unexpected guest in the gallery: Robert Kidd. Our performance today is likely to serve as an impromptu audition for our next job.

Showtime. The back of my throat constricts as Judge McDaniel taps her microphone. I still feel twinges of nervousness when the curtain is about to go up. "Mr. Daley," she says, "I understand Mr. Fairchild was injured last night."

Actually, he tried to kill himself. "Yes, Your Honor."

"Is your client able to proceed?"

I shoot a glance in Bobby's direction. He swallows and responds with a determined nod. I turn back and address the judge. "Yes, Your Honor," I say. "He welcomes the opportunity to demonstrate his innocence of these egregious charges as soon as possible."

"Thank you." She pretends to study her docket. In reality, she's taking a moment to gather her thoughts and show her unequivocal command of her courtroom. "The defendant has been charged with a violation of Penal Code Section 189: murder in the first degree. He has entered a not guilty plea. This is a preliminary hearing to determine whether there is sufficient evidence to move forward to trial."

That covers it.

The judge looks up. "Any issues before we begin?"

"Your Honor," I say, "the defense respectfully renews its request for bail."

"And we renew our opposition," McNulty says.

"Duly noted," the judge says. "Mr. Daley, as far as I can tell, nothing has changed since we last addressed this issue."

"Mr. Fairchild is not a flight risk or a threat to the community. We are willing to abide by reasonable restrictions. We are prepared to hire a private security firm to monitor his whereabouts twenty-four/seven."

"Denied."

"But, Your Honor—"

"Bail is still denied, Mr. Daley."

We're off to an inauspicious start. "Your Honor," I say, "we have submitted a motion to contest the prosecution's attempt to include a special circumstance with this charge."

"I will review your papers and rule in due course."

"But, Your Honor—"

"I will rule in due course," she repeats.

Damn it. "We also wish to inform the court that a suspect named Brian Hannah was killed this morning. His testimony was critical to our case."

"Your Honor," McNulty says, "there isn't a shred of evidence connecting Mr. Hannah to Judge Fairchild's death. He wasn't on our witness list."

"He was on ours," I say. "Mr. Hannah was in the vicinity of Judge Fairchild's house on Friday night. We also have proof that he received a telephone call from his employer, George Savage, a convicted felon who threatened Judge Fairchild in open court several weeks ago." It's a blatant play to the press.

The judge invokes a practical tone. "Mr. Daley," she says to me, "are you prepared to proceed without Mr. Hannah's testimony?"

"Looks like we have no choice, Your Honor."

"Fine." She turns to McNulty. "Do you wish to offer an opening statement?"

"Yes, Your Honor." He stands and buttons his charcoal suit jacket. He walks to the lectern, places a single note card in front of him, and adjusts the microphone. "May it please the court," he begins, "Judge Jack Fairchild was a talented lawyer, a respected jurist, a caring husband, and a loving father whose life was tragically cut short." He points an accusatory finger at Bobby. "What makes this situation even more tragic is the fact that Judge Fairchild's own son is responsible for his father's tragic death."

Everybody in this courtroom would agree Jack's death is a tragedy—even without McNasty repeating it a thousand times.

Bobby utters a guttural, "It isn't true."

"Stay calm," I whisper.

McNulty is still glaring at Bobby. "Did you say something, Mr. Fairchild?"

I answer for him. "No, he didn't."

McNulty's eyes are focused on Bobby's. "Do you *want* to say something, Mr. Fairchild?"

He's baiting us. "No, he doesn't," I reply. "Your Honor, would you please instruct Mr. McNulty to address the court?"

"You know better, Mr. McNulty."

"Yes, Your Honor." It takes him just a moment to summarize the most important pieces of evidence. Then he picks up his note card and lowers his voice. "Julie Fairchild has lost her husband. Sean Fairchild has lost his father. The legal community has lost a respected colleague and friend. We will demonstrate that there is sufficient evidence to bring Robert Joseph Fairchild to trial for the murder of his father. We must bring the person responsible for this great tragedy to justice."

The judge remains impassive as McNulty returns to his seat, where Ward gives him an obligatory nod of approval. On a scale of one to ten,

I'd give him an eight. He stayed on message and kept it short. I deducted a couple of style points for being melodramatic. Hyperbole doesn't play well in front of a smart judge.

Judge McDaniel looks at me. "Do you wish to make an opening statement, Mr. Daley?"

"Yes, Your Honor." I have the option of waiting until McNulty finishes his case, but I want to make a few points right away. I've never subscribed to the theory you win cases during opening statements. I do, however, believe you have only one chance to make a strong first impression.

I glance down at the note Rosie jotted on the pad between us. It instructs me to keep my remarks to two minutes. I walk to the lectern and wait for the courtroom to go completely silent. I start in the modulated tone I used when I presided at funerals. "Your Honor," I begin, "nobody disputes the fact that Judge Fairchild's death is a tragedy. However, it would be an even greater tragedy to try his son for a crime he did not commit."

The judge raises an eyebrow. At least she's listening.

"Your Honor," I continue, "Bobby Fairchild is not a killer. He's a victim. He hasn't been allowed to grieve for his father. He's been attacked in jail. He became so distraught that he attempted to injure himself last night. He will bear the burdens of this egregious mistake for the rest of his life."

McNulty stands to raise a legitimate objection, but reconsiders. It's unseemly to interrupt during an opening.

"Your Honor," I continue, "we take the killing of a judge very seriously. We also understand the prosecution's desire for swift justice. On the other hand, it doesn't give Mr. McNulty carte blanche to do whatever it takes to resolve this case. If anything, we should proceed with caution to ensure our rules and procedures are followed. It's the right thing to do. It's what Judge Fairchild would have wanted. We will demonstrate that Bobby Fairchild is the victim of a rush to judgment. We will show there is insufficient evidence to bind him over for trial."

I look up at the judge for a reaction, but none is forthcoming. She turns to McNulty and says, "Please call your first witness."

"The prosecution calls Officer Philip Dito."

# # #

Phil Dito is sporting a pressed patrolman's uniform as he sits in the witness box. "I've been a San Francisco police officer for twenty-seven years," he says. He's the embodiment of a competent career cop.

McNulty is standing at the lectern. The conventional wisdom says you should give a strong witness plenty of room. "Officer Dito," he says, "where do you work?"

"Park Station." He says it with pride.

"That includes Cole Valley and the Haight, doesn't it?"

"Objection," I say. "Leading." I'm trying to break up their rhythm.

"Sustained."

McNulty shoots a snarky glance my way, then turns back to the matters at hand. "Officer Dito," he says, "does Park Station cover Judge Jack Fairchild's house at the corner of Belvedere and Grattan?"

"Yes."

"Were you on duty in the early morning of Saturday, June eighteenth?"

"Yes."

Good prosecutors ask short, easy-to-follow questions.

"Did you respond to a 911 call at two ten a.m.?"

"Yes. There was a report of a homicide at Judge Fairchild's house."

The first points are quickly on the board. We have a body and a crime scene.

"Who made the call?" McNulty asks.

"The defendant. He was at his father's house."

Now he's placed Bobby at the scene.

"Officer Dito," McNulty continues, "how long did it take you to get there?"

"Less than five minutes."

"Did any other officers accompany you?"

"No. My partner was out sick, so I went by myself. I requested backup. Additional units arrived within minutes."

"What did you do when you arrived at Judge Fairchild's house?"

The creases in Dito's weather-worn face become more pronounced. "I followed standard procedure." He says he surveyed the exterior of the house and concluded he was in no imminent danger. "I knocked on the door and identified myself as a police officer. The defendant answered."

"Would you please describe the defendant's demeanor?"

"He was extremely agitated and upset."

"Do you know why?"

"He had killed his father."

Nice try. "Move to strike," I say. "Foundation. There are no facts in evidence to support Officer Dito's assertion that Bobby Fairchild killed his father."

"Sustained."

McNulty is unfazed. "Was the defendant holding anything?"

"A hammer."

McNulty walks over to the evidence cart and picks up the hammer wrapped in a clear plastic evidence bag and tagged. "Is this it?" he asks.

"Yes."

McNulty goes through the customary recitations to introduce the hammer into evidence. "Did you notice anything distinctive about this hammer?"

"It was covered with blood. The defendant tried to hand it to me, but I instructed him to place it on the floor. I wanted to avoid contamination."

"Did the defendant tell you how he came to have this object in his possession?"

"He said he used it to kill his father."

Bobby can barely contain himself. "That's a lie," he whispers to me. "I said it was the hammer that *somebody else* used to kill my father."

"Objection, Your Honor," I say. "Hearsay."

"Overruled."

"Exception."

"Noted."

I'm not finished. "Your Honor," I say, "Officer Dito is intentionally mischaracterizing his conversation with my client. There was no confession."

"You'll have to take it up on cross, Mr. Daley."

I will. Legally, it's the correct call. Morally, it's appalling that the rules of evidence permit the admission of such a highly inflammatory statement. My only remaining recourse is to whine. "But, Your Honor—"

"I've ruled, Mr. Daley."

Julie leans forward and whispers, "We're getting killed."

Thanks for bringing it to my attention. "The prosecution always scores points at the beginning," I tell her. Especially when you have a smart prosecutor like McNulty and a well-trained cop like Dito.

The gallery sits in rapt attention as McNulty leads Dito through a quick and damaging description of the gruesome crime-scene photos. Dito notes there were no signs of forced entry. He describes the overturned coat rack and table in the foyer. He confirms that nothing was missing from the house. A triumphant McNulty returns to his seat a mere five minutes after Dito took the stand.

"Cross-exam, Mr. Daley?" the judge asks.

"Yes, Your Honor." Robert Kidd always used to say you need the mindset of a heavyweight fighter when you cross-examine a strong witness. You get in close and try not to let your opponent breathe. "May we approach?"

"Yes, Mr. Daley."

I move in front of Dito, who leans forward. My father taught him to meet an uppity defense lawyer head on. "Officer Dito," I begin, "you testified that Bobby Fairchild was upset when he answered the door."

"Yes."

"You realize he had just found his father's body."

"I had no way of verifying that information at the time."

"You now understand Bobby had just turned eighteen."

"That's old enough to commit murder."

"It's also young enough to be very upset when you find a body—especially your own father's. How many times have you been called to the scene of a homicide?"

"About a dozen."

"How many times were you met by the children of the deceased?"

"Including this case, three."

"How did they react?"

"They were very upset."

Big surprise. "Wouldn't it therefore be fair to say Bobby's behavior wasn't unusual?"

McNulty is up. "Objection, Your Honor. Calls for speculation."

"Sustained."

"I'll rephrase. Given your experience," I say, "was Bobby's reaction unusual?"

"Probably not."

"It certainly shouldn't have been surprising he was visibly upset when you arrived a few minutes after he had discovered his father's body, right?"

"Objection," McNulty says. "Asked and answered."

"Sustained."

"Officer Dito," I continue, "did you see Bobby kill his father?"

"No."

"Have you or your colleagues found any witnesses who saw him kill his father?"

McNulty is up again. "Your Honor," he says, "we'll stipulate to the fact that the police have found no witnesses who saw the defendant kill his father."

"Thank you, Mr. McNulty," the judge says.

Good enough. I was simply trying to establish that this is a circumstantial case. "Officer Dito," I say, "you testified a moment ago that Bobby was holding a hammer when he answered the door."

"Correct." Dito flashes a hint of irritation. Cops hate it when defense lawyers try to use their own words against them.

"You also testified that he told you he had used the hammer to kill his father."

He's trying to figure out where I'm heading. "Correct."

"In other words, you're saying he confessed."

"Not in so many words."

"Either he did or he didn't. Yes or no?"

Dito thinks about it for an instant. "Yes."

"You filed a detailed police report regarding the events of Saturday morning, didn't you?"

"Of course."

"There was nothing in it about a confession."

"Yes, there was."

"You didn't use the word 'confess,' did you?"

"The defendant didn't use that word."

"That's because he didn't confess."

"Yes, he did."

"Then why didn't you put it in your report?"

"I did."

The hell you did. I flip open the report. "I'm quoting page two: 'Defendant acknowledged that a hammer was used to kill his father.'"

"Correct."

"That isn't a confession."

"Objection," McNulty says. "We're going in circles."

That's the whole idea. "Your Honor," I say, "Mr. McNulty is trying to stretch Officer Dito's testimony to suggest Bobby confessed. In reality, he didn't."

"Your Honor," McNulty says, "Mr. Daley is intentionally mischaracterizing Officer Dito's testimony."

"That's precisely what Mr. McNulty is doing." I can play semantic games, too.

"Your Honor—"

I cut McNulty off. "Your Honor," I say, "Bobby told Officer Dito that the hammer was used to kill his father. Notwithstanding Mr. McNulty's clever attempts at parsing, Bobby did not say *he* used the hammer to kill his father. There's a big difference. That's why Officer Dito's report made no mention of a confession."

McNulty's voice rises. "Your Honor," he says, "now Mr. Daley is testifying."

"No, I'm not." Yes, I am.

"Mr. Daley is also calling Officer Dito a liar."

"I'm not doing that, either." Well, sort of.

"Mr. Daley is trying to put words in my mouth."

I'm *definitely* doing that. "Now Mr. McNulty is testifying. I'm simply trying to provide the court with a truthful account of what Officer Dito saw and heard based solely upon the contents of his own police report. If Bobby had confessed to killing his father, a highly esteemed veteran such as Officer Dito would have mentioned it."

"He did," McNulty says.

"No, he didn't."

"Your Honor—" McNulty says.

Judge McDaniel stops him with an upraised hand. "You've made your position abundantly clear, Mr. McNulty. Anything else for this witness, Mr. Daley?"

The irritation in her tone suggests she may be leaning our way, but it's impossible to know for sure. I decide to stop while I'm ahead. "No, Your Honor."

"Please call your next witness, Mr. McNulty."

"The People call Dr. Roderick Beckert."

Wednesday, June 22, 10:18 a.m.

"How long have you been the Chief Medical Examiner of the City and County of San Francisco?" McNulty asks. Rod Beckert has ditched his starched white lab coat for a starched gray Armani suit. "Thirty-eight years," he says.

Judge McDaniel knows he's the real deal. "Your Honor," I say, "we'll stipulate to Dr. Beckert's expertise."

"Dr. Beckert," McNulty continues, "did you perform the autopsy on Judge Fairchild at approximately seven thirty on the morning of Saturday, June eighteenth?"

"I did."

McNulty clutches the autopsy report to his bosom as if it were the Holy Grail. "Your Honor," he says, "we would like to introduce Dr. Beckert's autopsy report into evidence."

"No objection," I say.

McNulty walks across the well of the courtroom and hands a copy of the thin volume to Beckert. "Doctor," he says, "would you please confirm that you prepared this report?"

"I did."

"Did you conduct the autopsy in accordance with the highest professional standards?"

There's no reason to give Beckert fifteen minutes to read his résumé into the record. "Your Honor," I say, "Dr. Beckert is an authority in his field. We will also stipulate that he conducted the autopsy in accordance with recognized standards."

I feel a tap on my shoulder. I turn around and see the fire in Julie's eyes. "Aren't you going to challenge his credibility?" she whispers.

I don't have time for this. "He's as good at his job as you are at yours."

McNulty is still hovering in front of the witness box. "Doctor," he says, "were you able to determine the cause of Judge Fairchild's death?"

"A blow from a blunt object caused a massive head wound and a fractured skull."

"And time of death?"

"Between eleven forty-five p.m. and twelve thirty a.m."

"It's possible to make that determination with such precision?"

"The body was still warm when I arrived at the scene. As a result, I was able to take very precise temperature readings of various organs. I performed other tests relating to the state of rigor mortis, lividity, and the degree of digestion of the food in his stomach."

That's good enough for McNulty. "No further questions."

"Cross-exam, Mr. Daley?" the judge asks.

"Yes, Your Honor." I button my jacket and walk over to the evidence cart. I pick up the hammer and hold it up in front of Beckert. "Doctor," I say, "is it your contention that this hammer was used to inflict the fatal blow?"

"Yes."

"Did you find any traces of metal in Judge Fairchild's skull?"

"That would have been almost impossible, Mr. Daley."

"Yes or no—did you find any such traces?"

"No."

"Were you able to match the contour of the hammer to the injury in the judge's skull?"

"Not precisely."

"So you can't say for sure whether the killer hit the judge with this hammer, can you?"

"It was covered with his blood, Mr. Daley. The implication is clear."

"Implications aren't evidence, Dr. Beckert."

"Objection," McNulty says. "There wasn't a question there."

No, there wasn't. "Withdrawn. Dr. Beckert," I continue, "is it possible Judge Fairchild's blood could have found its way onto the hammer in some way other than as a result of the defendant having hit him?"

"Objection," McNulty says. "Speculation."

"I'm asking for an informed opinion based upon Dr. Beckert's expertise, to which I've already stipulated." I'm also asking him to speculate.

"Overruled."

"It's unlikely," Beckert says.

"But it's possible?"

"It's unlikely," Beckert repeats.

"I'm going to take that as an affirmative answer. Is it also possible the blood could have found its way to the hammer when the defendant tried to help his father? Or somebody else hit him?"

McNulty's decision not to object to my blatantly speculative questions shows his confidence in Beckert. It also reflects the practical reality that Judge McDaniel is going to give Beckert the benefit of the doubt.

"Mr. Daley," Beckert says, "it is also possible that I came to court this morning on the Starship Enterprise. Even *you* would acknowledge it's highly unlikely."

Judge McDaniel taps her gavel to silence the gallery.

"What time did you arrive at the scene?" I ask Beckert.

"Two thirty-seven a.m."

"According to your own calculations, that would have been more than two hours after the judge was killed?"

"Yes."

"Was the body still in the laundry room when you arrived?"

"Yes."

"Had the paramedics administered CPR and other first aid?"

"Of course."

"Had they moved the body?"

"A little. It was a tight space. They needed room to work."

"Had they opened the garage door?"

"Yes."

"What about the door leading from the garage into the house?"

"It was still propped open by the body."

"Isn't it therefore possible that the jostling of the body and the exposure to the cold night air may have impacted the precision of your measurements in determining time of death?"

"Perhaps slightly, but only to an inconsequential degree."

"How inconsequential?" I ask.

"I can't say for sure."

Every second matters. "Two minutes? Five minutes? Ten minutes? An hour?"

Beckert invokes a professorial tone. "It didn't have any substantial impact on my calculations in this case."

# # #

McNulty is behind the lectern a few minutes later. "Sergeant Jacobsen," he begins, "how long have you been an evidence specialist with the SFPD?"

"Twenty-seven years."

Kathleen Jacobsen has been plying her trade in the bowels of the Hall longer than anybody except Beckert, Roosevelt, and the blind man who's run the sandwich cart in the lobby since the Kennedy administration. She spends her free time providing expert testimony in high-profile cases in other parts of the country. Though she steadfastly eschews the limelight, she became an unlikely media darling when she added her understated gravitas to CNN's coverage of the Scott Peterson trial. She's one of the few members of the media who emerged from that frenzy with her reputation and dignity intact.

"Sergeant," McNulty continues, "you supervised the collection of the evidence at Judge Fairchild's house, didn't you?"

"Yes."

To the untrained eye, the paunchy prosecutor and the stoic lesbian criminalist look like a couple of middle-aged bureaucrats going through their paces. To those of us who have had the privilege of admiring their work for the past two decades, they're the legal profession's counterpart to Astaire and Rogers.

McNulty walks over to the evidence cart and picks up the hammer Jacobsen meticulously wrapped and tagged. "Sergeant," he says, "can you identify this item?"

"It's the murder weapon," she says.

Well played. "Objection," I say. "Move to strike the witness's characterization of this exhibit as the 'murder' weapon. It assumes facts not yet admitted into evidence."

"Sustained."

McNulty and Jacobsen feign contrition as the judge halfheartedly admonishes them for trying to introduce evidence without the proper foundation. It's a lovely gesture, but everybody knows Fred and Ginger had it planned in advance.

"Were you able to positively identify the victim's blood on this hammer through DNA?"

"Yes."

I could make the usual—and futile—objection about the unreliability of DNA tests. Thanks to *CSI*, everybody believes they're infallible. In fairness, they're about as close as you can get to a sure bet. Studies have shown that jurors now expect prosecutors to pull a DNA rabbit out of a hat sometime during trial, just like on TV. In academic circles, it's called the *CSI* Effect.

"How were you able to conclude the tests so quickly?" McNulty asks.

"There is a common misperception that DNA tests take days or weeks. In reality, they can be concluded within a few days."

That much is true. It just takes money and clout.

"Were you able to positively identify any fingerprints on the hammer?" McNulty asks.

"Just the defendant's."

"What about smudged prints or unidentifiable prints?"

"None."

"No further questions."

I head straight for the witness box and park myself right in front of Jacobsen. "Sergeant," I say, "did Bobby Fairchild try to hide the bloody hammer?"

"No."

"If he was guilty, why didn't he get rid of it?"

"Objection," McNulty says. "Speculation."

"Sustained."

"Sergeant," I say, "Dr. Beckert placed the time of death between eleven forty-five p.m. and twelve thirty a.m., didn't he?"

"Yes."

Good. "Do you have any forensic evidence placing Bobby inside his father's house between eleven forty-five on Friday night and twelve thirty on Saturday morning?"

"His fingerprints were on the hammer."

Not good enough. "He admitted he picked up the hammer when he returned home at two a.m."

"We found his fingerprints all over the house."

"Everybody knows fingerprints have an indefinite shelf life and could have been weeks or months old. I'm going to ask you one more time: Did you find any forensic evidence placing Bobby Fairchild inside his father's house between the hours of eleven forty-five p.m. last Friday night and twelve thirty a.m. last Saturday morning?"

"No, Mr. Daley."

Okay. "Did you find any fingerprints in the house or the garage other than Bobby's?"

"Many. We found Judge Fairchild's fingerprints along with those of his son, Sean. We found the fingerprints of the defendant's girlfriend. We also found prints from Judge Fairchild's wife and several of the defendant's friends." She reads off a list of friends, relatives, cleaning people, and other hangers-on who had visited the Fairchild residence from time to time.

"Did you find any unidentifiable prints?"

"We found two smudged prints in the laundry room and a partial print on the inside knob of the front door. We ran the partial through the available databases. There were no matches with anybody with a criminal record. We've also ruled out relatives, friends, neighbors, and the defendant's girlfriend."

"Which means the smudged print could have belonged to anybody—including the person who killed Judge Fairchild."

"We have no evidence to that effect."

It opens up some possibilities, but it's all I can do for now. "No further questions."

Wednesday, June 22, 11:36 a.m.

"Mrs. Osborne," McNulty begins gently, "you taught at Grattan Elementary School for many years, didn't you?" I could object to the leading question, but I'll look petty.

Evelyn Osborne sits up a little taller and answers in her best school-teacher voice. "Forty years," she says.

McNulty has quickly established her as a credible and sympathetic witness. "How well did you know Judge Fairchild?"

"Not very well. He moved in next door just a few months ago. He was a good neighbor."

"And his children?"

"Bobby and Sean are nice boys. They've helped me around the house."

"Did they ever argue with their father?"

"Occasionally. You know how it is with teenagers."

"Yes, I do."

No, you don't. McNulty doesn't have any kids.

"Mrs. Osborne," he continues, "did you overhear an argument between Bobby Fairchild and his father on the morning of Friday, June seventeenth?"

"I'm not an eavesdropper, Mr. McNulty."

"Of course not, but did you hear them arguing?"

"Yes."

"What were they arguing about?"

"Teenage stuff."

"Could you be more specific?"

"Objection," I say. "Hearsay. This line of questioning is also an impermissible attempt to bring in evidence of Bobby's character."

"Overruled. Please answer the question, Mrs. Osborne."

"Judge Fairchild thought Bobby was spending too much time with his girlfriend."

"How did Bobby react?"

"He was very upset. He left the house and slammed the door behind him."

"Do you recall whether he said anything else to his father?"

I'm on my feet again. "Objection," I say. "Hearsay."

"Overruled."

She clutches her reading glasses tightly. "He told him he was going to make him pay."

"Those were his exact words?"

"Yes."

"No further questions."

I'm in a delicate spot. I need to discredit her testimony without coming off as a jerk. I address her from my seat. "Mrs. Osborne," I say, "how long have you lived on Belvedere Street?"

"Forty-seven years."

"You mentioned Judge Fairchild's sons have been helpful neighbors."

"Yes, they have."

"Have they ever given you any trouble?"

"Not really. They play their music a little too loud sometimes."

"Where were you when you heard the conversation between Bobby and his father?"

"In my kitchen. My window looks directly into Judge Fairchild's kitchen."

"How close is your window to the judge's?"

"About ten feet."

"Was your window open?"

"No."

"Was his?"

"I don't think so."

"Was your TV on?"

"Yes. I was watching *Mornings on Two*."

"I see. Were you eating breakfast?"

"I was having coffee."

"Mrs. Osborne," I say, "I apologize for asking about a personal matter, but I couldn't help noticing that you're wearing a hearing aid today."

"Yes, I am."

"Does it work pretty well?"

"I think so. My daughter says it might need to be adjusted a little."

She's incapable of lying. "Was the TV pretty loud?"

"Loud enough."

"Was it hard to hear Judge Fairchild and Bobby?"

"They were pretty loud, too."

"Louder than your TV?"

"Loud enough for me to hear them."

"Mrs. Osborne," I say, "I mean no disrespect, but is it possible that you may have misheard the judge and his son?"

She invokes the tone of someone who sent countless ill-behaved children to the principal's office. "I know what I heard, Mr. Daley."

I take a chance. "Do you think Bobby would have hurt his father?"

"Objection," McNulty says. "Calls for speculation."

"Overruled."

I didn't think Judge McDaniel would give me that one.

Evelyn Osborne fingers the gold chain that holds her reading glasses. "I don't think so, Mr. Daley. Bobby's a good boy who did very well in school."

"Thank you, Mrs. Osborne. No further questions."

Rosie leans over and whispers, "You did everything you could, Mike. If you had pushed any harder, she would have given you a detention."

# # #

Treadwell is up next. Sporting a charcoal going-to-court suit, he's sitting in the witness box with his hands clasped in front of him. "I was walking my dog on Belvedere when I saw Bobby Fairchild running down Grattan at twelve ten on Saturday morning," he says.

McNulty is addressing his former colleague from the prosecution table. "You're sure it was the defendant?" he asks.

"Yes. I've known him since he was a boy."

"No further questions."

I'm on my feet right away. A retired teacher was entitled to kid gloves. A former prosecutor isn't. I approach the witness box and gesture toward an enlarged satellite photo of the area surrounding Jack Fairchild's house. "Mr. Treadwell," I say, "could you please show us where you were standing when you saw somebody running down Grattan Street?"

He points to a spot near the corner of Belvedere and Grattan, across the street from the Fairchild house. "Right here," he says.

"That was about a hundred feet away from where the individual was running?"

"I'd say a little less."

"It was pretty dark, wasn't it?"

"There are streetlights."

"And foggy?"

"A little."

"And cold?"

"Chilly."

"And you were probably walking pretty quickly, weren't you?"

"Yes."

"Was your dog on a leash?"

"Yes."

"But you needed to keep an eye on him, right?"

"He's very smart."

Just like his master. "Were you wearing an iPod or other electronic device?"

"No."

Too bad. "Do you recall what kind of clothes this person was wearing?"

"I didn't notice."

"How about shoes?"

"I don't recall."

"A hat?"

"I don't remember."

"Did you see any blood on his clothes?"

"I didn't notice."

"Was he running toward you or away from you?"

"Away."

"Then how were you able to see his face?"

"I saw him from the side."

"Was he running fast?"

"I'd say a medium jog."

"So you probably saw him for just a second, right?"

"I'd say a couple of seconds."

"Did you call out to him?"

"No. I was busy."

"Walking your dog."

"Correct."

"You weren't concerned that your neighbor's son was out after midnight?"

"It happened very quickly. I didn't have time to react."

"So," I say, "from a distance of a hundred feet on a cold and foggy night while you were walking your dog, you were able to positively identify Bobby Fairchild from behind even though he was running away from you and you saw him for just a second or two?"

"Yes, Mr. Daley."

You're full of crap. "Did you see where he came from?"

"No."

"Was he inside Judge Fairchild's house?"

"I don't know."

I change course. "What did you do prior to your retirement, Mr. Treadwell?"

"I was a felony prosecutor with the San Francisco District Attorney's Office."

Impressive. "You worked on some cases with Mr. McNulty, didn't you?"

"Yes."

"In fact you trained him, didn't you?"

"Yes."

"And you're friends, right?"

"Yes."

"Friends try to help each other, don't they?"

He shakes his head. "I wouldn't lie to help a former colleague, Mr. Daley."

"But you might be inclined to give him the benefit of the doubt."

"Objection," McNulty says. "Argumentative."

"Withdrawn. No further questions, Your Honor."

The judge turns to McNulty. "Any other witnesses?"

"Just one, Your Honor. The People call Inspector Roosevelt Johnson."

44/ HOW MANY HOMICIDES HAVE YOU INVESTIGATED?

Wednesday, June 22, 11:48 a.m.

McNulty is standing at the lectern. "Inspector Johnson," he begins, "how long have you been with the San Francisco Police Department?"

Roosevelt taps the microphone. "Forty-eight years."

"How many homicides have you investigated during that time?"

"Hundreds."

"Your Honor," I say, "we will stipulate as to Inspector Johnson's experience."

"Thank you, Mr. Daley."

"Inspector," McNulty continues, "are you heading the investigation of the murder of Judge Jack Fairchild?"

"Alleged murder," I interject.

"Alleged murder," McNulty mutters.

"Yes," Roosevelt says.

"When did you arrive at the scene?"

"Two twenty-eight on Saturday morning." McNulty is deferential as he leads Roosevelt through a crisp minute-by-minute description of what transpired in the wee hours, making compelling use of the graphic crime scene photos. By the time they're finished, there is little room to challenge the procedures used to secure the crime scene or the chain of custody of the evidence.

"When did you first talk to the defendant?" McNulty asks.

"As soon as I arrived. He was very upset."

"That shouldn't have been surprising in the circumstances."

"It wasn't."

"When did you first consider the possibility that the defendant could have been involved in his father's death?"

"At first I thought it might have been a botched robbery. I also thought it was possible the judge might have been killed by somebody who had a grudge. That sort of thing is all too common nowadays. The longer that I spoke to the defendant, the more suspicious I became. He had difficulty describing where he had been on Friday night. Then the physical evidence started pointing in his direction."

"What physical evidence was that?" McNulty asks.

"Among other things, the defendant was holding a bloody hammer when the first officer arrived on the scene."

It takes Roosevelt and McNulty just a few minutes to go through a carefully rehearsed description of the physical evidence. Finally, McNulty walks back to the evidence cart and picks up four sealed plastic bags. "Can you identify these items?" he asks.

"They're the defendant's shirt, pants, socks, and tennis shoes. They found in the washer in the room where the body was found. Through DNA testing, we were able to identify traces of Judge Fairchild's blood in the clothing."

They'll be making *CSI: San Francisco* soon.

"Who put these items in the washer?" McNulty asks.

"The defendant."

"How do you know?"

"He admitted it."

"Did the defendant say when he put the items into the washer?"

"He said he did it while he was waiting for the police to arrive."

"Did it strike you as odd that the defendant was worried about washing his bloody clothing while his father lay dying a few feet away?"

"Objection," I say. "Calls for speculation."

"Sustained."

McNulty keeps pushing. "Inspector," he says, "did the defendant tell you why he decided to launder his clothing?"

"He said he didn't want to wear clothing covered with his father's blood. I believe the defendant was trying to hide his bloody clothing before the police arrived."

"Move to strike," I say. "Inspector Johnson's opinions—however well-informed—are not evidence."

"Sustained. Anything else, Mr. McNulty?"

"Just one more thing, Your Honor." McNulty walks back to the evidence cart and picks up a small plastic evidence bag. "Inspector," he says, "where did you find the contents of this bag?"

"A few feet from Judge Fairchild's body on the floor of the laundry room."

Rosie leans over and whispers, "What's going on?"

"I don't know."

McNulty holds up the baggie. "Would you please tell us what's inside this bag?"

"Two grams of marijuana."

What the hell? "Objection," I say. "This evidence did not appear in any police report. Furthermore, we were not given an opportunity to examine it or conduct our own tests to confirm the nature of this substance."

McNulty can't contain a smile as he responds in a patronizing tone. "Your Honor," he says, "the rules of criminal procedure require us to make evidence available to the defense only if it would tend to exonerate the defendant. I can assure you this does not."

That's for sure. "Your Honor," I say, "we strenuously object to the introduction of this evidence. This is without foundation and highly inflammatory."

"Overruled."

"Your Honor—"

"I've ruled, Mr. Daley. Anything else for this witness, Mr. McNulty?"

"One final question, Your Honor." He turns back to Roosevelt and lays it on the line. "Inspector," he says, "would you please summarize what happened at Judge Fairchild's house late last Friday night and early Saturday morning?"

"Certainly, Mr. McNulty." Roosevelt clears his throat and addresses Judge McDaniel. "The defendant went to dinner and a movie with his girlfriend. Then they went over to Judge Fairchild's house to pick up the defendant's car. It also appears the defendant was going to pick up some marijuana to share with his girlfriend."

Bobby leans over and whispers, "Not true."

"Quiet," I whisper. "The judge is watching. Let me handle it on cross-exam."

Roosevelt is still talking. "I believe the defendant was looking for his stash in the laundry room when his father came home. The defendant spilled some of the marijuana onto the floor. He and his father argued. The defendant grabbed a nearby hammer and hit his father, killing him on the spot. The defendant vandalized the foyer in an attempt to make it look like a botched robbery. He placed his clothes in the washer. He changed clothes and went out to the car, where his girlfriend was waiting for him. He drove her home, knowing she could provide an alibi."

At least he didn't implicate Grace.

"A seemingly perfect alibi," McNulty says.

"Not quite," Roosevelt says. "Mr. Treadwell saw him running down the street. We found traces of his father's blood in his laundered clothes. We found the marijuana in the laundry room. The staged vandalism of the foyer was little more than a clumsy attempt at a cover-up." Roosevelt invokes a fatherly tone. "I've been doing this for a long time. The sad reality was obvious: Bobby Fairchild killed his father."

"No further questions, Your Honor."

"Cross-exam, Mr. Daley?"

I need to talk to Bobby. "Your Honor," I say, "we request a brief recess to consult with our client."

Judge McDaniel looks at her watch. "We'll pick up with Inspector Johnson's cross-exam after lunch," she says.

45/ IT WASN'T MINE

Wednesday, June 22, 12:04 p.m.

"It wasn't mine," Bobby insists. His face is ashen, but his tone is adamant. He's staring at an uneaten turkey sandwich on the metal table inside the windowless holding pen behind Judge McDaniel's courtroom.

"Whose dope was it?" I ask.

"I don't know."

"How did it get inside the laundry room?"

"I don't know that, either."

"We can't afford any more surprises, Bobby."

"What are they trying to prove?" he asks.

Rosie answers him. "It's about appearances," she says. "We're trying to portray you as an honor student who has been unjustly accused. They're implying you're a doper who got into a fight with your father about drugs. It's an attempt to undercut our argument that you're a Boy Scout who is heading for an Ivy League school. It also suggests a motive."

"But it isn't true," Bobby pleads.

"It still looks terrible," I say, "It's also a distraction. By itself, the dope may have nothing to do with this case. Even so, we're going to have to deal with it."

"It wasn't mine," he repeats.

"What about your friends?" I ask. And your girlfriend?

"No."

Julie had been listening in simmering silence. "Are we done with the inquisition now?" she snaps. She's desperate to believe her son.

"It's on the record," I say. "It's going to be in the papers. It would help if we had an explanation."

"We do. It wasn't Bobby's. End of story."

"We can't put Bobby on the stand to testify that it wasn't his."

"Why the hell not?"

Because McNulty will eat him for lunch. "You never put a defendant on the stand unless you're desperate."

"Why don't you believe my son?"

Because there are holes in his story. "It's our job to be skeptical," I say. "It would be very helpful if we could figure out how the dope got there."

"Put me on the stand," Julie says. "I'll say it was mine."

Gimme a break. "That isn't true."

"How do you know?"

"It wouldn't take a rocket scientist to figure out that you were making it up to try to protect him. It will destroy your credibility—and his."

A sarcastic sneer crosses her face. "I love it when you lawyers try to take the moral high ground. What would *you* suggest?"

I can't imagine how she thinks it's helpful to excoriate us in front of our client. "We can ask for a continuance to try to figure out how it got there."

"That's out of the question."

"Unless you can tell us where the dope came from, our only option is to go after Inspector Johnson on cross-exam."

"That won't be enough."

"Then you can hire another lawyer."

Before she can respond, she's interrupted by the piercing sound of Bobby's voice. "Stop it," he shouts. "Stop it right now."

The cramped room goes silent as we turn to face him.

"I'm sorry to interrupt your little pissing contest," he says, "but my ass is on the line. I think my opinion should count for something."

Julie and I glare at each other for an instant. "It does," I say to Bobby.

"Then here's how it's going to come down. First, we aren't going to ask for a continuance. Second, you're going to do whatever you can on cross-exam. Third, I'm not going to hire another lawyer. Not today. Not tomorrow. Not the next day."

"Bobby—" Julie says.

"I've made up my mind, Mother. Maybe now we can get back to work."

Julie stares at the floor.

Rosie chooses her words with care. "Bobby," she says, "do you have any idea how that dope found its way into your father's house?"

"No."

"What about Sean?" she asks.

"No."

"Are you sure?"

"As far as I know, he's clean."

It's a more equivocal answer than I had expected. I decide to play a hunch. "Are you protecting him?"

Julie answers for him. "No, he isn't."

"I didn't ask you."

Her eyes fill with anger.

Bobby places his hands on the table in front of him. "No," he says softly. "I'm not protecting Sean."

"This isn't a time to be a hero."

"I'm not."

Julie interjects again. "Are we done?"

"We'll meet you back in court at one o'clock," I say. "I want to talk to Grace."

# # #

Grace's dark brown eyes are on fire, her voice full of exasperation. "Now they're saying Bobby's a pothead?"

"That's the gist of it," I reply.

We're meeting in the moldy file room in the basement of the Hall where one of Rosie's high school classmates works. Grace and Sylvia have been cooling their heels down here, away from the prying eyes of the media. Grace has been passing the time in our inelegant command center, skipping between CNN and the local news websites on her laptop. Sylvia is reading the online version of the *Chronicle*.

Our daughter's expression transforms into a pronounced scowl. "It isn't true," she says.

"Has Bobby ever offered you anything?" I ask.

She's becoming more agitated. "No."

"Ever been to a party where people offered you drugs or alcohol?"

She shakes her head a little too emphatically. "No."

"Grace?"

She waits a beat. "A couple of times."

No surprise. "Ever tried anything?"

Another hesitation. "Once or twice. Everybody does it, Dad."

"That doesn't make it right." I realize I sound just like my parents as I say it.

Grace fires right back. "As if you never did anything when you were in high school."

"That has nothing to do with this."

"It does if you're going to judge me."

"I'm allowed to judge you. I'm your father."

"You set a great example. Don't blame me for doing the same stuff you did."

"I'm not blaming anybody."

"Yes, you are."

Yes, I am. "There are consequences, Grace."

"Don't lecture me. We've been inundated with anti-drug programs since second grade. We understand the issues a lot better than you did."

That much is true. "You're only sixteen."

"That's old enough to make my own decisions. It isn't as if I'm going to develop a drug problem. I'm an athlete. I have too much respect for my body and myself."

"Don't be naïve, Grace."

"Don't be judgmental, Dad."

My throat is burning. "This isn't just about drugs or booze," I say. "You could get into serious trouble if you hang out with the wrong people."

"Come on, Dad."

It feels as if I'm reciting from one of those canned public service announcements on TV. "Have you ever been to a party where somebody called the cops?"

"Once. Nobody got arrested. Besides, it has nothing to do with Bobby's case."

Rosie can't hold back any longer. "Do you know what can happen if you get drunk at a party?"

"Yes. I wouldn't do it."

"It happens all the time. You or your friends could get in a car. You could end up in jail. You could get hurt—or worse."

"That isn't going to happen, Mother."

"That's what everybody says—until it happens to them."

"I have better judgment."

"Like showing up an hour after curfew on Friday night?"

Grace is indignant. "We weren't drinking. We just lost track of the time."

"That isn't the point, Grace."

"What *is* your point, Mother?"

"You're old enough to understand the ramifications of your actions for yourself and the people around you—including your father and me. With privileges come responsibilities."

"Come on, Mother."

"You're smart enough to get it, Grace. If you or your friends do something stupid, it could ruin your life."

Grace glares at her for a long moment. "Are you done now?" she asks.

Rosie can't mask her frustration. "We'll finish this conversation later. We're due back in court."

# # #

"Can we talk to you for a minute, Mike?" Julie's tone is uncharacteristically subdued as she and Sean approach me in the hallway outside Judge McDaniel's courtroom.

"Sure," I say. I lead them into the nearby stairwell.

"Sean has something to tell you," Julie says.

Bobby's brother swallows hard. "That dope was mine," he whispers.

My anger is tempered by the fact that this information can only help us. "It would have made things easier if you had told us about it a couple of days ago," I say.

"I know. I didn't want to get in trouble. I'm sorry."

"How did it get on the floor?"

"I spilled it."

"When?"

"Right before I left for Kerry's house on Friday night. Am I going to get in trouble?"

"Only if you've withheld any other information."

"Possession is illegal."

"It's a tiny amount. You're a juvenile. You have no prior record. If you agree to testify, I'll get it cleared up."

"Will it help Bobby?"

"Yes."

"I'm in."

Good. "For now, I'm going to have you sign a sworn statement saying it was yours. We'll have to leave it up to the DA as to whether she wants to bring charges. My guess is she has more important things on her plate than prosecuting a fifteen-year-old for having a little stash in his house."

"Okay."

"Were you anywhere near your father's house later on Friday night?"

"No, Mike. I swear to God."

I'm inclined to believe him—for now. "You should stay away from that stuff," I tell him. "It isn't good for you."

"I know."

"Sean?"

"Yes?"

"Thanks."

46/ DID YOU CONSIDER ANY OTHER SUSPECTS?

Wednesday, June 22, 1:08 p.m.

"Inspector Johnson," I begin, "you testified earlier that you found traces of marijuana on the floor of Judge Fairchild's laundry room."

"Correct."

I button my jacket and take my place directly in front of him. It's time to go toe-to-toe. "Did you find Bobby Fairchild's fingerprints on the marijuana?"

"You can't lift prints off organic material."

"How about DNA?"

"No."

"Did you try?"

"No."

"Why not?"

"It would have been very difficult to extract a usable sample."

"And you may not have liked the results."

"Objection," McNulty says. "Argumentative."

"Sustained."

I keep pushing. "Did you find any marijuana on Bobby's person?"

"No."

"In his clothing? In his room? In his car?"

"No."

"Did you find traces of marijuana anywhere else inside Judge Fairchild's house?"

"No."

"Did you administer a drug test to Bobby Fairchild?"

"He was given a screening after he was arrested."

"Did you find any traces of marijuana in his system?"

"No."

"Inspector," I say, "do you have any evidence the marijuana belonged to Bobby?"

"Objection," McNulty says. "Asked and answered."

"Overruled." Judge McDaniel casts a pointed look at McNulty as if to say, *If you're going to insinuate marijuana possession, you'd better be able to prove it.*

Roosevelt shoots a scornful glance at McNulty. "No," he says softly.

Good. "Did you find any evidence Bobby had any contact with this marijuana?"

"No."

"In fact, you have no idea whose it was or how it got into the laundry room, do you?"

"Objection," McNulty says. "Argumentative."

The judge holds up a hand. "We get the message, Mr. Daley. The objection is sustained."

Good enough. "Your Honor," I say, "at this time we would like to introduce a sworn statement signed by Sean Fairchild, who is Bobby Fairchild's younger brother."

McNulty is back up. "We had no notice of this, Your Honor."

"It just came to our attention during the lunch break," I say.

"What's the nature of this statement?"

I'm glad you asked. "Sean has admitted that the marijuana found in the laundry room belonged to him. He spilled it as he was leaving the house at eight o'clock on Friday night. Although he understands that he may be charged with a misdemeanor for possession of a controlled substance, he has courageously stepped forward to tell the truth."

"Has he been advised by counsel of the consequences of this admission?"

"Yes."

"Objection," McNulty says. "There is no foundation for any of this. In addition, Sean Fairchild isn't on any witness list. We've had no chance to interview him and we will have no opportunity to cross-examine him."

"Overruled," the judge says. "I will allow the statement to be entered into evidence."

McNulty sits in stone-cold silence as I read Sean's statement onto the record. A moment later, I pick up again with Roosevelt. "Inspector," I say, "given Sean Fairchild's statement, are you now prepared to change your conclusion that Bobby Fairchild got into an argument with his father about the marijuana that was found in the laundry room?"

"I'm prepared to consider it."

It's as much as I'll get. "Inspector," I say, "are you aware that the Medical Examiner concluded that Judge Fairchild died between eleven forty-five p.m. on Friday night and twelve thirty a.m. on Saturday morning?"

"Yes."

"Are you also aware that a witness named Keith Treadwell purported to have seen Bobby Fairchild outside his father's house at twelve ten a.m.?"

"Yes."

"Does that mean you believe Judge Fairchild was killed sometime before twelve ten?"

"Based upon the evidence available to me at this time, that would appear likely."

It may seem like a small point, but I just shaved twenty minutes off Bobby's window of opportunity. Now I need to keep chipping away. "Inspector," I continue, "you testified that you believe Bobby killed his father, took off his bloody clothes, put them in the washer, changed into clean clothes, vandalized the hallway to make it look like a robbery, and then ran outside to his car, correct?"

"Yes."

"How long do you figure it took him to do all of that?"

McNulty's up. "Objection," he says. "Speculation."

"Overruled."

"It probably happened very fast," Roosevelt says.

"A minute? Five minutes? Ten minutes?"

"I'd guess two or three minutes."

"I might have guessed longer. For purposes of discussion, let's say it took three minutes."

"It may have been less."

"And it may have been more. If it was three minutes, and Bobby really was seen outside at ten after twelve, the process must have started no later than seven minutes after twelve, right?"

"So it would appear."

"Which means Bobby must have entered the house no later than twelve-oh-seven, right?"

"Based upon the information available to us at this time, that appears to be correct."

"Realistically, he probably entered the house at least a few minutes earlier, right?"

"Objection," McNulty says. "Speculation."

"Sustained."

"Inspector," I say, "have you located any witnesses who saw Bobby enter his father's house on Friday night or Saturday morning?"

"No."

"So you have no proof that he was inside his father's house between eleven forty-five p.m. and twelve thirty a.m., do you?"

"Objection," McNulty says. "Asked and answered."

"Sustained."

"Inspector," I continue, "if we assume Bobby entered the house at twelve-oh-seven, it would follow that you believe he must have killed his father immediately thereafter, right?"

"So it would appear."

I just took another three precious minutes off the clock.

McNulty stands. "Your Honor," he says, "this line of questioning is pure speculation."

No it isn't. "Your Honor," I say, "on direct exam, Inspector Johnson testified as to the timing of Judge Fairchild's death. We have the right to question him about his conclusions."

"I'll give you a little leeway, Mr. Daley."

I still have a little more work to do. "Inspector," I continue, "did you interview a private investigator named Kaela Joy Gullion?"

"Yes."

"Did she inform you that she was keeping Judge Fairchild under surveillance on Friday night?"

"Yes."

We'll get into the reason she was tailing him a little later. "Did she explain that she followed Judge Fairchild to his house?"

"Yes."

"According to her eyewitness account, what time did he pull into his garage?"

"Midnight."

"I trust he was very much alive at that time?"

"Of course."

"Did you find her statement to be credible?"

"We have found no evidence to the contrary."

That takes fifteen minutes off the front end. "That means you believe Judge Fairchild must have been killed sometime between midnight and twelve-oh-seven a.m., right?"

"Based upon the evidence available to me at this time, that appears to be likely."

Dr. Beckert's forty-five minute window of opportunity is down to seven minutes. "Inspector," I say, "do you have any physical evidence placing Bobby inside his father's house between midnight and twelve-oh-seven a.m.?"

"We found the defendant's fingerprints inside."

"But we've already established that the fingerprints you found could have been weeks or even months old. Do you have an eyewitness account or any forensic evidence conclusively placing Bobby inside his father's house during that seven-minute window?"

"We only have circumstantial evidence."

"So," I say, "if we can demonstrate that he wasn't inside his father's house during that seven-minute window, you would agree he couldn't have killed his father, right?"

"I'll need to look at the rest of the evidence before I can make any final judgments."

I expected him to hedge. "Likewise," I say, "if we can demonstrate that Bobby wasn't inside his father's house at all on Friday night or Saturday morning, you'd have to agree that he couldn't have killed his father, right?"

"Yes."

He couldn't disagree with that one. "Inspector," I say, "you interviewed the defendant's girlfriend, didn't you?"

"Yes."

"And she told you she was with the defendant on Friday night, didn't she?"

"Yes."

"In fact she told you she and the defendant returned to the defendant's car around twelve fifteen, didn't she? And he drove her home to Marin County, didn't he? And they arrived at her house around one o'clock on Saturday morning, didn't they?"

"Yes."

"He didn't return to his father's house until two o'clock on Saturday morning, right?"

"That appears to be correct."

"If he killed his father between eleven forty-five and twelve thirty, doesn't that mean he must have been wearing the bloody clothes when he took his girlfriend home?"

"We believe he put the bloody clothes in the washer before he drove her home."

"In other words, he changed clothes?"

"Correct."

"Did you question his girlfriend about it?"

"Yes."

"Did she confirm that Bobby had changed clothes?"

"No."

"Do you have any reason to doubt her veracity?"

"We believe she was lying to protect her boyfriend."

"Do you have any specific forensic evidence to prove that assertion?"

"No."

"So that's speculation on your part, isn't it?"

"My conclusion is based on the evidence available to us at this time."

"Not to mention the fact that it certainly helps your case to call the defendant's girlfriend a liar, doesn't it?"

"Objection," McNulty says. "Argumentative."

"Sustained."

I'll deal with it when Grace is on the stand. For now, I simply want to lock Roosevelt into a time frame. "Inspector," I say, "just so we're clear, is it your belief that Bobby killed his father between twelve o'clock and twelve-oh-seven, quickly changed clothes, and drove his girlfriend home?"

"That explanation would fit the evidence, Mr. Daley."

"Then he called the cops shortly after he got home?"

"Yes."

"Why in God's name would he have called the cops if he was guilty?"

"Objection," McNulty says. "Speculation."

"Sustained."

I've shortened the time frame and set up Grace's testimony. Now I need to give the judge some options. "Inspector," I say, "Judge Fairchild had a high-profile position in the legal community, didn't he?"

"Yes."

"He handled several highly publicized cases, didn't he?"

"Yes."

"He received several death threats, didn't he?"

"Yes."

"He was so concerned at one point that he obtained a permit to carry a gun, didn't he?"

"Yes."

McNulty stands. "If you would instruct Mr. Daley to get to the point, Your Honor."

"Please, Mr. Daley."

"Inspector," I say, "did you consider the possibility that somebody who had threatened Judge Fairchild carried out his intention?"

"We considered many possibilities, Mr. Daley."

"Yet you arrested Judge Fairchild's son within minutes after you arrived at his father's house, right?"

"All of the evidence pointed to the defendant."

"Did you consider any other suspects?"

"Yes. All of the evidence pointed toward the defendant."

"Does the name George Savage mean anything to you?"

"Yes. He's the owner of Bayview Towing."

"Judge Fairchild recently presided over a case in which Mr. Savage was convicted of racketeering, didn't he?"

"Yes."

"Mr. Savage paid a substantial fine, didn't he?"

"Yes."

"And he threatened Judge Fairchild in open court, didn't he?"

"Some of his statements could have been interpreted that way."

"Did you take that threat seriously?"

"Absolutely. We interviewed Mr. Savage several times. We found no evidence of any connection to Judge Fairchild's death."

"Does the name Brian Hannah mean anything to you?"

"Yes. He worked for Mr. Savage's towing company."

"He's also dead."

"He was killed last night."

"Before he died, Mr. Hannah admitted his tow truck was parked down the block from Judge Fairchild's house on Friday night, didn't he?"

"Yes."

"Telephone records indicated a call was placed from Mr. Savage's private cell phone to Mr. Hannah's cell phone at eleven o'clock on Friday night, didn't they?"

"Yes. Our investigation concluded Mr. Savage called Mr. Hannah on a legitimate and unrelated business matter."

"Like killing a judge?"

"Like picking up a package the following morning."

"You took Mr. Savage's word for it?"

"We interrogated Mr. Savage and Mr. Hannah."

"You understand they were both convicted felons."

"Yes."

"Yet you gave them the benefit of the doubt?"

"We had no evidence to cast doubt upon their stories, Mr. Daley."

"Have you arrested anybody in connection with Mr. Hannah's murder?"

"We are still investigating."

I feign exasperation as I turn back to the judge. Her skeptical expression suggests my attempt to invoke the legal doctrine of "blaming it on the dead guy" wasn't terribly well-received. "Your Honor," I say, "we reserve the right to recall this witness to discuss additional evidence concerning the circumstances surrounding Mr. Hannah's death." It's a bluff.

"That's fine, Mr. Daley. Any further questions for this witness?"

"No, Your Honor."

"Redirect, Mr. McNulty?"

"No, Your Honor. The prosecution rests."

"I take it you would like to make a motion, Mr. Daley?"

"The defense respectfully moves to have the charges dropped as a matter of law."

"On what grounds?"

"Lack of evidence."

"Denied. Please call your first witness, Mr. Daley."

"Yes, Your Honor." You always lead with strength. "The defense calls Kaela Joy Gullion."

Wednesday, June 22, 1:27 p.m.

All eyes are focused intently on the back of the courtroom as Kaela Joy Gullion—all six-feet-two of her—stands erect, tosses back her flowing chestnut locks, and does her best imitation of a high-end fashion model strutting down the runway. She winks at the reporter from the *Chronicle*, who nods appreciatively. The sketch artists in the back row are furiously attacking their pads.

Defense lawyers should never forget we're in the business of telling stories. We'll use every tool at our disposal to do it as effectively as we can.

The bailiff holds up a Bible that Kaela Joy touches seductively with her left hand as she raises her right. She swears to tell the truth and takes her seat in the witness box. I look at her admiringly from the lectern. I give her a moment to adjust the microphone and get her bearings—as if she really needs the extra time. McNulty and Ward feign disinterest from their seats at the prosecution table. They try to give the impression that our presentation will have as much drama as taking your car in for an oil change.

"Ms. Gullion," I begin, "how long have you been a private investigator?"

"Almost twenty years."

"I understand Julie Fairchild hired you to watch her husband."

"She did." Kaela Joy pauses to milk the moment—just the way we rehearsed it. "Dr. Fairchild was suspicious that her husband was cheating."

"Was he?"

"Absolutely."

I shoot a quick glance over at Bobby, who is staring straight ahead. "Did you inform Dr. Fairchild of your findings?" I ask.

"I did. She hired a lawyer and filed for a divorce."

I move in closer. "Ms. Gullion," I continue, "did Judge Fairchild have a mistress?" I could have chosen a softer term such as girlfriend or significant other. This exercise is intended to portray Jack Fairchild as a serial adulterer.

"Judge Fairchild was seeing a young woman named Christina Evans. She's a staff attorney at the court."

"Was he seeing anybody else?"

"Yes, he was." Her eyes dart apologetically toward Bobby. "Judge Fairchild had a 'thing' for certain young women."

"What sort of a 'thing?'"

"He liked to have sex with underage Asian girls."

I let the answer hang. I take another look at Bobby, who hasn't moved. Sean, on the other hand, has a disgusted expression. He's holding his palms up and glaring at his mother in the front row of the gallery. I turn back to Kaela Joy and ask, "How young?"

"Girls under the age of eighteen—preferably with small bodies and developing breasts."

Bobby remains stoic, but Sean is whispering heatedly to his mother. The judge's icy glare silences the murmurs in the gallery.

"Ms. Gullion," I continue, "did Judge Fairchild find a place to procure the services of such girls?"

"The Sunshine Massage Spa in the Tenderloin."

"He went there for massages?"

"No, Mr. Daley. He went there for sex."

Her delivery is impeccable. It also causes Bobby to elicit a pronounced sigh. Julie is unable to calm a visibly distraught Sean. She leads him out of the courtroom.

"How long had this been going on?" I ask Kaela Joy.

"At least a couple of months."

I've succeeded in engaging the prurient curiosity of the gallery. The newspaper scribes have more than enough to portray Judge Fairchild as a member of the Pervert Hall of Fame in tomorrow morning's headlines. Hopefully, this will generate some sympathy for Bobby, but I need to tread cautiously. It could also engender the sort of revulsion suggesting Bobby had a motive to kill his father.

I ask Kaela Joy if she was keeping the judge under surveillance on Friday night.

"Yes." She confirms that he went to dinner at the Bohemian Club. "He was supposed to go over to Ms. Evans's apartment after dinner. He went to the Sunshine instead."

"What time did he get there?"

"Eleven o'clock. He left at eleven forty-five."

"What was the purpose of his visit?"

McNulty finally decides to try to stop our flow. "Objection," he says. "Speculation. Unless Ms. Gullion went inside, she has no way of knowing."

"Overruled."

Kaela Joy keeps her voice modulated. "Judge Fairchild went to the Sunshine Massage Spa to engage in sex with underage prostitutes."

I can't resist a swipe. "Not especially dignified behavior for a judge, eh?"

"Objection," McNulty says. "Argumentative."

"Withdrawn. Ms. Gullion," I continue, "where did Judge Fairchild go after he left the Sunshine?"

"Straight home."

"Did you follow him?"

"At a discreet distance."

Of course. "What time did he arrive at his house?"

"Midnight. I watched him pull into his garage. He opened the door with his remote and parked inside. He closed the door behind him."

"How long were you there?"

"Just a moment. I had what I needed."

Yes, you did. "Did you see Bobby Fairchild enter or exit his father's house while you were there?"

"No."

"Did you see anyone else?"

"No."

"Ms. Gullion," I say, "did you notice anything unusual inside Judge Fairchild's house?"

"No."

"What about outside?"

"There was a gray Crown Victoria without license plates parked illegally in front of the fire hydrant on Grattan."

"Had you ever seen it before?"

"No."

"Was anybody inside the car?"

"No."

"And because there was no license plate, there was no way you could have identified the owner of that vehicle, right?"

"Correct."

"And it may have been stolen."

"I have no way of knowing."

"And it may have belonged to the person who killed Judge Fairchild, right?"

"Objection," McNulty says. "Speculation."

"Sustained."

"Ms. Gullion," I say, "did you drive down Grattan on your way home?"

"Yes."

"Did you see a truck from Bayview Towing?"

"Yes. It was double-parked down near Cole."

"Was anybody inside?"

"No."

"Do you know where the driver was?"

"No."

I've placed her at the scene around the time of the killing. She's raised questions about the Crown Vic and the tow truck. She's testified she didn't see Bobby—although her vantage point was imperfect. "No further questions, Your Honor."

"Cross-exam, Mr. McNulty?"

"Just a few questions, Your Honor." McNulty strides to the witness box. "Ms. Gullion," he says, "did you know there's a back door to Judge Fairchild's house that opens into the yard?"

"Yes."

"There is also a gate leading from the yard directly onto the sidewalk on Grattan Street, isn't there?"

"Yes."

I try to break up his flow. "I don't understand the point," I say. "We've already established Ms. Gullion's location and the geography surrounding Judge Fairchild's house."

Judge McDaniel addresses McNulty. "Get to the point, Mr. McNulty."

"Yes, Your Honor." He turns back to Kaela Joy. "Ms. Gullion," he says, "is it possible the defendant could have entered and exited his father's house through the back door?"

"Yes."

"Is it also possible he could have done so without your having seen him?"

"Objection," I say. "Speculation."

"Overruled."

"It's possible," Kaela Joy says.

"No further questions."

"Redirect, Mr. Daley?"

"Yes, Your Honor. Ms. Gullion," I say, "just so we're clear, did you see Bobby Fairchild or anyone else anywhere near his father's house early Saturday morning?"

"No."

"No further questions, Your Honor."

"Please call your next witness, Mr. Daley."

I'm about to respond when I feel a tap on my shoulder. "One moment please, Your Honor." I turn around and look straight into the eyes of an irate Julie Fairchild, who has returned to the courtroom without Sean. "What the hell was that all about?" she snaps.

"Lower your voice," I say. "The judge will hear you."

"Why did you have to make Jack look like a pervert?"

Because he was. "I told you this was coming, Julie. We needed to show where Jack was on Friday night—and when he got home."

"You didn't have to do it in front of my children."

"You promised me that you were going to tell them."

"I didn't have time."

"Then don't blame me."

"Who's up next?" she asks.

"Lenny Stone."

"Terrific. My son's life is on the line and your star witness is a homeless guy."

48/ MY NAME IS LEONARD STONE

Wednesday, June 22, 1:36 p.m.

Lenny is gulping water and tugging at the sleeves of the ill-fitting blazer Pete bought for him yesterday. We got him a room at a fleabag motel near the Hall last night where Pete kept an eye on him. With a fresh shave and shower, he could almost pass for a college professor.

"My name is Leonard Stone," he says tentatively. "Everybody calls me Lenny."

"Where do you live?" I ask.

"The Haight."

"Where in the Haight?"

He shifts in his chair. "It changes from day to day."

Don't get cute. "Where do you spend most of your time?"

"In the daytime I'm in Golden Gate Park and on Haight Street. I spend the nights in the Muni tunnel between Cole and Clayton."

"How long have you been living on the street?"

"About ten years."

"How do you get money to eat?"

"I hit people up for change. I collect bottles and cans and take them to the recycling center."

"Have you ever thought about staying in a shelter?"

"I tried it a couple of times. Too many rules. No dogs."

Fidel is relaxing at our office and guarding the shopping cart with his master's worldly belongings. It took all of my persuasive skills to convince Lenny his possessions would be safe with us. "Lenny," I say, "did you take your dog for a walk on Friday night?"

"Yes."

"What time did you leave the Muni tunnel?"

"Around midnight."

"That's pretty late."

"Nobody bothers us at night."

"Where did you go?"

He says he took Clayton to Parnassus. "We turned onto Belvedere and walked up to Alma."

"Do you know where Judge Jack Fairchild lived?"

"At the corner of Belvedere and Grattan."

"How did you know?"

"There were police cars in front of his house during the Savage trial. That made it a no-fly zone for a few months."

"Did you walk by Judge Fairchild's house on Friday night?"

"Yes."

"What time was that?"

"I would say around twelve-oh-five a.m."

"Did you see anybody inside the judge's house?"

"Nope."

"What about outside?"

"Nope."

"Do you recall seeing a gray Crown Victoria parked in front of the fire hydrant next to the judge's house?"

"Yes."

"How did you happen to notice it?"

"It had tinted windows and no plates. I thought it might have been an unmarked cop car."

"Was anybody inside?"

"I didn't stop to check."

"Where did you go from there?"

"We went over to the playground behind the grammar school. I let my dog run around for a few minutes. I can't do it during the day when the children are around. We stayed there for about ten minutes. Then we walked back home."

"What route did you take?"

"We took Grattan to Belvedere. Then we headed over to Parnassus."

"So you walked by the Grattan Street side of Judge Fairchild's house on your way back?"

"Yes."

"What time was that?"

He looks up at the clock in the back of the courtroom. "Around a quarter after twelve."

"Did you see anybody outside Judge Fairchild's house?"

"Nope."

"What about inside?"

"Nope."

"Did you notice anything else in particular as you were passing the judge's house?"

"The Crown Vic was gone."

"No further questions, Your Honor."

McNulty buttons his jacket and moves in front of Lenny. "Mr. Stone," he says with exaggerated politeness, "you've been living on the street for a long time, haven't you?"

"Objection," I say. I need to show Lenny that I'm watching out for him. "Asked and answered. We have already established that Mr. Stone has been living on the street for ten years."

"Sustained."

"Mr. Stone," McNulty continues, "you worked as an auto mechanic for a while, didn't you?"

"Yes. It was after I got out of the army."

"Why was your employment terminated?"

"Objection," I say. "Relevance."

"Your Honor," McNulty says, "Mr. Stone's employment history—or lack thereof—goes directly to his credibility."

No, it doesn't. "Your Honor," I say, "Mr. Stone's employment history has nothing to do with his credibility or this case."

"Sustained."

McNulty is nonplussed. "Mr. Stone," he says, "you have a drug problem, don't you?"

"Objection," I say. "Relevance."

"Your Honor," McNulty says, "Mr. Daley opened the door when he brought up the fact that Mr. Stone lives on the street. We should be able to probe the reasons why."

"He lives on the street because he's unemployed and he can't afford an apartment," I say. It's my turn to invoke a little self-righteousness. "Mr. Stone is a veteran of the first Gulf War. It is a disgrace our country doesn't do more to help its veterans. Mr. McNulty's personal attacks on Mr. Stone are offensive and mean-spirited."

Judge McDaniel nods. "Move along, Mr. McNulty."

"Mr. Stone," McNulty continues, "a little while ago, you expressed concern that you and your dog might have run into a police officer when you were out for your walk last Friday night."

"That's true."

"Is that because you've been arrested?"

"Objection," I say. "Relevance."

"Your Honor," McNulty says, "Mr. Stone brought up his desire to avoid contact with police officers. He opened the door. We have the right to cross-examine him about it."

"Overruled."

Legally, it's the correct call.

Lenny's tone turns indignant. "I've been arrested several times, but—"

McNulty cuts him off. "Thank you, Mr. Stone."

"Your Honor," I say, "Mr. McNulty didn't let Mr. Stone finish his answer."

"Did you wish to add something, Mr. Stone?"

"Yes. I was going to say I've done a few things that I'm not especially proud of, but I've never hurt anybody."

Sometimes you get help from unexpected sources.

McNulty moves in closer. "Mr. Stone," he says, "Mr. Daley paid for a hotel room last night, didn't he?"

"Yes."

"And he bought you those new clothes, didn't he?"

"Yes."

"And he paid for your dinner last night and your breakfast this morning, didn't he?"

"Yes."

"Did he promise to help you with your legal problems?"

"No."

"Did he promise to find you a place to live?"

"No."

"What else has he promised you, Mr. Stone?"

"Nothing."

I warned Lenny this onslaught was coming. It will only look worse if I interrupt. So far, he's holding his own.

"Mr. Stone," McNulty says, "it seems to me you would say just about anything to stay on Mr. Daley's good side."

"I'm telling the truth."

"But you'd be willing to fudge it a little to get another hot meal, wouldn't you?"

"No, I wouldn't."

"And you might be willing to fudge it a lot—maybe even to change your story completely—if Mr. Daley found you a place to live, right?"

"No."

"Come on, Mr. Stone. Perjury is a felony."

Enough. "Objection," I say. "Argumentative."

"Sustained."

"No further questions," McNulty says.

Rosie leans over. "Should we put on Savage?" she whispers.

"It won't help," I say. "He'll deny everything. So will Newsom."

I can hear the judge's voice from behind me. "Any more witnesses, Mr. Daley?"

"Just one, Your Honor. If we might have a brief recess to confer."

"We'll reconvene in fifteen minutes."

When it will all come down to Grace.

Wednesday, June 22, 1:44 p.m.

"Y ou need to talk your daughter," Sylvia says. She makes no attempt to conceal her frustration as she stands guard outside the file room in the basement of the Hall, where she and Grace have been holed up since early this morning.

"What now?" Rosie asks.

"She doesn't want to testify."

We don't have time for this. "Why not?" I ask.

"Maybe she's tired of being browbeaten by her own parents."

Arguing with Sylvia is even more difficult than arguing with Rosie. "That's not fair, Sylvia."

"Sure it is. While you've been giving Bobby all of your time and energy, you've ignored your own daughter."

"That isn't true."

"Yes, it is."

"We're doing our job."

"That's crap, Mike. You take everything he says at face value, yet you question everything she says."

Rosie's left hand balls up into a tight fist. "That isn't true, either, Mama."

"Isn't it?" Sylvia's voice gets louder. "You barely know this boy. You certainly don't know anything about his parents. It's obvious they weren't the All-American couple—far from it. Yet you've accepted everything his mother has said as gospel."

Rosie flashes anger. "No, we haven't, Mama. We've spent the last week taking unending grief from her. We've talked about withdrawing from this case more than once. Julie has threatened to fire us."

"Maybe that would be in everybody's best interests."

"Maybe it would."

Sylvia isn't finished. "You need to decide whose side you're on, Rosita."

There is no hesitation. "Grace's."

"From where I'm sitting, it doesn't look that way to me."

"You don't know the whole story, Mama."

"Clearly, neither do you."

"You're overreacting."

"No, I'm not."

Rosie drums her fingers against her thigh. "We don't have time for this now, Mama. Grace is going on the stand in a few minutes. If you have something you want to say to us, just say it."

Sylvia Fernandez looks intently into her daughter's eyes as she invokes the quiet gravitas of her seventy-nine years. "You never should have taken this case, Rosita. I know your intentions are good, but you're enabling the Fairchild boy to try to get out of trouble while you let Grace twist in the wind. He'll never understand the consequences of his actions." She pauses before she adds, "Neither will Grace."

"Are you suggesting Grace is involved in Judge Fairchild's death?"

"I don't think so, but I don't know for sure. I do know for sure that she used horrible judgment by staying out until one o'clock on Saturday morning."

"It isn't the first time she's broken curfew," Rosie says, "and it won't be the last. At the moment, that's the least of our problems."

"If that's all it was," Sylvia says.

"What are you saying, Mama?"

"You're far too willing to believe Grace and her boyfriend."

"You think they're lying?"

"I don't know that, either."

Rosie pushes out a frustrated sigh. "What do you want us to do, Mama? They're entitled to a lawyer. They'll get eaten alive by the legal system if we don't help them."

"I expect you to teach them that their actions have consequences."

"It isn't that simple, Mama."

"Yes, it is, Rosita."

"No, it isn't. Don't you understand? Their lives are already changed forever. If they end up in jail, their lives will be over."

"You're enabling them."

"We're helping them. That's what lawyers do." Rosie takes a deep breath. "That's what parents do."

"You aren't doing your children any favors by teaching them that their actions have no consequences if they hire a smart lawyer."

"Thanks for your input, Mama. I'll try to keep that in mind."

# # #

"What's bugging you?" I ask Grace.

"Everything." She's sitting in an uncomfortable wooden chair with her legs crossed. Her laptop is turned off. Her cell phone is silent. Her iPod is sitting on the table. "I can't do this, Dad."

It isn't unusual for a key witness to get cold feet shortly before they have to testify. "Sure you can," I say.

"No, I can't."

She's scared. "Why not?"

"I just can't."

Life with a teenage daughter is frequently an exercise in mind reading. It also requires a knack for making life-altering decisions on an instant's notice. "Did something happen?" I ask.

"No."

"I thought we had everything worked out."

"We did."

"What's changed since earlier today?"

"Nothing."

"Talk to me, Grace."

"Nothing," she repeats.

"Are you mad at us?"

She shrugs. "No more than usual."

"What about Bobby?"

"A little." Her eyes fill with tears as the frustrations come pouring out. "Why did he have to pick up that hammer? Why did he have to put his clothes in the washer? Why did he have to get into that argument with his father on Friday morning?"

"He was upset."

"It was stupid."

"He was under a lot of stress."

"It makes him look guilty."

Yes, it does. It's also an opening. "Is he?" I ask.

"Of course not."

"Then you have to help him."

"It isn't that easy."

"I never said it was."

She doesn't respond.

"Grace?"

She's looking down when she says, "Yes?"

"If there's something you haven't told us, this would be a good time."

"There's nothing."

"We won't get mad at you, honey. I promise."

She's more emphatic this time. "There's nothing."

"Did Bobby go inside his father's house?"

"No."

"Then you have nothing to worry about."

"If I screw this up, Bobby is going to be in more trouble."

"It will be worse if you don't testify."

"I guess." She's trying to hold back tears.

"You'll do fine, Grace. Just follow my lead and keep your answers short."

"I wish it were over."

So do I. "It'll be over soon."

My baby-daughter-turned-young-woman looks up at me through glassy eyes. "Thanks for helping Bobby, Daddy."

I can feel a lump forming in the back of my throat. "You're welcome, honey." I realize it sounds more hollow than reassuring when I add, "Everything is going to be fine."

Wednesday, June 22, 2:02 p.m.

"My name is Grace Fernandez Daley." Her voice is soft, but clear.

"How old are you, Grace?" I ask. The acid in my stomach boils like molten lava.

"Sixteen."

She's wearing a simple white cotton blouse and no makeup. Her straight hair cascades down her back. Her hands have a choke hold on the arms of the straight-back chair in the witness box. The courtroom is silent.

"Where do you go to school?" I ask.

She shoots a quick glance at Sylvia, who is providing moral support from the second row of the gallery. "I just finished my sophomore year at Redwood High School."

"Are you a good student?"

"I'm near the top of my class."

I take a moment to walk her through her multitude of activities: shortstop on the softball team, drama club, debate team, freshman orientation committee. I want to show she's a solid citizen. More importantly, I want to give her time to get her bearings.

I move in closer and get down to business. "Do you know Bobby Fairchild?"

"Yes. He's my boyfriend."

"How long have you been seeing each other?"

"About six months."

"Are you happy with your relationship?"

"Yes."

"You'd met Bobby's parents, hadn't you?"

"Yes."

"You knew they were getting divorced, right?"

"Objection, Your Honor," McNulty says, trying to disrupt our flow. "Mr. Daley is leading his daughter."

Yes, I am. I can also do without the attitude.

"Please, Mr. Daley," the judge says.

"I'll rephrase." I haven't taken my eyes off Grace. "Did you know Bobby's parents were getting divorced?"

"Yes."

"Was it acrimonious?"

"Yes."

"Was Bobby upset about it?"

"Wouldn't you be upset?"

McNulty tries to fluster her. "Your Honor," he interjects, "would you please instruct the witness not to ask questions of counsel?"

His pettiness elicits a hint of annoyance from Judge McDaniel. She addresses Grace in a maternal tone. "Ms. Daley," she says, "please answer your father's questions."

"Yes, Your Honor." She looks at Bobby for an instant. "I would say that he was more frustrated than upset. Bobby's parents were fighting for a long time."

Good enough. "Did Bobby get along with his father?"

"Yes."

"Did they ever argue?"

"A little."

"About what?"

"Stuff that parents argue about with their teenage kids."

Don't play games, Grace. "Grades?"

"No. He's a straight-A student."

"Girls?"

"A little."

"Alcohol or drugs?"

"Absolutely not."

So far, so good. "Grace," I say, "did you and Bobby go out on Friday night?"

"Yes."

"What time did you get together?"

"Bobby picked me up at six o'clock." She methodically recites the story Rosie has been drilling into her for the past two days. They drove to Cole Valley and parked on Grattan next to the judge's house. They walked over to Zazie.

"Did you go inside Judge Fairchild's house before dinner?"

"No. There wasn't enough time."

"Where did you go after you finished eating?"

"We went to see *Waiting for Guffman* at the Red Vic. Then we took a walk down Haight Street to Amoeba Music, where we looked at CDs. We walked back to get Bobby's car when they closed at midnight."

"What time did you get back to the car?"

"A quarter after twelve."

"You were out late."

"We lost track of the time."

"Did you get in trouble?"

"Yes."

"Did you see Bobby's father when you got back to the car?"

"No."

"Was he home?"

"I don't know."

"Did you see anybody inside Judge Fairchild's house?"

"No." She confirms she didn't see anybody outside, either.

"Grace," I say, "were you and Bobby together for the entire evening?"

"Yes."

"You walked back to the car together?"

"Yes."

"And you got right into the car when you got there?"

"Yes. Bobby drove me straight home."

Hang with me, Gracie. We're almost done. "Grace," I say, "did you or Bobby go inside Judge Fairchild's house at any time on Friday night or Saturday morning?"

"No."

"Is there any chance Bobby went inside his father's house without your having seen it?"

"No."

I have what I need. "No further questions." I give Grace a subtle nod and return to my seat.

Rosie whispers to me, "She did a nice job."

"Yes, she did."

"So did you."

"Thanks." The easy part is over. Now we'll see how she holds up on cross.

51/ DO YOU LOVE YOUR BOYFRIEND?

Wednesday, June 22, 2:24 p.m.

McNulty invokes a respectful tone as he addresses the judge from the prosecution table. "May we approach the witness, Your Honor?" he asks.

"Yes, Mr. McNulty."

Instinctively, I give Grace a reassuring nod. As McNulty moves forward, Rosie leans over and whispers, "Protect her."

"I will." The knot in my stomach has grown to the size of a tennis ball.

McNulty parks himself in front of Grace and flashes a transparently phony smile. "Ms. Daley," he begins, "I am Assistant District Attorney William McNulty. I need to ask you a few questions about what happened Friday night and Saturday morning."

Grace squeezes the armrests of her chair more tightly. Stay the course, honey.

"Ms. Daley," McNulty continues, "do you understand that you're under oath?"

"Yes."

"You know that means you're required to tell us the truth, right?"

"Yes."

"You were telling the truth when your father was asking you questions, right?"

He's trying to intimidate her. "Objection," I say. "The witness has already acknowledged she's under oath."

"Sustained. Let's get moving, Mr. McNulty."

He places a hand on the rail of the witness box and never takes his eyes off Grace. "Ms. Daley," he continues, "you testified earlier that you and the defendant went out to dinner and a movie last Friday night, correct?"

"Yes."

"The defendant's car was parked on Grattan Street next to Judge Fairchild's house, correct?"

"Yes."

Good girl, Grace. Short answers.

"And the defendant drove you straight back to your mother's house, right?"

"Right."

I can't stop McNulty from leading her on cross. Nor can I keep him from referring to Bobby as "the defendant." He hasn't raised anything new that could get us into trouble—yet.

"Ms. Daley," he continues, "I want to focus on the time after you and the defendant left the movie. You said you walked down Haight Street to Amoeba Music, right?"

"Yes."

"And you left that store when it closed at midnight, right?"

"Yes."

"And you went back to retrieve the defendant's car, right?"

I need to show Grace that I've got her back. "Objection," I say. "Asked and answered."

"Sustained."

McNulty doesn't fluster. "Ms. Daley," he says, "did you see anybody when you and the defendant walked down Haight?"

"There were people on the street. Amoeba was pretty crowded."

"Can you give us any names?"

"No."

"Can anybody corroborate your whereabouts on Friday night?"

Grace shows her first hint of being flustered. "I don't know," she says.

"Your story would be more credible if somebody other than your boyfriend could confirm it."

"Objection," I say. "There wasn't a question there."

"Sustained."

"Ms. Daley," McNulty continues, "have you ever been inside Judge Fairchild's house?"

"Yes."

"How many times?"

"A few."

"How many is a few?"

"Maybe five."

"When was the last time you were there?"

"Last Monday."

"So it's your testimony that you weren't inside Judge Fairchild's house last Friday night, right?"

"Right."

"And neither was the defendant, right?"

"Right."

"So you say."

"Objection," I say. "Argumentative."

"Withdrawn." McNulty inches toward Grace. "Ms. Daley, have you ever been inside your boyfriend's bedroom?"

"Yes."

My antenna goes up. Until now, McNulty has referred to Bobby as "the defendant." Suddenly, he's morphed into Grace's boyfriend. To a casual observer, this might appear to be a minor semantic detail.

Knowing McNulty, there's a reason for the subtle switch in terminology.

McNulty keeps going. "Were you inside his room on Friday night?"

"No."

"You and your boyfriend didn't sneak over to his father's house for a little time alone?"

"Objection," I say. "Asked and answered. The witness testified that she wasn't inside Judge Fairchild's house on Friday night."

"Sustained."

Rosie is leaning forward. I can barely hear her when she whispers, "Watch out."

"Ms. Daley," McNulty continues, "are you and your boyfriend close?"

"Yes."

"Very close?"

"Yes."

"Do you love your boyfriend?"

Grace looks at me for an instant before she answers. "Yes."

As her lawyer, I'll always take a truthful answer—even if it suggests she has a motive to protect Bobby. As her father, I'm not nearly as ecstatic.

"Do you love him a lot?" McNulty asks.

"Objection," I say. "Asked and answered."

"Sustained."

"Do you love him enough that you'd lie to protect him?"

"Objection," I say. "Argumentative."

"Overruled."

Grace is glaring straight into McNulty's eyes as she lowers her voice a half-octave. "No, Mr. McNulty," she says. "My parents are lawyers. I know better than to lie in court."

For an instant, McNulty seems taken aback by her understated forthrightness. He moves in front of her and purposely blocks my view.

"Ms. Daley," he says, "are you and your boyfriend sexually active?"

What the hell? Rosie and I leap out of our seats. "Objection!" I shout. "That question is irrelevant and offensive."

McNulty responds in an even tone. "Your Honor," he says, "the question speaks to the fundamental credibility of this witness."

The hell it does. "Your Honor," I say, "this is a grandstand play to try to intimidate our daughter."

Judge McDaniel taps her gavel once to silence the murmuring in the gallery. "Counsel will approach," she says. Rosie and I walk to the front of the courtroom. The judge covers her microphone and addresses McNulty out of Grace's earshot. "I'm not going to allow you to brow-beat a sixteen-year-old girl," she whispers.

"This witness is lying to protect her boyfriend."

"No, she isn't," I snap. "This is just a desperate attempt to intimidate her because her testimony is destroying his case."

"No, it isn't," McNulty insists.

The judge arches an eyebrow. "It's starting to look that way to me, Mr. McNulty."

"I can assure you that it isn't."

"I don't deal in assurances, Mr. McNulty. I deal in evidence."

"We're working on it, Your Honor."

"He's stalling," I say.

"No, I'm not. We are trying to confirm some additional information that will have a direct and significant bearing on this case."

"What information would that be?" the judge asks.

"I'm not at liberty to discuss it at this time."

"That's because it doesn't exist," I say.

"Yes, it does."

The judge glares at him. "I need evidence, Mr. McNulty."

"Your Honor," he says, "we respectfully request a recess to follow up on this new and highly compelling information."

"Your Honor," I say, "this is nothing more than a stalling tactic to give them more time to go on another fishing expedition."

"Your Honor," McNulty says, "I can assure you it is not."

The judge looks at the clock in the back of her courtroom. "I'll give you until ten o'clock tomorrow morning," she says. "You'd better have something really good to show me, Mr. McNulty. If not, I'm going to dismiss the charges and hold you in contempt."

"It'll be good, Your Honor."

"Your Honor—" I say.

"Step back, counsel." The judge uncovers her microphone. "We're adjourned until ten o'clock tomorrow morning," she announces.

52/ YOUR CLIENT IS LYING TO YOU

Wednesday, June 22, 3:07 p.m.

Immediately after court is adjourned, Rosie and Sylvia hustle Grace downstairs while I make a beeline for McNulty. I corner him in a stairwell outside the prying eyes of the media. My heart is pounding when I say, "What the hell do you think you're doing?"

"My job."

"You're stalling. You have nothing."

"Yes, we do."

"Then you have a legal obligation to tell us what it is."

"I have a legal obligation to disclose evidence that might exonerate your client. I can assure you this does not." He reaches for the door and adds, "Your client is lying to you. So is your daughter."

# # #

Grace is tugging nervously at her collar when I arrive in the dungeon of the Hall a few minutes later. "Why do we have to wait until tomorrow?" she asks.

"The prosecutors claim they have some additional evidence."

She eyes me warily. "What is it?"

"I don't know." I take her hand. "We can't afford any surprises,

Grace. If there's something you need to tell us, this is your last chance."

"There isn't."

A furious Sylvia is struggling to contain her emotions in front of her granddaughter. "This is ridiculous," she says. "They're trying to intimidate her. Their case is falling apart."

Rosie tries to mask her anxiety, but I can hear the tension in her voice. "Mama," she says, "Mike and I need to go to the office to prepare for tomorrow. I'd like you to take Grace home. We'll meet you there as soon as we can."

# # #

"Have you heard anything from Pete?" Rosie asks. We're sitting in my office at five minutes to seven on Wednesday night.

"I just talked to him. Nothing new," I say.

"Damn it. Where is he?"

"Parked across the street from the Sunshine."

"What for?"

"He didn't have any better ideas. At the moment, neither do I."

Rosie exhales heavily. "Were you able to reach Roosevelt?"

"I've left three messages," I say.

"Is he avoiding us?"

"Maybe."

Rosie temples her fingers in front of her face. The strain of the past week is taking its toll. "Do you think they've found something?" she asks.

I answer her honestly. "I don't know. Maybe they're trying to buy time to keep fishing."

"They're going to look foolish if they don't bring something to the party tomorrow morning."

"People have short memories. Nobody will be talking about this by the end of the week."

She strokes her chin. "Do you think my mother was right about us representing Bobby?"

My first instinct is to deflect. "Let's not go there tonight, Rosie. We shouldn't second-guess ourselves in the middle of a case."

"That rule doesn't apply when your daughter is involved."

I can't avoid this discussion. I try not to sound too defensive when I say, "I don't know what else we could have done."

"We could have brought in another lawyer."

True. "Hindsight is always twenty-twenty, Rosie. We can't change it now."

We look at each other with the silent understanding that we made a mistake by taking this case. We're interrupted when our receptionist, process server, and occasional bodyguard, Terrence "the Terminator" Love, taps on my open door. The seven-foot-tall former prizefighter and recovering alcoholic was once one of my most reliable clients at the PD's Office. He retired from boxing after losing four bouts to pursue an equally undistinguished career in theft. The gentle giant took great pride that he stole only necessities and never hurt anybody. When he was about to be sent away for good after his third serious felony, Judge McDaniel gave us two options: watch him go to jail for life or hire him as our receptionist. We opted for the latter, and he hasn't missed a day of work ever since. He now lives in a modest studio apartment not far from Savage's impound lot in the Bayview.

"Your case was the lead story on the news," he says. "They said Grace did a nice job."

"She did," I say.

For a guy with little formal education who spent his formative years trying to earn a living by beating the daylights out of people, Terrence has a firm grasp of current events. He quickly adds, "They said McNulty is promising something spectacular in the morning."

"Did they mention what it was?"

"No, but it might explain why you have a visitor."

"McNulty?"

"Roosevelt."

Wednesday, June 22, 7:00 p.m.

Roosevelt's baritone is subdued. "You did a nice job on cross today," he tells me.

"Thanks." I study his poker face for any hint of the reason for his visit, but I can't read him. "Sorry for beating you up."

"Part of the process. I'm too old to take it personally."

He's jammed his large torso into one of the uncomfortable swivel chairs opposite my desk. In what passes for business casual attire for him, the Windsor knot in his tie is slightly loosened. Rosie is sitting on my windowsill. Outside my office, First Street is quiet. The bell at the Ferry Building tolls seven times.

"You got any scotch?" he asks.

I pull out a fifth of Johnnie Walker Red and three shot glasses from my bottom drawer. "Pop used to say a lawyer's office isn't complete without a bottle."

"He said the same thing about a homicide cop's desk. Is that the bottle he bought you when you graduated from law school?"

"Yes." Twenty years later, it's still more than half full. "I'm more of a Guinness guy."

"So was your dad." He gets a faraway look in his eyes. "He was proud of you, Mike. So am I."

"Thanks, Roosevelt."

I line up the glasses and pour a shot for each of us. Roosevelt downs his drink in a single gulp. Then he takes off his glasses and rubs his eyes. I'm familiar with this gesture. He's taking a moment to sort out his thoughts.

"I have two grandchildren in high school," he finally says. "Stay close to your kids. They'll be gone before you know it."

He knows. He rarely talks about the son he lost in a drive-by shooting in the Bayview thirty years ago. "That's good advice," I say.

"I know."

Rosie sets down her empty glass. "What brings you here tonight, Roosevelt?" she asks.

The deep lines in his leathery face become more pronounced as his expression contorts into a frown. "Family," he says.

"Yours or mine?"

"Ours." He puts his glasses back on and pours himself another shot. "This conversation isn't taking place."

"Understood."

We wait.

"I didn't like the way McNulty went after Grace in court," he finally says. "It violated my sense of fair play."

"Mine too," Rosie replies uneasily.

"I'm trying to level the playing field. You'd do the same for my kids."

"Yes, we would."

He clears his throat. "McNulty wasn't bluffing. They found Grace's prints on a drinking glass in Bobby's bedroom. It was a perfect match."

"We never agreed to provide a sample of her prints," I say.

"They were already in the system. They took her prints when she did an internship at the Marin County Public Defender's Office last summer."

Rosie never loses her composure, but there is heightened concern in her voice. "Fingerprints have an indefinite shelf life. Grace was in Bobby's room last Monday. She could have gotten her prints on that glass when she was there. For that matter, she could have picked up that glass a month ago. You'll never be able to tell for sure."

"The glass was half full of water. There were no signs of evaporation."

"It doesn't prove anything, Roosevelt."

"There's more—a lot more."

His ominous tone sends a shiver up my back.

Roosevelt's voice turns melancholy. "We found a spent condom under Bobby's bed," he says. "We ran DNA tests. We didn't get the results until earlier this evening. That's why McNulty was stalling in court."

Oh, hell.

"We found two matches," he says. "Male and female."

My stomach is now churning uncontrollably.

"You can figure out the rest," he says. "The male was Bobby. The female was Grace."

The room is starting to spin.

Rosie's lips form a tight line across her face as she strains to keep her emotions in check. "We never agreed to provide a DNA sample for Grace," she says.

"We already had a sample from her fingerprint on the glass."

The nightmare is now complete.

Rosie lays it on the line. "Are you suggesting she was involved with Judge Fairchild's death?"

"Honestly, I don't know."

"Is she a suspect?"

"I'm not going to jump to any conclusions. We're still investigating."

"Are you planning to arrest her?"

"At the moment, she's just a person of interest. For obvious reasons, her status could change precipitously in the next few hours." Roosevelt takes a deep breath and lets it out slowly. "I know this sounds harsh, but you need to look up the word 'gullible' in the dictionary. Your client and your daughter have been lying to you from the start. I know your intentions have been honorable, but you've been hearing what you've wanted to hear. That isn't especially helpful in your role as a lawyer or a parent. Now Grace and Bobby are going to have to deal with the consequences."

The only sound in the room is the buzzing from the light above my desk.

"At this point," he says, "there isn't much that I can do to help you."

"Then why did you come?" I ask.

"To warn you that it's all going to come down tomorrow morning. I didn't want you to get blind-sided in open court. I don't know for sure what happened inside Judge Fairchild's house on Friday night. I do know for sure that Grace and Bobby were there—having sex. As a cop, I think he's already guilty of statutory rape and she's already guilty of perjury. Depending upon what else we find, we may charge her as an accomplice or an accessory-after-the-fact. As a parent, I think it's a bad idea for a sixteen-year-old girl to be sleeping with her boyfriend and lying about it to the cops and her parents. As a friend, I would encourage her come clean as soon as possible. I would also suggest you give serious consideration to cutting a deal before this gets out of hand."

I'm going to be violently ill. "Do you have anything that might help us?" I ask.

He reaches into his breast pocket and takes out a folded piece of paper. "This is a copy of the unidentified partial print we found on the inside handle of Judge Fairchild's front door. It's the only one we haven't been able to match through the system."

I stare at the photocopy. "So," I say, "all we have to do is match this print and we've found the killer?"

"Not necessarily. For all I know, it could belong to a plumber or an electrician. I can tell you it isn't Brian Hannah, George Savage, or Dr.

Derek Newsom. I'm sorry, Mike."

"So am I."

He glances at his watch. "I don't know if you can fix this tonight," he says. "You need to place somebody other than Bobby and Grace inside Judge Fairchild's house on Friday night. By my reckoning, you have about fifteen hours to try."

"You lied to us," I say to Bobby, making no attempt to modulate my voice.

He leans back defensively and reacts with a combination of surprise and indignation. "What are you talking about?"

My head feels as if it's about to implode. "You lied to us," I repeat more emphatically.

"About what?"

"Everything."

We're gathered in the consultation room at the Hall at eight fifteen on Wednesday night. We had Terrence call Bobby's mother to tell her to meet us here, but we didn't say why. She's seated next to Bobby. She's wearing no makeup. Her arms are folded. Her expression is grim.

"What's going on?" Bobby asks.

Rosie's voice fills with unfiltered raw emotion. "It's been nothing but lies from the start," she says. "All lies. One after another."

Julie's protective instincts kick in. "What the hell are you talking about?"

Rosie fires right back. "Don't you dare try to protect him. You'll just be enabling him even more." She turns to Bobby. "You were there on Friday night." It isn't a question—it's a statement of fact.

"Where?" he asks. His attempt at feigned innocence has suddenly turned utterly unconvincing.

"Your father's house."

"No, I wasn't."

"Yes, you were." Rosie's empties both barrels. "Don't play dumb with us, Bobby. We spent the past hour getting our asses kicked by Inspector Johnson. It's over. They know you were there. They have proof. You're going to make it even worse if you keep lying."

The color leaves his face. "I don't know what you're talking about."

"Yes, you do," Rosie snaps. My father used to say the most effective way to yell at somebody is not to raise your voice. Rosie invokes a venomous whisper. "They found a condom under your bed. The DNA tests matched you and Grace. They've got you, Bobby. Dead to rights. You were there. You had sex with my daughter. You lied about it from the start. You've turned a difficult situation into a full-blown disaster—not just for yourself, but for Grace."

Julie leaps to his defense. "You have no right to talk to him that way."

I jab a finger at her. "Yes, we do."

"The hell you do."

"The hell we don't. We've been working our asses off around the clock to help your son. He lied to us. He lied to you. He lied to the cops. He's done irreparable damage to his own defense. He has no credibility. He's already guilty of perjury and statutory rape. Now Grace may be guilty of perjury, too."

"It isn't Bobby's fault your daughter chose to lie under oath."

"She did it in a misguided attempt to protect your lying son. Now she may be arrested as an accomplice to murder."

"That's her problem."

"That's *our* problem," I say.

Julie's blue eyes are on fire. "It takes two to tango. You should have expected this after your exemplary parenting. You can't be surprised that you have a promiscuous daughter."

"And you can't be surprised that you have a promiscuous son."

"Now you're judging me, too?"

"Damn right. The apple didn't fall far from the tree. On Friday night, you were busy boinking your boy toy while your son was having sex with his underage girlfriend—who happens to be my daughter."

"My personal life is none of your business."

"It is now."

Bobby turns to his mother. "What the hell is he talking about, Mother?"

She takes a deep breath. "I've been seeing someone, Bobby."

"You, too?"

Julie swallows hard. "I was going to tell you, Bobby."

"When?"

"Soon."

"How long has this been going on?"

"A couple of months."

"Who?"

"Dr. Newsom."

Bobby's eyes light up. "He's one of your students."

"It happens, Bobby."

"And now you're judging me?"

"I meant to tell you."

He's too angry to reply.

I turn my anger back to Julie. "Your boyfriend threatened your husband," I say. "For some reason, you keep trying to protect him."

Julie's last pretense of civility disappears as she takes the offensive. "That's bullshit, Mike. Derek has nothing to do with this. Your daughter wasn't an innocent victim. And you were on the other side of the Bay when she was seducing my son."

"You and your husband set a terrific example. He was sleeping with underage hookers. You're sleeping with one of your students."

"You two aren't model parents, either."

"What the hell is that supposed to mean?"

"Before you start casting stones, you ought to look in the mirror."

Rosie holds up a dismissive hand and invokes a tone I haven't heard since the darkest days of our divorce. "We aren't going to take any more shit from you and your son," she hisses. "We're done, Julie. We quit. You can find another lawyer."

"You're fired," Julie says.

"Fine. Either way, we're out of here."

"Great."

"On our way to the car, we're going to ask Inspector Johnson to file charges against Bobby for statutory rape."

"No, you won't."

"Yes, we will."

"You're bluffing."

"The hell I am."

"You'd have to admit your daughter was at Jack's house on Friday night."

"They already have proof. We're going to come clean and cut the best deal we can—even if it means your son is going to jail for the rest of his life."

"You can't do that."

"Yes, we can. You're a better doctor than a lawyer, Julie. Everybody knows the first one to sing gets the best deal."

"You have a conflict of interest."

"Not anymore. You just fired us, remember?"

"You still have a fiduciary duty to Bobby."

"It's trumped by our paternal duty to Grace."

Julie's mouth is open as she glares at Rosie. She realizes this isn't a negotiation and Rosie isn't going to budge. There is desperation in her voice when she says, "I'll go to the papers. I'll ruin your reputation."

"We can play that game, too," Rosie says. "You're out of your league. Nobody gives a shit about two small-time defense lawyers who practice law around the corner from the bus terminal. The press will have a field day when they find out a hotshot surgeon at UCSF has been sleeping with her intern. The Board of Trustees at UCSF will have something to say about it, too."

"I'll file a complaint with the State Bar."

"Be my guest. Bobby will be sleeping in orange pajamas for twenty years before they get around to investigating your claim."

"I'll hire a lawyer. I'll get you disbarred."

"Let me make it easy for you," I say. I pull out my wallet and toss my State Bar card down on the metal table. "Here's my ticket. Knock yourself out. Hire an army of lawyers to go after me. I don't give a damn about you, your lying son, the State Bar, or the entire legal profession. I'm going to do what's best for my daughter."

"You can't just walk."

"Yes, we can."

"You'll never get Grace to testify against Bobby."

"Yes, she will." I turn to Bobby, who has been observing this exchange in terrified silence. "You're in a world of trouble, son. Now that I'm no longer your lawyer, let me give you some free advice. Hire the best defense lawyer you can find and cut the best deal you can get."

The former high school baseball player and honor student looks as if he's going to cry.

Rosie and I stand and head toward the door. I'm about to call for the guard when I hear the sound of unvarnished panic from behind me.

"Please don't leave," Bobby wails. His voice is choked with raw fear. "I'm sorry," he says. "I'm so sorry."

Rosie and I turn around slowly. "It's too late for apologies," Rosie says to him.

"I'm so sorry for everything."

"The damage is done, Bobby. It's over."

Fear and desperation overwhelm him and he bursts into tears. "You can't go," he howls.

"Yes, we can."

He collapses forward onto the metal table. "Please don't go," he begs. "Please. I didn't kill my father. You're my only chance."

"Not anymore," I say. "We aren't going to represent you. We just can't."

"I promise to tell you everything—the whole truth—I swear to God."

Julie moves over and puts her arm around her son's shoulder. "You don't have to say anything to them, Bobby."

"Yes, I do."

"They aren't your lawyers anymore. They'll use it against you."

"I don't care. I want to tell the truth, Mother. I *need* to tell the truth—which is more than you've done."

"Don't say another word, Bobby. You're only making it worse."

"It's my choice, Mother. I'm trying to make it right." He turns to me and says, "Will you help me if I tell you everything? I'll tell you the truth. I swear to God."

Rosie and I look at each other. We're treading in murky ethical waters. In a perfect world, we would tell him to hire another lawyer and not say another word. Then again, the real world is highly imperfect—especially when you daughter may be charged with murder in fourteen hours. He may tell us something that could help Grace—or incriminate himself—or both. Either way, it can't hurt to listen. "Do you promise to tell the truth?" I ask.

"I swear to God."

"We're listening."

Wednesday, June 22, 8:28 p.m.

"The movie started at nine," Bobby says, desperately trying to find a modicum of composure. "It ended at eleven."

"So you never went to Amoeba, did you?" Rosie says. Her tone is modulated for now. She'll revert to her lawyer voice if necessary.

"No," Bobby says. He darts a glance at his mother, who is sitting next to him in frozen silence. "We decided to go to my father's house."

"Because you knew he wouldn't be home?"

"Yes."

"And you knew Sean was staying at a friend's house?"

He nods.

Rosie takes a deep breath. "What time did you get there?"

"A quarter after eleven."

"Was anybody home?"

"No." He swallows hard and adds, "I'm really sorry."

"Sorry you had sex with my daughter or sorry you got caught?"

"Sorry about everything."

"Was it your first time with Grace?"

He doesn't respond.

"Bobby?"

His voice is barely audible. "No."

"How many other times?" Rosie asks.

"Twice."

"Where?"

"My father's house—when he was with Christy."

Or when he was at the Sunshine.

Rosie's tone fills with sarcasm. "Whose brilliant idea was this?"

"Both of us, I guess."

"Grace was a willing participant?"

"Yes."

Rosie leans forward. "Did you use a condom every time?"

"Yes."

"You'd better be telling the truth."

"I am."

"Have you slept with any other girls?"

Julie interjects. "You don't have to answer that, Bobby."

Rosie hasn't taken her eyes off Bobby. "Yes, you do," she says.

"Two others," he says. "Before I met Grace."

"Does Grace know about this?"

"No."

"She will now. Did you use a condom every time?"

"Yes."

"Are you lying to me, Bobby?"

"No."

"Is there any chance you've been infected with AIDS or an STD?"

"No. Grace and I got tested just to be sure. You can do it confiden-tially."

The world has changed since I was sixteen.

"I'm glad you were so responsible about sleeping with my underage daughter," Rosie says.

Bobby looks straight down. "I'm sorry," he whispers. "I'm really, *really* sorry."

Rosie nods to me. It's my turn. I try not to let my imagination run wild as I think about my baby daughter and her boyfriend having sex in his room in the middle of the night. My parental instincts make me want to leap across the table and pound the crap out of him. However, this isn't a good time for me to play the role of the irate father of a teenage daughter. If I can hold it together, Bobby might impart some useful information.

"What time did your father get home?" I ask.

"Midnight."

"Where were you?"

"In my bedroom in the basement."

"Having sex with my daughter?"

"I'm sorry, Mike."

"So am I. What happened next?"

"We heard the garage door open. Grace and I jumped out of bed and put on our clothes. It was hard because it was dark."

I'm sure. "Did your father see you?"

"No."

"How did you get out of the house without him seeing you?"

"We left through the back door."

"Is it possible somebody else was in the house?"

"I don't know. Maybe."

"Did you hear anybody?"

"Other than my father, no." He adds, "It's hard to hear from downstairs."

We need to prove somebody else was there. "Did you go straight to the car?"

"Yes." He says they ran through the yard and out the gate that opens onto Grattan.

"What time was that?"

"A couple of minutes after twelve."

"Did you see anybody?"

"No."

"Did you see a gray Crown Vic parked by the fire hydrant?"

"Yes."

"Did you leave right away?"

"Not exactly," he says.

"What do you mean?"

"When we got to the car, I realized I left my keys in my room. I went back to get them."

"Did Grace go with you?"

"Yes, but she waited in the yard while I was inside the house."

"So you were alone inside the house with your father?"

"Yes."

This information may be enough to throw Bobby under a bus. I start firing questions more rapidly. "Did you see your father when you were inside?"

"No."

"Did you see anybody else?"

"No."

"Did you hear anything?"

"No."

"How long were you inside?"

"Just a couple of minutes. I had trouble finding my keys."

"Did you change your clothes?"

"No. I didn't put my clothes into the washer until after I found my dad." He reads my skeptical expression and adds, "I swear to God, Mike."

"Then what?"

"I went out through the back door again. Grace was still in the yard. We went to the car and I drove her straight home. That was it."

"What time was that?"

"Around ten after twelve."

"Did you see anybody outside?"

"No."

"Was the gray Crown Vic still parked by the fire hydrant?"

He thinks about it for a moment. "I don't think so. I don't remember for sure."

"Were you and Grace together the entire time after you came back outside?"

"Yes." There's another pause. "Except for just a minute."

Huh? "How's that?"

"Grace dropped her cell phone in the bushes as we were going out the gate. I ran over to the car by myself. I didn't realize she had stopped until I got to the car. I went back to help her find it."

Which means Treadwell could have seen Bobby jogging west on Grattan by himself. "Are you leaving anything out?" I ask.

"No."

"Are you absolutely sure?"

"Yes. I'm really sorry, Mike."

"So am I. We're going to talk to Grace to make sure her story matches up with yours."

"It will, Mike. I swear to God."

"If you've lied to us about anything—even the smallest detail—I'm going to make sure you never see the light of day."

#

"We're idiots," Rosie says.

"Yes, we are," I reply.

Her hands have a vise-like grip on the steering wheel as we drive north on Van Ness at nine fifteen on Wednesday night. Our mood matches the heavy summer fog.

"We should have seen it," she says.

"I know."

"How could we have been so stupid?"

"We believed our daughter."

Her jaw clenches. "After all these years, are we really so naïve?"

"We aren't the only parents who gave their kid the benefit of the doubt."

"That doesn't make it right. It certainly doesn't make us good parents. We've been lawyers for twenty years, Mike. We've represented murderers, rapists, drug dealers, and armed robbers. I think I'm pretty good at figuring out when somebody's lying. Now, I can't even tell with my own daughter."

"Evidently, neither can I." I reach over and touch her hand. "We can't afford to get angry about it tonight."

"Damn right we can, Mike. I'm angry at Grace. I'm angry at Bobby. I'm angry at you. I'm ready to kill Julie. Most of all, I'm furious at myself."

"We'll have plenty of time to beat ourselves up after this case is over, Rosie."

"How can you be so calm?"

"Believe me, I'm not." My stomach feels like a vat of hot acid. "We have no choice. We have to keep our heads on straight."

"Why?"

"Because we have to talk to Grace. And we have less than thirteen hours to figure out a way to keep her out of jail."

Wednesday, June 22, 9:40 p.m.

Rosie's living room is deathly silent. Grace is sitting on the sofa with her legs crossed. Her arms are clenched tightly around her stomach as she stares intently at the coffee table. We asked Sylvia to wait in Tommy's room. For the next few minutes, we need to be absolutely sure that everything we say is covered by the attorney-client privilege.

"We have a serious problem," I say to Grace. My priest voice is soft but firm.

There is genuine concern in her eyes. "What is it?"

Here goes. "Roosevelt found evidence placing you and Bobby at Judge Fairchild's house on Friday night."

Her eyes dart across the room. "Have you talked to Bobby?"

"Yes. He told us everything."

"Everything?"

"Everything."

Grace tugs at the sleeves of her pink sweatshirt. "Are you going to yell at me?"

"Eventually." This exercise is going to be difficult enough without high-level histrionics. "At the moment, I'm more interested in hearing your version of what happened. This time, I need the truth."

"You said you already talked to Bobby."

"We did. Now we want to hear it from you."

Grace takes a deep breath. "Bobby didn't kill his father."

"I really hope that's true, Grace. On the other hand, you understand why we're reluctant to take your word for it."

Tears appear in the corners of her eyes. "What did they find?"

"For starters," I say, "your fingerprints were on a drinking glass in Bobby's room."

"I was there on Monday night," she says.

I hold up a hand. "Stop it right now. You aren't fooling anybody. You'll only make it worse if you lie."

"I'm not."

"Yes, you are. Cut the shucking and jiving, Grace. Bobby told us you went over to his father's house on Friday night. He admitted you had sex. He admitted you were still there when Bobby's father came home."

There is resignation in her eyes. "What else did they find?"

"A condom under Bobby's bed. They did a DNA test. They matched both of you."

The tears start streaming down her cheeks.

"We trusted you," I say. "You violated that trust. You've been sneaking around. You've been sleeping with your boyfriend. I'm most disappointed that you lied to us."

Grace's delicate features contort into a vision of pure anguish. "I couldn't tell you," she whispers.

"You can come to us with anything, Grace. Now you and Bobby are going to have to deal with the consequences."

Her glassy eyes fill with panic as she starts to sob uncontrollably. "You have to do something, Daddy. You have to fix this." She takes a couple of deep breaths. "You just have to."

"We don't know where to begin until you tell us what really happened."

"Why do you have to be so mean?"

"Things are going to get a lot meaner if you're arrested. At the moment, I'm not just your father. I'm your lawyer."

"Bobby didn't kill his father," she repeats.

"Then you have to help us prove it."

"How?"

"You can start by telling the truth." There is no reason to hold back. "Putting aside the fact that you and your boyfriend were sleeping together, there are serious legal ramifications for both of you. There's a good chance you're going to be arrested in the morning. At a minimum, you're already guilty of perjury and Bobby is already guilty of statutory rape. They may charge you as an accomplice or an accessory to murder. You've already destroyed your credibility. Any way you cut it, everything is going to get a lot more difficult."

The unthinkable gravity of the situation is finally sinking in. My baby daughter is a suspect in a murder case.

Grace takes a moment to compose herself. She never looks up as everything comes pouring out in a hushed monotone. "Bobby and I went to his father's house after the movie," she says. "We were just going to watch TV and listen to music."

Sure you were.

"And make out?" Rosie asks.

Grace waits a beat. "Probably."

"And have sex?"

A longer pause. "Maybe. I wasn't sure when we got there. Then it just happened."

"It didn't *just happen*," Rosie snaps.

"Yes, it did," Grace insists.

"No, it didn't. Sex doesn't just happen. Bobby admitted it wasn't your first time."

Grace's lips form a tiny ball. Her web of lies has imploded. She's backed into a corner. "It's happened a couple of times," she says.

"No, Grace," Rosie says. "You and Bobby made it happen."

"That's one way of looking at it."

"Don't give me that crap. You and Bobby made a conscious choice."

"Maybe we did. What's the big deal? Everybody does it."

"That doesn't make it right."

"That doesn't make it wrong."

"Are you proud of yourself?"

"You expect me to apologize for having sex with a boy that I love?"

"You have no idea what love is."

"Yes, I do."

"You're only sixteen."

"I'm entitled to have feelings."

"Maybe, but you aren't entitled to have sex."

"Why not?"

"Because you're too young."

"Give me a break, Mother."

"You're too immature to understand the consequences."

"No, I'm not. Your generation invented casual sex. Don't blame us."

"Don't throw it back at me, Grace."

"Then don't put it all on me."

Rosie is seething. "This isn't just about party sex with your boy-friend. You could get sick. You could get AIDS. You could die."

"Bobby and I went together to get tested for AIDS and STDs."

"That was terribly responsible of you. You could also get pregnant."

Grace isn't backing down. "I'm well aware of that, Mother. I'm also old enough to know you and Dad didn't exactly plan on having Tommy."

Rosie is taken aback for an instant. "Tommy has nothing to do with this."

"Maybe not, but you guys aren't exactly poster children for abstinence, either."

"Your father and I understood the risks and the responsibilities."

"So do I. Bobby used a condom. I have a diaphragm."

"Where the hell did you get a diaphragm?"

"Welcome to the twenty-first century, Mother."

"Have you slept with any other boys?"

Grace is unapologetic. "Just one."

She's *sixteen*. She's had more partners than I had by the time I was thirty.

"Who?" Rosie asks.

Grace reveals the name of one of her classmates—a senior honors student who going to Princeton in the fall.

"When did this happen?"

"After a party at school. It wasn't a big deal, Mother."

"It is to me. Did he use a condom?"

"Of course, Mother. I used my diaphragm."

Rosie can't contain her exasperation. "You're still too young," she insists.

"No, I'm not."

"Yes, you are."

"Things have changed since you were in high school."

"They haven't changed that much."

"How old were you when you first had sex?"

"That's none of your business."

"Maybe it is now."

The room goes painfully silent as Rosie contemplates how much she wants to reveal. "On the night of my quinceañera," she finally whispers.

Grace looks at her mother in disbelief. A quinceañera is the traditional coming-of-age event for Latina girls—part birthday party and part debutante ball. "You were only fifteen?" Grace whispers.

"Yes."

It takes our daughter a moment to process this new information. "Really?" she finally stammers.

"Really," Rosie says.

"Who was it?" Grace asks.

"A senior at St. Ignatius," Rosie says. "He was so handsome. He was on the football team. I was absolutely certain he was the love of my life."

I judiciously decide not to mention that he may have been one of my classmates.

"What's the big deal?" Grace asks. "You couldn't have been the only girl in your class who slept with her boyfriend. Nothing bad happened."

"I got pregnant," Rosie says.

This time, there is no glib response from our daughter.

Rosie's voice is tinged with bitterness. "When I told the love of my life that he was going to be a dad, he decided he never wanted to see me again."

Grace sits in stunned silence.

"So you see," Rosie continues, "I'm familiar with this scenario."

Grace wipes the tears from her eyes. "I'm not pregnant," she says. "Bobby and I have been very careful."

"And very lucky. You're still way too young to be having sex. Believe me, I know."

Grace looks at Rosie. "Did you keep the baby?" she asks.

"I had a miscarriage." Rosie sighs heavily. "I wouldn't wish that experience on anyone—especially you."

The tears are now rolling freely down Grace's cheeks. "Did Grandma and Grandpa know about it?"

"Of course." Rosie gestures toward Tommy's bedroom, where Sylvia is camped out. "They said I was too young for sex. They were right."

My daughter and my ex-wife look at each other for a long, anguished moment. It's Grace who finally speaks. "I'm so sorry, Mama," she whispers.

"So am I."

Grace swallows hard. "Not just for you and your baby, Mama. For everything."

Rosie's eyes fill with tears, too. "Me, too, honey."

Grace tugs at her long black hair. "Are you going to yell at me?"

"Not now, honey." Rosie says.

Grace turns to me. "What about you?"

This topic wasn't covered in the parental playbook I was issued sixteen years ago. Nor was it ever covered adequately at the seminary, where I learned all sorts of useless advice to dispense to strangers, but very little about dealing with my own problems. At times like this, I have little faith in my own instincts, so I revert to lawyer mode. "At the moment," I say, "we have other more pressing issues."

"Like what?"

"Like what happened on Friday night and Saturday morning."

"So you're not mad?"

"I'm furious. We'll have a much longer discussion about this later. Mom just came clean to you, Grace. It's time for you to come clean to us."

The game is over. "Where do you want to start?" she asks.

"What time did you get to Judge Fairchild's house?"

"Eleven fifteen."

We let her talk without interrupting. To my relief, her story lines up precisely with Bobby's. They went to Judge Fairchild's house after the movie ended. They were having sex downstairs in Bobby's room when they heard the garage door open. They put on their clothes and sprinted out the back door. When they got to the car, they discovered Bobby had left his keys inside the house. Grace waited for Bobby in the yard while he went back inside to retrieve them. Bobby did, in fact, run to the car by himself while Grace was trying to find her cell phone in the bushes. Then he came back to help her. They left for Rosie's house by twelve fifteen. They drove straight there.

When she's finished, I start probing gently. "Grace," I say, "is it possible somebody else was inside the house when Bobby's father got home?"

"I guess. We were downstairs in the back." She says she didn't see anybody.

"Did you hear anything?"

"No, but it's hard to hear from Bobby's room."

Especially if the intruder was trying to remain quiet. "How long were you out in the yard while Bobby was looking for his keys?" I ask.

"A couple of minutes."

I'm desperately grasping for anything that might help. "Did anybody walk by while you were waiting?"

"I think I heard somebody, but I couldn't see him. I ducked down behind the gate."

That might explain why Lenny didn't see her. "Was Bobby wearing the same shirt when he came back outside?"

"Of course. There wasn't any blood on it."

"Did you see anybody else while Bobby was inside?"

She thinks about it for a moment. "I saw a man get into the Crown Vic."

It's an opening. "Where did he come from?"

"Around the corner from in front of the house."

"Why in God's name didn't you tell us about him?"

"I didn't want you to know that we were there."

"We might have avoided a week of hell if you had. Is it possible he was inside the judge's house?"

"It's possible. I don't know for sure."

"Did he see you?"

"I don't think so. I was behind the fence."

"Did you get a good look at him?"

"No. It happened too fast."

"Think hard, Grace."

"I'm sorry, Dad. I don't remember."

Rosie takes our daughter's hand and opens her bag of tricks. "Close your eyes, honey," she says. "I need you to relax."

Grace does as she's told.

"Visualize Grattan Street early Saturday morning. It's dark and foggy. You're standing behind the fence. You're nervous and excited. You see the man coming around the corner from in front of Bobby's house. Can you picture him in your mind?"

"Kind of."

"What's he doing?"

"He's running toward the car. He's looking over his shoulder."

Rosie squeezes her hand a little tighter. "I need you to think carefully. What does he look like?"

"I don't remember."

"Yes, you do. Tell me, Grace."

"I don't know. I'm scared."

"Stay with me, honey. Is he tall?"

"No."

"Is he skinny?"

"No, he's muscular."

"White? Black? Asian?"

"Asian—I think."

"Dark hair or light hair?"

Grace's eyes are still shut tightly. "Dark. He's wearing a baseball cap."

"What else is he wearing?"

"A black shirt. Big boots."

"Any noticeable marks?"

"Tattoos on his arms."

"Do you see any blood on his arms or clothes?"

"I don't remember."

"Do you remember anything else? Any detail might be important."

Grace's eyes are closed tightly. "He smelled," she finally says.

"Bad? Like a homeless guy?"

"No. Like perfume."

"What kind?"

"Sort of like lavender."

My antenna shoots up. "Are you absolutely sure about that smell?"

"Yes."

Rosie gives me a perplexed look. "What is it, Mike?"

I pull out the paper with the unidentified fingerprint Roosevelt gave us and study it intently. "We need to call Pete."

"Why?"

The pieces are starting to fit together. "I think I know who killed Judge Fairchild. I need Pete to help me prove it. Grace may be the perfect alibi after all."

Thursday, June 23, 12:52 a.m.

The lights are turned down and the back room of Dunleavy's is silent as Big John pours Roosevelt a cup of freshly brewed coffee. "Thanks," Roosevelt says to him.

My uncle tries to break the tension with a little forced levity. "We aren't Starbucks," he says, "but we make up for it with exceptional service."

Roosevelt responds with a weary smile. He, Rosie, Pete, and I are sitting at one of the small round tables. The dark setting matches our somber mood. The room still smells of the cigarette smoke baked into the paneled walls decades before San Francisco banned smoking in restaurants and bars.

"Can you give us a moment?" I say to Big John.

"Of course, lad." He leaves the coffee pot on the table and heads into the front of the bar to add up the day's earnings.

"So," Roosevelt says to me, "when do I get to talk to Grace?"

"Soon," I say.

"Is she prepared to come clean?"

"Yes."

"What's with all the cloak-and-dagger stuff?"

"We're being extra careful," I tell him. "When it's your kid, you gotta get it right."

"Understood."

I nod to Pete, who hands Roosevelt his fancy digital camera. "I spent the evening parked across the street from the Sunshine Massage Spa," he says. "I've been taking pictures of the patrons. You might recognize a few of them."

Roosevelt takes off his glasses and squints at the tiny images. "Who?" he asks.

Pete provides a running commentary as he pushes the button to advance the photos. "An Assistant City Attorney. A member of the Board of Supervisors. A judge. A fire captain." He can't contain a smile when he gets to the last one. "That's my old lieutenant at Mission Station. He was recently promoted to Assistant Chief."

He may not be serving in that capacity for long. "Pretty high-brow clientele," I observe.

"Even ranking members of the SFPD have needs, Mick."

Roosevelt isn't amused as he sets the camera down. "It's very late and I'm very tired," he says. "This better not be some half-baked attempt to shake down the SFPD."

"It's nothing of the sort," I say.

"Are you suggesting some connection to the Fairchild case?"

It's Pete who responds. "Precisely," he says.

Roosevelt gives my kid brother a long look. "I'm listening."

Pete goes to his cop voice. "I talked to several of the Sunshine's patrons. As you might expect, they were reluctant to chat with me. My old boss was particularly unpleasant."

"I'll bet."

"We came to a friendly understanding. He agreed to provide information. I promised not to give his name and photo to the press."

Roosevelt is growing impatient. "Are you planning to get to the point anytime soon?"

Pete nods. "In addition to purchasing sexual gratification from the young women who work at the Sunshine, several of the patrons had something else in common. Their houses had been burglarized during the past six months. Coincidentally, the break-ins all took place while they were, uh, having their needs fulfilled at the Sunshine."

Roosevelt takes a sip of scalding coffee as he begins processing the information. "You're saying the people who run the Sunshine were stealing from their customers?"

"You might say it's a full-service operation."

Roosevelt gives him a puzzled look. "Why are they still patronizing the Sunshine?"

Pete can't contain a smirk. "Maybe they liked the service."

"It's late, Pete."

"They didn't know the Sunshine was ripping them off. For that matter, they didn't know the other customers had been burglarized, too."

"SFPD couldn't put two and two together?"

"There was no obvious connection. Not surprisingly, nobody admitted they'd been at the Sunshine while their houses were being ripped off."

"How did *you* manage to figure this out?"

"I used to be a pretty good cop. Frankly, it wasn't that complicated once I started putting the pieces together. The MO was the same. The burglars were professional. They worked fast. They hit houses when nobody was home. There were no signs of forced entry. They grabbed small, easy-to-find valuables and got the hell out."

"How did they know where their customers lived?"

"It isn't hard to find anybody nowadays. Ms. Amanda probably checked their drivers' licenses while they were getting their massages."

"How did they get inside the houses without breaking in?"

Pete gives him a knowing smile. "There's a locksmith shop downstairs from the Sunshine that's owned by the people who run the massage parlor. They made duplicate keys while their customers were upstairs."

"How do you know?"

"I have sources inside the Sunshine."

Roosevelt is now fully engaged. "I take it this means you believe somebody from the Sunshine went over to rip off Judge Fairchild's house on Friday night?"

"Yes. The MO was exactly the same."

"Except nothing was missing."

"The burglar didn't have time to take anything. The judge came home early and surprised him."

"He didn't have to kill him."

"He panicked."

"You still haven't given me any proof."

It's my turn to interject. "Off the record, Grace told us she saw a muscular Asian guy with tattoos leaving the judge's house early Saturday morning. He got into the Crown Vic and drove away."

"Is she prepared to admit she was there on Friday night?"

"Off the record, yes."

"Can she positively identify him?"

"Probably not. But she noticed he smelled of lavender. They use lavender-scented candles at the Sunshine."

"How would you know?"

"I was there Saturday night."

Roosevelt takes a sip of his coffee. "I need a name," he says.

Pete's expression transforms into a triumphant grin. "Louis Park," he says. "He's their muscle guy. He's also the nephew of the owners."

"You got a photo?"

Pete hands Roosevelt his camera again. "Check it out."

Roosevelt studies the shot of the hulking young man who escorted me upstairs. "When did you take this?" he asks.

"A couple of hours ago. Park left the building shortly after Judge

Weatherby arrived. If my guess is correct, some of the judge's jewelry was missing by the time he got home."

"We'll check it out," Roosevelt says, "but you still haven't given me any definitive proof that Park was at Judge Fairchild's house on Friday night."

Pete reaches under the table and pulls out a white coffee mug enclosed in a zip-lock bag. "His prints are on this," he says triumphantly.

"Where the hell did you get that?" Roosevelt asks.

"Like I said, I have sources inside the Sunshine."

Thank you, Jasmine.

Pete's getting excited. He starts talking faster in clipped cop dialect. "The prints on this mug match the unidentified partial you found on Judge Fairchild's front door."

"When did you become a fingerprint expert?"

"Jeff Lowenthal used to play shortstop on my softball team. He owed me a favor."

Next to Kathleen Jacobsen, Lowenthal is the SFPD's best fingerprint guru. He also has excellent range, a strong throwing arm, and power to all fields.

"Is Jeff prepared to testify that it's a match?" Roosevelt asks.

"Absolutely." Pete grins triumphantly. "If you have any doubts, you'll find a gray Crown Vic with no license plates parked inside the garage of the Sunshine."

Roosevelt nods. "I still need a little more," he says.

It's my turn. "We've given you everything you need. You can go over to the Sunshine and arrest Park and shut down their operation."

"I need to meet the person who lifted this coffee mug."

"We can arrange it," I say, "but I have some conditions."

"I'm listening."

"In exchange for her cooperation, you won't press charges for her activities at the Sunshine."

"Agreed."

"Second, she won't be prosecuted for being here illegally."

"You know I can't speak for INS."

"You can't deport her if you expect her to testify."

"I'll make it happen."

"Third, she's going to need a new identity and passage to Korea after she testifies."

"I'll figure out a way to do it. Anything else?"

"Finally," I say, "you'll provide round-the-clock protection for her. I can persuade her to cooperate only if you can assure her safety."

"You're asking for a lot."

"We're giving you a lot. You're going to get credit for solving the murder of a judge and shutting down one of the most egregious exploiters of underage sex slaves in the Bay Area. You'll be a big hero. I can't think of a better way to conclude your long and distinguished career with the SFPD."

Roosevelt eyes me intently as he does a mental calculation of the countless ramifications. "If you're wrong," he says, "your client is going on trial for murder and your daughter is going on trial for perjury—or more."

"We aren't wrong, Roosevelt."

"I need to talk to the witness first. I can't derail a murder case without evaluating her credibility."

"As her lawyer, I can't let you do that until I have assurances you'll be able to fulfill all of my conditions."

"You have my word."

"I need more."

"You have my word," he repeats.

I have no cards left to play. "Everything is off the record until you can provide protection and confirm you'll comply with the rest of my conditions," I say.

"That's fair," he says.

"Then we have a deal."

"Fine. What's her name?"

"Jasmine Lee."

"Where is she?"

"Downstairs in Big John's office. I'll bring her up to meet you."

#

It takes Roosevelt a few minutes to get Jasmine talking. Once she starts, she doesn't stop. It's surreal to watch the waiflike Asian girl pouring out her heart in stilted English to the imposing African American man in the back room of an empty saloon in the City of St. Francis in the middle of the night. She's relieved to find somebody who's willing to listen. In response to Roosevelt's gentle questioning, she confesses that she's an undocumented alien. She confirms that she's engaged in illicit sexual activities. She admits to pilfering Park's coffee mug. Most importantly, she confirms the Sunshine's scheme to burglarize the homes of their customers while they were having their needs fulfilled.

It's after three a.m. when Roosevelt finally closes his notebook and places it on the table in front of him. "It's going to take a little time to verify her story," he says to me.

"We have until ten o'clock this morning."

He flips open his cell, punches in a series of numbers, and starts issuing orders. "I need three units to the Sunshine Massage Spa on the corner of Eddy and Leavenworth immediately. No lights or sirens. Do not enter until I arrive." He snaps his phone shut. He turns to me and says, "There's a black and white parked in front for protection. I want you to sit tight. I'll be back as soon as I can."

Thursday, June 23, 5:30 a.m.

"Mind if I ask you something?" I say to Rosie.

"Sure," she says.

We've been drinking coffee in the back room of Dunleavy's for the past two hours, anxiously waiting to hear from Roosevelt. It feels like a hospital waiting room. We haven't said much, except for our frequent phone calls to update Grace and Sylvia. Pete and Big John are passing the time watching ESPN on the TV in the front of the bar. Jasmine dozed off on the sofa in my uncle's cluttered office downstairs.

"How come you never told me you got pregnant when you were in high school?" I ask.

Rosie tenses. "A little mystery is healthy for a relationship. I never asked you about your old girlfriends. I didn't think you needed to know about my old boyfriends."

"Have you kept any other secrets from me?"

"A few. Have you kept any from me?"

"A few. Why didn't you tell me about it?"

Rosie takes a sip of coffee. "It was the worst experience of my life."

"Worse than our divorce?"

"Absolutely."

"Worse than this week?"

"About the same."

We look at each other intently. "There's more to the story than you told Grace, isn't there?"

"You know me too well, Mike."

"You know me even better."

She sets her mug down. She seems to want to get something off her chest. "If I tell you the whole story, do you promise we'll never talk about it again?"

"Absolutely."

"Are you going to judge me?"

"Absolutely not."

She takes a deep breath and speaks slowly. "The circumstances surrounding the termination of my pregnancy were more complicated than the way I described them to Grace."

Uh oh. "Did you get an abortion?" I whisper.

"No," she says. "I really had a miscarriage—the day before I was supposed to get an abortion."

Dear God. "I'm so sorry, Rosie."

"So am I." Her eyes are now filled with tears. "It didn't seem like the sort of thing you would share with a priest."

"Ex-priest," I correct her. "It wasn't your fault, Rosie."

"Yes, it was, Mike. It was no different than Grace and Bobby. I chose to sleep with my boyfriend. It was my responsibility. I knew the consequences."

"You were a kid. You made a mistake. I'm not going to let you beat yourself up about it now."

"You can't stop me. At the very minimum, I would assume you might have a problem with the fact that a nice Catholic girl was ready to have an abortion."

"Things happen. You were only fifteen."

"That doesn't matter. God took away my baby before I could do it myself."

"You know that isn't true."

"That's the way my priest explained it to me. He told me I was going to hell for killing my baby."

"Are you serious?"

"Yes."

"Then your priest was an asshole."

"You aren't going to get any argument from me about that."

As long as I've known her, Rosie has always referred to herself as a "lapsed Catholic" without elaboration. Now I finally understand why. "Is that when you stopped going to church?"

"Yes. It seemed rather pointless. My priest said my ticket to hell was already punched."

"He was wrong."

"That's little comfort to me now."

Maybe I don't know her as well as I thought—even after twenty years. "Did your parents know about it?" I ask.

"Of course. Who do you think made the arrangements for the abortion?"

My mind flashes to Sylvia. "Are you serious?"

"Yes. Surprised?"

"Yes. They were devout Catholics."

"They were also practical Catholics, Mike. I wasn't breaking new ground. Do you think I was the only girl in my class who got pregnant?"

"Nope." A couple of my classmates at St. Ignatius became fathers before they graduated from high school. "Your mother still goes to church every Sunday."

"She's more optimistic about the concept of redemption than I am."

"I think you finished your penance this week," I say.

"Things might have been a little easier if I'd had a priest like you."

I take a deep breath and ask, "Who else knows about this?"

"My brother and sister. My asshole boyfriend who dumped me. My asshole priest who told me I was going to hell." She pauses. "And now Grace and you."

My God. "You've been carrying this around for all these years?"

"Yep. And this is the last time I plan to talk about it."

"I'm so sorry, Rosie."

"Me, too." Her expression indicates this topic of discussion is closed—for good.

Big John walks in a moment later. The veteran barkeep reads our somber expressions and invokes an apologetic tone. "Sorry for interrupting," he says. "Roosevelt just pulled up."

Thursday, June 23, 5:45 a.m.

The sun is peeking through the early morning fog as Roosevelt takes a seat in one of the worn chairs the back room on Dunleavy's. His stoic expression gives no indication as to whether the news is good or bad. He clears his throat and gets down to business. "This conversation isn't taking place," he says.

Rosie, Pete, and I nod in unison. We lean forward and listen.

"The previously unidentified fingerprint found on the door to Judge Fairchild's house matches that of Louis Park, the facilities manager of the Sunshine Massage Spa. Mr. Park's fingerprints were also found on the steering wheel of a stolen gray Crown Victoria parked in the Sunshine's garage. Inside the trunk we discovered jewelry and other valuables belonging to several of the customers of the Sunshine, including Judge Sherman Weatherby. We believe Mr. Park was burglarizing the homes of the Sunshine's customers while they were enjoying the services at the spa. We have shut down the entire operation. We have taken Mr. Park and the owners into custody. Mr. Park will be charged with murder. The owners will face various other charges."

So far, so good. "Did Park confess to killing Judge Fairchild?" I ask.

"I can't comment on the details of an ongoing investigation. Off the record, he told us more than he would have if he'd been represented by competent counsel such as yourself. We are confident he will be receptive to a plea bargain for second-degree murder in exchange for his cooperation in providing information about the operation of the Sunshine. The federal authorities are also interested."

"What about the owners?" I ask.

"That will be harder," he says. "This isn't the first time they've been on our radar and they've already lawyered up. If Park cuts a deal, I'm hopeful his testimony will link them directly to the killing of Judge Fairchild. They will also be prosecuted for burglary, pimping, kidnapping, money laundering, and tax evasion. The DA intends to devote significant resources to this case. We may not get them for everything, but we'll shut them down and they'll do time."

Coincidentally, it will give a huge boost to Ward's re-election campaign. "Where does that leave Bobby?" I ask.

"Bill McNulty will be calling you shortly to tell you officially that all charges have been dropped. Your client should be home later this morning. For what it's worth, please extend my apologies to him for jumping to an incorrect conclusion."

"We will."

"Please also inform him that if he files a civil suit against the SFPD and the City for false arrest, I will personally place him under arrest for statutory rape in connection with his escapades with your daughter."

"I'll pass it along."

"In addition, I want you to tell him in no uncertain terms that if he ever engages in sex with your daughter again, I will rip out his internal organs with my bare hands."

I smile. "You'll have to take a number."

"Which brings me to Grace," he says. "I have it on good authority that in exchange for her full cooperation, no perjury charges will be filed against her."

The knot in my stomach starts to ease for the first time in a week.

"Thanks, Roosevelt."

He isn't quite finished. "I trust you will exert appropriate parental influence to remind her that some of her recent decisions did not evidence exemplary judgment. In particular, you may wish to point out that she was a few hours away from being charged as an accomplice to murder."

"I will."

"Finally," he says, "there's something I need from you."

"Name it."

"There are about two dozen soon-to-be-former employees of the Sunshine Massage Spa who have been brought into this country illegally—including Jasmine Lee. We're letting them stay at the Sunshine under our supervision until we can sort everything out. Many of them speak little or no English. Most have been held against their will and forced to work under abysmal conditions. It's likely many of them may be subject to criminal charges, and in some cases, deportation. Personally, I see little to be gained by arresting them, but the final call isn't mine."

"What do you want from us?"

"They're going to need lawyers. I want you to represent them—for free."

It's a small price to pay. "We will," I say.

"Thank you." He gives us the fatherly nod I've seen countless times over the past half-century. "There's something else I want you to know. This is my last case. I'm retiring for good."

"You've tried three times," I say. "You'll be bored."

"I don't think so. I've been chasing bad guys for a long time. I want to spend more time with my grandchildren."

Thursday, June 23, 11:15 p.m.

"**H**ow's Bobby?" I ask Grace. They just got off the phone for the fourth time in the last hour.

"Better than yesterday," she says. She's sitting on the corner of her bed. "Things are never going to be the way they were, but he's happy to be home."

"And you?"

She tugs at the sleeves of her worn Redwood High School sweatshirt. "I'll be okay, Daddy," she says bravely.

"It may be hard for a while."

"I know." She clutches the large teddy bear that came out of retirement earlier this week after spending the past couple of years on her dresser. "Can I ask you something?"

"Sure."

"When are you going to yell at me?"

"Not tonight, honey."

"You aren't mad?"

"I'm very mad, but yelling about it tonight isn't going to help. You made some bad decisions. You learned some hard lessons. Frankly, I'm more disappointed than angry."

"Why?"

"This exercise should have taught you that we always stick together and deal with whatever comes up—no matter what." It's a tired cliché, but it's one of those rare occasions where it lines up with the truth.

"Are you and Mommy going to ground me?"

"Yep."

"For how long?"

Until you turn fifty. "For the rest of the summer."

"That's pretty drastic."

"You were a couple of hours away from being arrested as an accessory to murder. You put everything at risk—for yourself and for Mommy and me. You could have lost everything, Grace."

"Then why aren't you giving me a harsher punishment?"

How much more can you take? "The purpose of punishing your kids is to remind them of the gravity of their mistakes—and their consequences. You hope it stays with them long enough that they won't make the same mistake again. Mommy and I are reasonably sure you understand the consequences. Grounding you for six more months won't add much to the lesson. We're going to keep a much closer eye on your extracurricular activities, though. And let me make one thing as clear as I can: If I catch you sleeping with Bobby or any other boy in the next five years, I will kill both of you instantly."

"Got it."

"Speaking of which, what were you and Bobby talking about for so long?"

"Stuff."

Not good enough. "What kind of stuff?"

She swallows hard. "We aren't going to go out anymore. He's going to college in the fall. I want to spend more time with other people. We're going to try to be friends, but I think I'm going to take a little break from boys."

It's the best news I've heard in a while. "I think that's a good decision."

"So do I." She clutches her teddy bear more tightly as her eyes fill with tears. "Daddy?"

"Yes?"

"I'm sorry I put you and Mommy through all of this."

"Me too."

"Daddy?"

"Yes?"

"Thanks."

# # #

"Did your mother finally go home?"

"Yes," Rosie says. "She's had a busy week."

"So have we."

We're sitting on the weathered redwood bench on Rosie's back porch in the cool, foggy air at two o'clock on Friday morning. We're each nursing a Guinness. There is always an emotional letdown after a big case is resolved and our mood is decidedly melancholy.

"We should get something for her," I say.

"She stopped accepting gifts when she turned seventy-five."

"How about a nice dinner?"

"That might work as long as it includes the kids. I think she'd appreciate it more if we promise not to take another murder case until Tommy starts college."

"So would I. Have you heard anything from Julie?"

"She paid our bill."

"Did she manage to say thank you?"

"It isn't in her vocabulary."

"Was she apologetic for all the nasty things she said to us?"

"Nope."

"Some things never change." I look up at the single street lamp struggling to provide a little illumination through the fog. "Is Grace asleep?"

"Finally." Rosie is in a contemplative mood. "How do you feel about our baby daughter sleeping with her boyfriend?"

"It means she isn't a baby anymore. We should have seen it coming."

"We haven't been setting an especially stellar example."

"No, we haven't."

"Does that make us crappy parents?"

Yes. "It's been a long week, Rosie. Let's not beat ourselves up even more tonight."

She won't let it go. "Our daughter was a few hours away from being charged with murder. She should have been convicted of perjury. She was sleeping with her boyfriend behind our backs. We need to talk about it."

I know she's right. "We need to keep a closer eye on her," I say. "There's a fine line between supporting and enabling. I'm not sure exactly where to draw it, but I know we crossed it this time."

Rosie's eyes turn to cold steel. "We can't let something like this ever happen again."

"I agree."

"How do we make sure?"

"We have to trust her a lot less and be around a lot more. Life with a teenage daughter is a war of attrition. Maybe we should set a goal of getting her to college before we kill her—or ourselves."

I get the smile I was hoping for. "Sounds pretty good to me," she says. "I hope it's realistic."

"So do I."

The light from the street lamp reflects off Rosie's jet black eyes as we take in the cool breeze. "You look tired," she says.

It's a welcome respite from talking about teenage problems. "I'm fine, Rosita."

"You're even worse than my mother. You'll never admit you're slowing down."

"I'm not."

"Yes, you are. So am I."

"Maybe a little," I say grudgingly. I quickly add, "It's been a long week, but we got a good result for our client and our daughter. We identified Judge Fairchild's killer and got the Sunshine shut down. Jasmine may be going home to her parents. Hell, we even got paid. All things considered, that isn't so bad."

"I guess." Rosie's smile disappears. "Jack Fairchild is still dead. Bobby and Sean won't see him again. The girls at the Sunshine will never have normal lives. Grace isn't going to be the same. Doesn't it bother you?"

"Of course. We can't fix everything, Rosie. There's no such thing as perfect justice."

"When did you become so practical?"

"I learned it from you. The past twenty years would have been a lot easier if I had been a quicker study."

"Maybe. Have you given any more thought to Robert's offer?"

"I haven't had a lot of time to think about it."

"Sure you have."

Yes, I have. "I'm inclined to do it. I'm ready to try something different. It might be a good time to start training the next generation of idealistic young defense lawyers before we get too old and cynical."

"You mean people like we *used* to be?"

"We aren't *that* old and *that* cynical yet."

"You'll miss trying cases."

"Robert said we can do a couple of cases a year. That's plenty. There are also health benefits, a retirement plan, and maybe even an occasional vacation. He said we could use the attorneys at the PD's Office to handle the cases for employees of the Sunshine. It'll be a good training opportunity. Most importantly, I persuaded him to buy us new furniture."

"We won't have to use the dented metal desks we had twenty years ago?"

"We're getting new metal desks."

She smiles. "You're one helluva negotiator."

"Thanks." I look into her eyes. "Does that mean you're in?"

There's a long pause. "I think so."

"I'll call Robert in the morning with the good news." I finish my beer and give her a thoughtful look. "You realize this is the first major decision we've agreed on in a long time."

Her smile broadens. "Given our history, that doesn't give me a great deal of comfort, Mike." She pecks me on the cheek. "I guess the circle is now complete."

I touch her cheek softly. "You just quoted Darth Vader."

"I thought it was Obi-Wan Kenobi."

"You'll have to ask Tommy when he wakes up. He's memorized all six *Star Wars* movies. Either way, it's probably a fitting epitaph for Fernandez and Daley."

"Maybe it is." Her expression turns wistful. "While we're talking about major lifecycle events, do you think we should consider any adjustments in our personal situation?"

This is where things have always gotten tricky. "What do you have in mind?"

"Maybe we could start by having you stay over here a couple of nights a week. It would give you a chance to spend more time with Tommy and Grace. You could even help with the dishes."

"I'd like that."

"So would I, but be careful what you wish for. Grace is still a teenager."

"I'm well aware of that. Do you want to revisit any other aspects of our relationship?"

"I think we've covered enough territory for one night, Mike."

Relief. "Probably the right call."

She leans over again and kisses me softly, then pulls back slowly. "You realize this is the first time in twenty years we've agreed on *two* major decisions in one night," she says.

"That's a new record for us."

"Maybe we're evolving. Maybe we're maturing."

"Or maybe we've finally run out of things to argue about," I say.

She squeezes my hand tightly as she looks out into the foggy night. I can feel her warm breath on the side of my face as she leans over and whispers, "I love you, Mike."

"I love you, too, Rosie."

ACKNOWLEDGMENTS

It takes a village to write a novel. For me, it takes a very large village. I get a lot of help writing these stories and I want to take this opportunity to thank the kind people who have been so generous with their time and expertise.

Thanks to my beautiful wife, Linda, who has remained unfailingly supportive and patient through the process of seven novels. It isn't always easy living with somebody who spends as much time as I do sitting in front of a computer. Thanks also to our twin sons, Alan and Stephen. You are excellent editors and I will miss your daily input as you head off to college.

Thanks to my publisher, David Poindexter, at MacAdam/Cage, for your encouragement and wisdom. Thanks to MacAdam/Cage's editor-in-chief, Pat Walsh, for your insights, friendship, and perseverance. Thanks to my editor, Guy Intoci, for your patience, perceptiveness, and good humor. Thanks to Dorothy Carico Smith for your exceptional art and design work.

Thanks to my extraordinary agent, Margret McBride, and to Donna DeGutis, Faye Atchison, and Anne Bomke at the Margret McBride Literary Agency. You are still the best! Thanks also to the incomparable Nevins McBride.

Thanks to criminal defense attorney David Nickerson for your insights into the criminal justice system. Keep fighting the good fight.

Thanks to the Every Other Thursday Night Writers' Group: Bonnie

DeClark, Meg Stiefvater, Anne Maczulak, Liz Hartka, Janet Wallace, and Priscilla Royal. Thanks to Elaine and Bill Petrocelli for your endless support.

Thanks my friends and colleagues at Sheppard, Mullin, Richter & Hampton (and your spouses and significant others) for your support and encouragement for so many years. I'm sorry that I can't mention all of you by name in this space, but I wanted to give particular thanks to those of you with whom I've worked the longest: Randy and Mary Short, Cheryl Holmes, Joan Story and Robert Kidd, Bob Thompson, Phil and Wendy Atkins-Pattinson, Sue Lenzi, Maria Sariano, Betsy McDaniel, Bill and Barbara Manierre, Donna Andrews, Geri Freeman and David Nickerson, Julie and Jim Ebert, Ron and Rita Ryland, Bob Stumpf, and Aline Pearl. Special thanks to Jane Gorsi for your superb editing and proofreading.

Thanks always to our ever-expanding family: Charlotte, Ben, Michelle, Margaret, and Andy Siegel; Ilene Garber; Joe, Jan, and Julia Garber; Terry Garber; Roger and Sharon Fineberg; Jan Harris Sandler and Matz Sandler, Scott, Michelle, Stephanie, Kim, and Sophie Harris; Cathy, Richard, and Matthew Falco; and Julie Harris and Matthew, Aiden, and Ari Stewart.

Finally, thanks again to all of my readers for your continuing kindness and enthusiasm. It means a lot to me and I really appreciate it.